A TASTE OF SAGE

A TASTE

of

SAGE

a novel

YAFFA S. SANTOS

HARPER

NEW YORK • LONDON • TORONTO • SYDNEY

HARPER

HarperCollins books may be purchased for educational, business, or sales promotional use. For information, please email the Special Markets Department at SPsales@harpercollins.com.

FIRST EDITION

Designed by Jen Overstreet

Library of Congress Cataloging-in-Publication Data has been applied for.

ISBN 978-0-06-297484-6 (pbk.)

20 21 22 23 24   LSC   10 9 8 7 6 5 4 3 2 1

A TASTE OF SAGE

PROLOGUE

"Are the plátanos ready, Magda?" Lumi Santana called to her sous chef. She stirred the cauldron at hand, turning over juicy sautéed shrimp, glossy slivers of bell pepper, and rings of sliced onion.

"Ready, Chef," Magda said, laying a tray of still-sizzling green plantain rounds on the butcher block table behind Lumi.

They mashed the plantains in a huge pilón, a mortar and pestle Lumi had received as a gift three years ago for her twenty-ninth birthday. Between strokes of the mortar, she browned a little garlic on the stove, inhaling the rich, buttery aroma. When it was done, she shook it out over the plantain mixture.

She folded in the sautéed shrimp and then, using a square bowl, made many little pyramids of mofongo. Each one was plated with a helping of shrimp sauce and an edible ginger flower.

"Chef, we have two tables," Giselle, Caraluna's only waitress, said.

"Okay. Send out the first course," Lumi told Giselle. To herself, she said, "We're missing something in this kitchen . . . Oh, music!"

She chose a Spotify playlist she'd made for cooking instead of playing the radio, despite the fact that turning the radio on to her favorite station felt to her like putting her finger on the pulse of her neighborhood.

Plates of beets on a bed of arugula sprinkled with finely chopped queso de hoja and sides of fresh plantain chips began their trip from the kitchen island to the two occupied round tables in Caraluna's dining room.

"Do we need another starter for tonight? I can make some alcapurrias, just like the ones we used to make back home in Puerto Rico," Magda said.

"I think we'll stay with the salad, because I still have a full crate of arugula that needs to go today. But another day, that would be amazing," Lumi said.

Minutes later, the dishes traveled back to the kitchen completely empty, and it was time for the shrimp mofongo to make the trek.

"Chef, we have two more tables," Giselle said.

"Great. There are more salads ready on the island."

Once she was done cleaning her station, Lumi peeked out the round window on the kitchen door into the dining room. At the first table, a woman took a bite of the mofongo, and Lumi watched as a smile spread across her face.

"This is amazing!" said a man sitting at the second table.

"Yes. Best mofongo I ever had. The taste is slightly different than traditional, but I like it even better," said his companion.

She could listen to them all night.

"Okay, the first two tables need dessert. And we now have a fifth," Giselle said.

Lumi gestured toward the kitchen island, where bowls of majarete, sweet corn pudding, infused with lavender extract, were lined up right behind the salads.

Minutes later, the empty bowls came back to the kitchen, and with them, more compliments for the chef.

After the first wave of guests dwindled, Lumi left Magda and Giselle to sit down at her tiny desk. She pulled out a sheaf of papers and smiled to herself as she reviewed the receipts from the day's seafood and vegetable deliveries. It was happening. Caraluna was finally real, just like she had dreamed all those years ago.

1

LUMI

When Lumi Santana got to her restaurant, she found Magda and Diego, the line cook, standing over a cauldron of sancocho, complaining that the earthy root vegetable stew just wasn't thickening. Lumi grabbed a bowl of squash puree left over from the previous weekend's wedding and stirred it in at an impressive clip.

"Stir with purpose, my friends," Lumi said. "Doors open in thirty-five minutes."

She pulled a lavender silicone oven glove off a stainless steel hook. Aside from the stainless steel utensils, everything in Caraluna's kitchen was purple: the walls, the appliances, the mixing bowls. A sole pop of yellow came from her aunt's cheery sunflower painting, which hung on the oak door leading to her back office. The only thing black in the whole place was the chalkboard Lumi put out for holiday specials. Caraluna ran specials on every holiday except Father's Day. No reason to offer specials on a holiday she'd never celebrated.

"What else are we making besides sancocho tonight, boss?" Magda asked as she stirred the cauldron with a well-muscled arm. Lumi ran Caraluna the same way the down-home Dominican and Cuban restaurants did during her childhood in Miami. These small, colorful establishments usually had only one chef and often no menu. The day's offerings were whatever the chef felt like making based on the ingredients on hand. The variety on the menu was smaller, but patrons could be sure that their meal was cooked fresh. Every day was as much of an adventure for the staff as it was for Lumi, as she stood in front of the pantry to see what she had and what she could create from it.

Together, Lumi and Diego picked out the ingredients for an avocado salad, saffron rice, and a spiced coconut pudding to accompany the sancocho, which Magda kept stirring. While Magda and Diego worked on the side dishes, Lumi pulled out a bag of flour and started making some fresh tortillas for an enchilada casserole. She loved that Caraluna fused the Dominican cuisine of her childhood with dishes from all over the world.

She scraped the griddle of the tiny burned scraps of dough that remained from last night's shrimp roti and placed the tortillas on the grill. She flipped the tortillas with a deft flick of her wrist. When they were done bubbling, she upended them onto a periwinkle earthenware plate. Next, Lumi layered the fresh tortillas into a glass dish, alternating layers of crumbled savory cotija cheese and tart homemade tomato salsa. She popped the dish into the oven, and thirty minutes later, gloves on hands, she removed the casserole just in time for the doors to open.

While Lumi prepared the food, Magda wrote the specials on the chalkboard in neon-green chalk. Within minutes, a gray-haired couple wandered in, the first guests of the night. The man was tall, with straight, well-combed hair parted to the side, and he wore a plaid lumberjack vest. The woman was of average height and wore a kukui nut necklace that matched her sepia skin. Giselle greeted them and allowed them to choose whichever table they liked. They chose a corner table and began perusing the specials board.

Next came a young woman with blue hair who was dining by herself. Giselle seated her at the table opposite the couple, and she promptly retrieved a dog-eared book from her messenger bag. Lumi pulled herself away from the window to the dining room and set her sights on the entrées waiting to be plated.

With the sancocho done, Magda and Diego ladled hearty portions into Caraluna's signature moon-print ceramic bowls. From her place in the kitchen, Lumi stole one more peek at her guests again.

She loved to see her customers relaxing in this space she had planned with exactly that goal. Glancing at the couple again, she thought she might recognize the woman and hoped she would get a moment later to say hello.

Giselle brought out the avocado salad first, followed by the enchilada casserole, the sancocho, and saffron rice. Her diners dug in at once, oohing and aahing over the brilliant array of colors, tastes, and textures. The enchiladas had taken on a toothsome crunch after being baked and provided a perfect balance for the wonderfully spiced stew, with its tender chunks of braised goat and roasted pumpkin.

The couple sent their compliments to the kitchen, and Lumi decided it was only right to come out and thank them herself. More than anything, she wanted to meet this couple who seemed so sophisticated. She smiled as she approached their table, and they smiled in return.

"I was just telling our waitress how excellent the meal was," the woman said. "I'm Glenda and this is my husband, Jonathan." She gestured to the man, and he nodded back with a kind countenance.

"Iluminada Santana," Lumi said. "Nice to meet you both."

"It's lovely to meet you, Iluminada. Tell me," Glenda asked, "do you do much business here?"

Lumi froze, staring blankly at her inquisitive guests. "W-why do you ask?" she said.

Glenda cleared her throat. "Well, I'm retired now, but I used to own Pesce di Mare, a seafood restaurant in Morningside Heights."

Lumi nodded as this new information registered in her brain. So that's where she'd seen her. She had been to Pesce di Mare a couple years back, when she was still in culinary school.

"As you can imagine," Glenda continued, "I know a couple of things about this business." She cast her gaze toward the rest of the restaurant with a sympathetic frown. "It's just that the food is too excellent for you to have this many empty tables on a Thursday night."

Lumi sighed. She was not in the mood to get schooled by one of her patrons, even if it was a fellow restaurant owner.

"Have you thought about working with a set menu?" Glenda asked.

Lumi backed up a step. "You know, I should check on the coconut pudding," she said.

"Please don't take it personally, honey. Look, here's my card if there's anything I can ever do for you," Glenda said, holding out a crisp white paper square.

Glenda and Jonathan exchanged glances as Lumi took the card, thanked her quickly, and hightailed it to the kitchen. She swung the door open and almost hit Diego and Magda, who were hurriedly shoving away a flask of rum.

"Wait. Give that to me," Lumi said.

The two watched in shock as Lumi poured herself a shot and downed it in one gulp. Magda peered out the kitchen window and then shrugged to herself and started preparing Lumi a small bowl of sancocho. She added a sprinkle of dried bacon and some sprigs of cilantro.

"Thank you, Magda," Lumi said with an appreciative sigh as Magda handed her the bowl and winked at her.

Lumi willed herself to sit down at the tiny wooden card table in her office and eat her stew. The table was the only vestige of her ex-boyfriend Colton left in her restaurant. He bought it for her at a yard sale he'd stumbled upon while in Newark for one of his slam poetry gigs. She commanded herself to stop that train of thought and focus on her bowl of stew. As she tasted the first spoonful, her shoulders softened and the tightness in her chest eased. Leave it to Magda to suffuse every stew with motherly concern. The warmth spread through her belly and gradually relieved the urge to scream, which had mounted in her throat during the conversation with Glenda and her husband. The subject was never far from her mind, but what else could she do when she was already giving it all she had?

LUMI'S SIMPLE SANCOCHO
Serves 8

1 tablespoon vegetable oil (not olive)

1 tablespoon brown sugar

6 cloves garlic

1 tbsp. black pepper

1 large red onion

1 pound beef cubes or oxtail

1 pound goat

10 cups water

1 cup auyama (West Indies squash), diced

3 carrots, peeled and diced

2 ears of corn, shucked and cut into 1-inch
 rounds

2 cups yuca, peeled and diced

1 cup yautia, peeled and diced

⅓ cup cilantro, chopped

juice of 1 bitter orange

salt, to taste

cooked white rice, to serve

Mash garlic in a mortar and pestle. Dice onion. Season the meats with the salt, pepper, cilantro, onion, and juice of the bitter orange. Heat the oil on medium high in a large Dutch oven or "caldero" and add the sugar. When the sugar is bubbling, add the meats and brown them on all sides. When they are thoroughly browned, add the water and the vegetables. Bring to a boil and then simmer until all the ingredients are cooked through, about 1 hour and 20 minutes. Serve with white rice.

Note: Chicken and pork are also commonly used instead of or in addition to beef and goat. Plátano is also a traditional addition that was left out here due to flavor preference.

AVOCADO SALAD
Serves 4

4 ripe avocados (not overripe)
$1/2$ red onion
$1/4$ cup olive oil
juice of 1 lime

Split each avocado, remove the pit, scoop out the flesh, and dice into bite-sized chunks. Dice the onion, setting aside some for garnish. Combine the avocado, onion, olive oil, and lime juice and toss. Sprinkle diced onions on top to serve.

2

JULIEN

Julien Dax wiped the sweat from his brow with one freckled forearm, sweeping back a stray crimson lock. There had been five steak au poivre orders in the last twenty minutes, and he had managed to churn them all out without missing a beat. Out of the corner of his eye he spotted his sous chef, Simon, sitting in a chair and checking the latest Instagram posts from Paris. He gritted his teeth.

Before he could ask Simon how the duck à l'orange was coming along, the door from the dining room swung open. In stepped Fallon, waitress par excellence, a puzzled look wrinkling her rosy forehead.

"What's wrong?" Julien asked.

Fallon sighed. "Chef, a diner has complained that there's no ketchup . . . again."

"Hmm." Julien nodded, and before she could say anything more, he barreled into the dining room. His gaze bounced off the cream-colored walls, from one fully seated round table to the next.

"Who asked for ketchup here?"

A bespectacled man stood up and raised his hand at the table nearest the door.

"Educate your taste buds, sir. This is a three-star restaurant; we don't carry that red abomination here. However, I will be happy to provide you with béarnaise, rouille, or tarragon rémoulade on the house. Does that settle this concern?"

The diner shook his head. "No. I want ketchup."

"Well, I want a gold boat," Julien replied, "but that doesn't seem to be happening anytime soon either."

The man narrowed his eyes. "I'm writing you a bad review on Yelp as soon as I get home."

"Do as you may, sir," Julien said. "No one I care about will be dismayed by the lack of ketchup on these premises. And please feel free to get out of my restaurant. What you ate of your meal is on the house."

The man stumbled back and then quickly ran for the door as the other diners gaped on.

"That's that," Julien said. He contemplated taking a small bow, but instead he strode back into the kitchen.

"It's true," Simon said without looking up, "that steak was dry."

Julien turned on his heel to face him. "How would you know?" he asked. "You didn't try it. You've hardly done a thing tonight besides check the headlines of *Le Monde*. You are *here*, Simon, you are here in New York. I'd advise you to get your head around that."

"What if I don't want to?" Simon sniffed, scrolling down his phone screen once more.

"After I spent two thousand dollars to bring you here and weeks helping you get set up? Well, then, I would say eat shit."

"The nerve! You know what? I've run out of reasons to put up with your attitude. Adieu, Julien," Simon said, snapping a nearby dish towel onto the floor and storming out.

Julien shrugged and went back to grinding the peppercorns. It wasn't until he texted Simon later that night and he replied with a knife emoji that Julien understood Simon was not coming back to DAX.

3

LUMI

At six o'clock on weekdays on West 218th Street, the pungent smell of doughnut grease hung heavy in the air. Lumi could not understand how the Twin Donut staff could be unaware that cheap oil being used to fry at too-low temperatures produced a nauseating stench. The worst part of it was that it covered up the smells of the other food that she loved being made on that same street, like the aroma of long-grain rice cooking to perfection in so many households.

The rice scent trickled in through her door, since she had her shutters closed tight, befitting the chilly November Monday. Getting used to the New York winters was a step that Lumi had skipped. She flicked on her natural light therapy lamp and settled onto the burgundy velour couch with a box of pistachio cream puffs that Magda had made her during the downtime that afternoon.

No sooner had she undone the purple grosgrain ribbon than her phone began to ring. She sighed, eyeing the cream puffs with longing. Rafelina, read the screen. She considered covering it with a pillow and telling her friend and accountant that she was in yoga.

Reluctantly, she pressed the "talk" button and raised the phone to her ear. "Hey, Rafi," she said, trying to sound upbeat.

"Hey . . . Lumi," Rafelina said with a heavy sigh. "Listen, I got a letter from the management company today."

"Ross and Greene?" Lumi asked. They both knew there was only one management company.

"They're raising the rent by ten thousand dollars a month," Rafelina blurted out.

A stray dab of pistachio cream had affixed itself to the side of the box, and Lumi brushed it away with a graceful finger. "Well, no big deal, right? We'll just need to sell more. Do a Groupon deal, maybe, or expand the bakery section. We'll make up the difference," she said, nodding emphatically to herself as she spoke and ignoring the quaver in her own voice.

The line was silent except for Rafelina's breathing on the other side. "Lumi . . . honey. I hate to be the one to put it this way, you know, I really do. But you're already going under as it is."

Shivering, Lumi pulled the sherpa throw she kept on the couch all the way up to her neck. "Well, yeah, it might be slow at first, but this is a good motivator. It's lighting a fire under our asses. I've been talking about expanding the bakery for months now; this will be my chance to actually do it. Once it's under way, I'm sure we'll start making up the difference—"

"Lu. This is a forty percent increase in your rent. And you haven't broken even since August."

Lumi frowned. "Well, that's not true, Rafi, you see—"

"You've been paying all the bills since September with your savings. You can tell anyone else that things are balancing out, but I'm your accountant, sweetie, remember?" she asked Lumi.

Lumi's heart sank. It was true. She hadn't wanted to focus on the bottom line and hoped things would get better after the winter. But with what Rafelina was telling her, even if they did, it wasn't going to be enough.

"I'm sorry, hon, but unless a miracle happens in the next thirty days, you are going to have to close Caraluna by the end of the year."

Lumi sank back into the couch. She no longer had a desire to talk. "Hey, let me call you back a little later, Rafi," she said.

"Lumi, are you okay? I know what this means to you, and—"

"Yup, I'm okay, talk to you soon!" she said, pressing the "end call" button as fast as she could.

The box of cream puffs slipped from the couch and landed on the hardwood floor with a thud, and she didn't notice. All she could hear was her mother Inés's voice in her head saying, *Following dreams is what stupid people do. And you know what they end up with? Nothing.* Lumi had heard that so many times . . . and choosing another reality for herself hadn't prevented her from ending up where she was now.

Her dream was dying. All the nights of hard work. The meticulous planning. The flourishes of creativity that came straight from her heart. Her small but devoted base of regulars, who came back time after time to be delighted and find new favorite meals. How would she face them and tell them she was no longer going to be able to share her offerings? Her throat felt like it was growing thicker, slowly closing. And what would she tell her staff?

She crumpled onto her burgundy couch. This next catering job had to go well. Caraluna needed it to. She needed it to.

4

LUMI

Lumi gazed out over the Hudson, the twinkling lights on the other side of the river distracting her from her monumental headache. From the burned flan to the beef in the ropa vieja that refused to soften, she had never catered a wedding where so many things had gone wrong. Just when she needed them to go right more than ever.

Of course it had to happen at the wedding of the most influential clients she'd ever had, famed violinist Oscar Rosario and renowned ballet dancer Carolina Urbaez. Hundreds of New York restaurateurs had coveted the gig, and yet it had gone to her because she was the only one Carolina trusted to pull off a perfect Dominican cake. At least that had gone right.

She sidled up to the bar and gave a nod to the bespectacled bartender, who acknowledged her with a small wave.

"I'll have a whiskey sour and a shot of Brugal," she said, and allowed her tired body to sink onto the cushioned seat. She stared down at the mirrored countertop, her amber skin and impeccably outlined brown eyes staring back at her. She had made peace with her long face a while back, but the counter mirror stretched it to almost comical proportions. Good. She could use a laugh the way things were going.

"Had a hard day?" a husky male voice said too close to her ear.

"Jesus Christ!" she said. "I didn't see . . ." Her voice trailed off as she came face-to-face with the most striking man she'd ever seen. The shock of crimson hair that fell onto his forehead cast broad shadows over his brow. His eyes were a deep brown, and even his eyebrows were a bright shade of red. His eyelashes were red too and longer than she would have expected a man's to be. A smattering of freckles dusted his nose and cheeks. She knew she'd seen him before somewhere, but she couldn't place him.

"Y-yes, you could say that," Lumi said, willing herself to stop ogling his square jaw and train her eyes on her drink, which the bartender had just set down on the gleaming countertop. She took a sip, feeling the stranger following her every move, and fixed her gaze on her glass until she felt him focus back on his own drink. A sideways squint revealed it was a bourbon on the rocks. A tiny metal fishhook caught her eye, and she noticed it was fixed to a black leather cord around his wrist.

He took a swig and, after a moment, began to speak. "I can't believe I lost the gig to this caterer. Those beef strips were so overcooked I could have tied shoes with them," he said, shaking his head.

Her shoulders dropped and she willed herself not to reply. So much for setting a trend.

"Honestly, I don't know why my friend Oscar would rather

have one of these artsy small-time caterers do his wedding than the preeminent French restaurant in Manhattan," he said with a snort.

Lumi felt heat rising around her collarbone, and she took another sip of her drink before turning to him. "And what, you think you could have done better?" she asked.

The dinner may not have been perfect, but it was far better than most. Only a delicate palate would've been able to detect the errors after her labored fixes, and no matter how pouty his bottom lip, she did not trust this man's palate. A faint aroma of wood and vanilla emanated from his person, and she fought the urge to fan it away with her hand.

"Think?" he asked. "I'm certain of it." His face was hard with smug assurance. "I could whip a horse with those beef strips."

She looked at him askance. "Well, I'm sorry, but I don't serve beef that looks like it could be a prop in a horror film."

The stranger studied her for a moment, his face neutral, and then raised his hand to cover his mouth. "Oh, my God. It's you," he whispered.

She pressed her jaws together.

"My stupid mouth." He flashed her an incandescent smile.

Her heart slowed its angered rhythm as her eyes met his . . . until she remembered his rude comments. She pushed her chair back and slapped a few bills on the counter.

An expression of alarm flashed over the stranger's features. "Wait! I didn't get your name."

Lumi narrowed her eyes. "Just ask for the caterer, you know, the one whose beef strips are used in horse training."

She rushed down the hall that led from the bar to the

ballroom, which was decorated with white roses and glittering mercury spheres. She grabbed the handle to the kitchen door and pulled it open, then tugged on her white coat and chef's hat as fast as she could. Her goal for the evening had been to make sure that the Rosario-Urbaez wedding went off without a hitch, but now she had a new goal: complete all the tasks without leaving the kitchen, so she never had to run into that man again.

On the kitchen counter, a chrome tray of dulce de leche tarts fresh from the oven was giving off feathery plumes of smoke. Lumi buried her head in her hands for a split second before raising it up to yell at her pastry chef.

"Holy . . . seriously, Brayden? Again?"

Brayden hung his head, his sandy bangs falling forward onto his sallow forehead. "I'm sorry, Chef, I just—"

Lumi grabbed the tray of scorched pastries in front of him and flung them into the trash. The sous chef and line cook suddenly found the pears they were chopping fascinating.

"It doesn't matter now. Let's just serve the wedding cake and poached pears and keep it moving," she said.

Brayden nodded and opened a new bag of sugar. As he shuffled off to the pantry, Lumi noticed a single tart had been saved from the garbage. She speared it with her pinkie, rubbing the dab of sugared cream onto her tongue. No sooner had she tasted it than a sinking feeling started to grow in her chest.

She wiped her pinkie on a clean patch of her grosgrain apron and felt her chest grow heavy. She could tell that something else was troubling Brayden besides the tarts. He lumbered back, a case of condensed milk cans in tow, and she sighed when she noticed him avoiding eye contact with her.

"Brayden," she began, "I apologize for throwing away your tarts."

Brayden gave a noncommittal shrug with his gangly shoulders. If Lumi remembered correctly, he was twenty-six, but could easily be mistaken for a teenager.

"It's okay, Chef. You were right. They were burned."

"You can leave early for the night if you'd like. I'm certain Magda, the event staff, and I can handle the rest of this job."

Brayden's eyes widened, and she tried her best to fashion her lips into an encouraging smile. He nodded slowly, still unsure, but Lumi could see a glimmer in his eyes. It was a crisp November evening, and she was sure he would rather be rehearsing with his band, the Puggles, than holed up in the kitchen baking desserts.

"Well . . . if you insist, Chef! The Puggles are rehearsing tonight, and my allergies are acting up, anyway." He fetched his leather jacket, and the glossy double doors of the kitchen swung shut behind him before Lumi or the staff could say goodbye.

"Okay, then," she muttered under her breath, and began drizzling the poached pears with guava syrup.

Her cell phone rang from within her purse. Turning down the heat on the boiling syrup and peeling off her gloves, she skipped over to check her messages. Her face twisted in dismay.

THOM: Hey babe, what's going on? I haven't heard from you since our second date and I was hoping this next one would be special! Send me a text when you get a chance. Kisses.

Lumi considered this for a moment, then tossed her phone back in her purse, message unanswered. She'd more than learned that lesson with Colton.

Lumi eased herself into her claw-footed tub. The water was hot, almost hot enough to boil a chicken. She started by dipping her toes in, then slid in her curvy, tanned legs, and finally allowed her entire body to sink into the waiting water.

"Ahh," she sighed in appreciation as the aroma of her gardenia-lime bubble bath reached her nose.

She leaned all the way back in the tub, resting her curly-haired head on the inflatable bath pillow she had pinioned with suction cups to the side of the bath. Her espresso-colored curls were twisted on top of her head, a tortoiseshell enamel hair clip holding them in place. Before she could sink farther into the depths of the bath, she paused. Something was missing.

Lumi glanced to the right. She'd left her bottle of cabernet and wineglass on her vanity table a few steps away.

"Damn it!" she muttered, annoyed at having to get out of the heavenly bath, even if it was to retrieve something that would only make it more blissful. She pushed against the smooth sides of the tub and rose, snatched the bottle and empty glass, and just as quickly dropped back into the water once she had them securely in hand.

She poured herself a glass and rested the bottle next to the tub, then settled back onto her bath pillow. As the warmth of the water washed over her skin, she allowed herself to get lost in thought, the lavender walls growing fuzzy in front of her. It was the perfect end to a hectic day of catering.

Lumi thought back on all the bride's demands, some of which bordered on insane. Carolina wanted the tuna tartare "three-fourths well done," whatever that meant, and had asked for a tiny wire swan on a toothpick to be inserted into each offering on the dessert plate. Thank God she had been none the wiser about the burned tarts and had even complimented the beef.

Unlike that man at the bar.

Who was that guy? Her hackles began to rise as she remembered his smile and then his words. Smug. Sexy. And he knew it. She could only hope never to run into him again.

The only thing mitigating her agita from working on this wedding was the $30,000 check making itself cozy in her bank account. If only business picked up in December, she could just scrape through, and in the New Year, she would add her bakery. If not . . . She shuddered and took a lingering sip from her goblet, pushing the remaining thoughts out of her mind. Everything could be dealt with tomorrow. For now, there was only her, her bath, and her wine.

5

JULIEN

Of all the ways to be lost at sea, being lost in a sea of blankets was Julien Dax's favorite. He stretched and flexed from the tips of his fingers overhead to his toes and eyed his bedside alarm clock. "Mon Dieu," he muttered under his breath. It was four in the morning. He shook his head, eyes still heavy from sleep. The glow radiating from around the outline of his bathroom door was the only light in the apartment.

He did not quite remember how he'd reached his bed, but he whistled a sigh of relief to see there was no one else in it, even as he shrugged off his slight disappointment. He'd had some wild dreams, no doubt assisted by the stellar libations from the Rosario-Urbaez wedding. Even the Manhattan, a drink he usually consumed under duress, such as the lack of other drinks, had been palatable.

What he did remember was the dark-haired chef at the bar, all curves and sass. A lazy smile spread across his face. He truly had not suspected she was the caterer. Although something about the fire crackling in her eyes when he teased her wiped away any regret he had over doing so. He would have liked to talk with her a little longer—see if that rapid-fire tongue held any other biting remarks.

Before he could sink into fantasy, Julien tore the navy tartan blankets away from his body and sprang from the bed. There was too much to be done to waste time lounging. And now that Simon, his sous chef, was gone, he needed to arrive at DAX even earlier than usual to get things in order.

He felt a pang of regret as he recalled Simon slamming the door of the kitchen. Maybe Simon hadn't been so wrong to side with that patron. Maybe Julien had overreacted. Asking for ketchup for the finest filet mignon in the city was a sin, but perhaps he didn't have to throw the man out. And then tell Simon to eat shit.

But it was too late. Simon was a proud French chef who had to be halfway back to Paris already. He would manage. DAX was Julien's restaurant, after all. He ambled into the bathroom, and as his eyes adjusted to the increase in light, his reflection came into focus before him in the mirror. A shadow of scarlet stubble had already grown over the planes of his cheeks and chin.

He poured some shaving cream and smoothed it between his square hands, the woodsy scent waking him up further as he spread it over his face. The lather melted away beneath the glistening blade, and his thoughts reverted to his restaurant. Perhaps he would start placing a few ads and, with luck, find a fine candidate before the New Year. Or at least a skilled one who could put up with his tyranny. He wouldn't have gotten to the top if he hadn't always demanded the best.

He wiped the remnants of the shaving cream off with a warm towel and went to the kitchen, making sure to stick to his rule of never going to DAX hungry. It messed with his focus. He pulled eggs from the fridge, and when the eggs hit the frying pan, they sizzled, diffusing their aroma throughout the apartment. There was some cretons pâté in the fridge that he made from Maman's recipe, but now was not the time for nostalgia. Smoked salmon covered toast, and eggs topped salmon. Bless the ease of acquiring good smoked salmon in Manhattan.

The hollandaise was exactly where he left it, thank Berta for that. He spooned it over the eggs and bit into the toast ensemble with an appreciative groan. The flavor balance was so glorious, it was almost a shame to eat it alone. It was one of those moments when he was struck with longing, wishing he had someone to cook for.

"Shut up. You have three thousand people a week to cook for," he said, interrupting his thoughts.

He focused his attention on his breakfast again. If his staff could cook this well, he would serve breakfast at DAX. But as it was, he had enough to worry about. He stuck his hand in the drawer and pulled out a fistful of lemon and ginger chews. His emergency palate cleansers went wherever he went.

Breakfast in belly, he was ready to begin the day and confront whatever challenges came his way.

6

LUMI

The most important discovery Lumi had made today was that the burgundy velour fabric of her couch had a delicate pointelle pattern invisible to the eye unless your face was pressed flush up against it.

She was also astounded by the number of split ends she had. It was outrageous. She riffled through the ends of her ponytail, turning it from side to side, growing frustrated when she couldn't find any more of them. Wasn't there anything left that needed fixing?

It had been four weeks since she'd shuttered Caraluna. Four weeks that seemed to stretch on into the abyss. Her daily schedule had become a cycle of avoiding breakfast, sinking into the couch, daring herself not to look at the bills that remained from Caraluna, skipping lunch, watching Netflix, and falling asleep in place on the couch.

And then there were the boxes. Oh, the boxes. Stacked into haphazard piles leaning toward her front door, as if they couldn't decide whether they were staying or going. Two cheerful hand-painted earthenware bowls taunted her every time she opened the lid to unpack them. They were a reminder of the kitchen accoutrements that came in every shade of violet that she didn't want to see.

For the first time in five years, she had been tempted to call Colton. In some ways, it felt like he was the only one who could fully grasp the magnitude of her downfall. He was the one who had refilled her coffee at two o'clock in the morning when she was feverishly scratching out her business plan and, later, rewriting it for the twenty-seventh time. The one who had driven her to warehouses in Long Island City to find the best wholesale spices.

Sometimes, when she allowed herself, she could recall the feel of him leaning over her shoulder, one of his black curls brushing her cheek; see his easy, unfettered smile. But then the thought of the ballerina answering his phone and having to ask her if Colton Peralta was there burst that bubble of desire. Lumi wondered if they were still together after all this time. The truth was that she didn't want to know if they were.

It was the first time in Lumi's life that she had ever given herself the berth to simply do nothing. But deep down, she knew she needed it. She needed this time, to learn the intricacies of her couch, to hunt down split ends, to practice a rant at Colton's ballerina (only to end up smothering her phone with a pillow), and to do anything else that would keep her from thinking about what a spectacular bust Caraluna had been.

One comfort to Lumi was that all her staff members had found new jobs since the closing. Even better, Magda and Brayden had gotten positions at better paying, more prestigious establishments. They had called Lumi several times, and she loved hearing from them, but when they offered to visit, she found ways to politely decline.

She had a sinking feeling she knew what they'd say about her appearance upon seeing her. They'd notice that the one thing that Lumi had being doing the least of was eating. Her clothes hung on her, and her high cheekbones were beginning to create an almost ghoulish contrast with her hollowing cheeks. She might have been being unkind to herself, but she didn't want to taste, not for a while.

She hadn't talked to Inés since New Year's Day. She just wasn't ready to hear her say "I told you so." Especially when the message Inés had given her time and again about dreams and dreamers was playing out before her. She stared at the door and conjured in her mind's eye a holographic Inés milling around her apartment, clucking her tongue at the piles of bills, shaking her head at her pathetic daughter burrowing into the couch.

The image roiled her insides, and suddenly she could no longer stand to be where she was.

"This is bullshit!" she said aloud. "There has to be something I can do."

She pushed herself off the couch and went straight to her refrigerator.

"Habichuelas con dulce for sale!" Lumi yelled as loudly as she could. The January weather had rendered her street desolate, the sidewalks ashy from the dustings of salt they had received to ward off the ice. Even so, she had made a few sales of the sweet cream of beans she'd whipped up in her kitchen. As a result, fifty dollars in small bills lined the pocket of her peacoat.

She stirred the enormous orange cooler she had snapped up at the dollar store. The wooden spoon dipped down into the viscous sienna-colored mix, and she absentmindedly watched the swirls it made as if another hand were guiding them. After two hours out in the blistering twenty-degree weather, it took much effort to keep up her spirits.

Men and women hurried down the street, bundled up, rushing to escape from the biting cold. *Two more hours*, she told herself as she blew warm breath into her cupped, gloved fingers.

If she had made fifty dollars in only two hours, perhaps with two more she could go grocery shopping for the week.

She spooned some beans for herself into a small plastic cup and wrapped her fingers around it the best she could despite the encroaching frost. Inhaling the tantalizing vapors, she raised it to her lips and sipped. Immediately the flavors of evaporated milk, red beans, vanilla, and cloves washed over her tongue, and the heat of the liquid warmed her chest.

A portly figure in a knee-length black puffer jacket turned the corner of Broadway and began to approach, sights clearly set on Lumi's apartment building. When the person came to a full stop in front of her table, Lumi saw that it was not just another customer.

"Lumi?" Jenny's shocked voice emerged as a muffled croak from under her scarf.

"Oh, hey, Jenn!" Lumi replied as casually as she could.

Reluctantly, Jenny pulled her hands out of her pockets and yanked down the scarf, exposing her ruddy cheeks to the frost. Strands of her blond hair fell over her forehead, and she shoved them back into place with her fingers.

"It's freaking freezing out here, what are you doing?" she asked, her tone incredulous.

"Just making some money," Lumi said, her gaze trained on the cooler.

Jenny eyed the small stand, and her face fell just a fraction. "I see. Well, can we go upstairs for a little bit? I'm sure you could use some time to warm up."

Lumi looked up and down the street. She didn't want to miss any customers, but if she was being honest with herself, she could barely feel her toes anymore.

"Okay. Let's go in," she said, hoisting up her steaming cooler while Jenny folded the table.

Lumi cringed as she undid the lock on her door and removed her peacoat. She already knew what Jenny was going to say.

"Jesus! Lumi, are you starving yourself?" Jenny gasped as she took in her friend's now-spindly frame.

Lumi gave her a short hug and stepped back just as quickly. "No, of course not, Jenn," she fibbed.

Jenny's hazel eyes were frantic with worry. "You must have lost twenty pounds since I saw you last!" she said. "I'm going to have to bring you to work with me!"

Lumi tried to fake a laugh. Jenny had become a receptionist at the French Culinary Institute while they were both students there, and shortly after graduation she had moved to the alumni relations department, where she was now junior director.

Jenny marched over to Lumi's refrigerator and swung open the door. She covered her eyes with her hand after she saw the cartons of coconut water and two or three stray grapes that were the sole denizens of that space. After ten years of friendship, she knew that food was everything to Lumi.

"Oh . . . honey." She sighed, turning to Lumi and looping her arm around her. "This is bad."

It had been years since Lumi had cried in front of anybody, but now, after being alone with her grief for so long, the sobs just spilled out. The women sank onto the couch, and she let Jenny hold her until the tumult subsided and she could speak. She leaned her curly head on Jenny's round shoulder.

"I don't know what I'm going to do," she whispered, waving in the direction of her growing stack of bills.

Jenny patted her arm and passed her some tissues from her purse, a pained look on her face. Jenny had been following Lumi's career trajectory since the inception of her idea for Caraluna; she had been witness to many of the coffee-fueled all-nighters it took Lumi to get her place open. Lumi, Jenny, and all their culinary classmates knew the NYC restaurant business was rough, and Lumi was certain that was why Jenny had opted for a desk job at the institute while she worked on her cupcake catering business after hours. But Jenny had always voiced her support as well as her hope that Lumi's eclectic flair and unbreakable work ethic would carry her through.

"Hey, why don't we go down to Eataly to get a cappuccino and a cannoli?" Jenny asked.

Lumi shook her head and sighed. "Thanks, hon," she said, "but I don't feel like going anywhere."

She cringed as Jenny appraised the empty packages of saltines on the floor and the empty bottle of lavender body wash that lay just shy of the garbage bin.

"Well, at least you're showering, lady," Jenny said.

Lumi chuckled mirthlessly. "I love that about you, Jenn . . . always focusing on the positive."

Jenny shrugged with an apologetic smile. "So, what's next?" she asked.

Lumi stared blankly at the coffee table. "I don't know." She exhaled. "But I am going to have to figure out something soon. My savings have all but run out."

Jenny frowned and reached out to squeeze Lumi's shoulder. "I have an idea. But first, we're going on a little field trip," she said.

"But what about my habichuela stand?" Lumi asked.

"We'll be back with enough time for you to catch the evening crowd, if there is one in this godforsaken weather," Jenny said.

"Where are we going?"

Jenny winked at her. "To Fairway, to get some duck eggs, pancake batter, and wild boar bacon. Well, at least wild boar bacon for you. I'll get turkey bacon for myself. I am trying to keep kosher these days. But anyway! This is about you. It's high time you had a good meal."

The last carton of coconut water landed in the trash can with a bang. Jenny's meal of fried duck eggs, truffle hollandaise, and pancakes with boar bacon had been just the thing to lift Lumi's spirits and give her the energy to get her life in order.

She thought back on their afternoon together and decided to call Jenny just to say thanks. She was glad it had been Jenny and not Rafelina, because Rafi probably would have beaten her with a shoe until she came back to her senses.

Jenny answered on the second ring. "Lumi!" she said. "Perfect timing. I am just scrolling through the job postings on the alumni site, and I found something that doesn't sound all that bad."

"Oh," said Lumi. She hadn't expected the job search to start this quickly. She knew her friend was simply trying to be helpful, though, and after tasting her care and affection and feeling uplifted by it, she couldn't let her down. "Oh, yeah?" she asked, feigning interest. "What's the position?"

Jenny hummed to herself as she moved her cursor down the page. "Sous chef at DAX on Forty-Second Street," she answered calmly.

Lumi furrowed her brow. "DAX . . ." she thought aloud.

"Yup," Jenny said. "As in Julien Dax, the chef who has been written up on Page Six for punching a food critic in the face and kicking a patron out of his restaurant for asking for ketchup to put on his cooking." She snickered.

Lumi sighed. "Sounds charming."

"I know what you mean. But he's paying thirty dollars an hour for a sous chef. Not bad at all," Jenny said.

Lumi bit her tongue.

"Plus," Jenny continued, "it's all traditional French cooking. Same stuff we learned in school. You wouldn't have to learn anything too elaborate to get started."

Lumi's shoulders drooped the slightest bit. "I would like to learn something elaborate."

"I hear you, honey, but are we really in the position to pick and choose right now?"

The air whooshed out of Lumi's lungs, making her feel deflated. But she knew Jenny was right. "I guess not. So, tell me, what would I need to do?"

"That's the spirit. There's an email address here. Send me your résumé and I'll forward it to them so it is coming from the French Culinary Institute alumni office," said Jenny.

Lumi exhaled. "Thank you, Jenny. You're a lifesaver. I don't know how to repay you," she said.

Jenny clucked her tongue. "I'm not doing anything you wouldn't do for me! And if you insist, you can make me some of your famous fish balls when things are more settled."

Lumi grinned. "Fish balls? It's a deal," she said. Lumi

could hear the sunshine edging back into her voice. "I'll get on it right away."

She brushed the saltine crumbs off her laptop and flipped it open, the screen bright as it whirred to life.

LUMI'S FAMOUS FISH BALLS
Serves 2 (makes about 8 fish balls)

1 pound ground white fish
½ cup bread crumbs
¼ cup parsley, finely chopped
½ teaspoon ground cilantro
¼ teaspoon ground ginger
2 cloves garlic, finely chopped
1 egg white, lightly beaten
kosher salt, to taste
freshly ground black pepper, to taste
frying oil of choice (canola and avocado
   are two of many options)

Stir together the fish, bread crumbs, parsley, cilantro, ginger, garlic, egg white, and salt and pepper in a bowl. Form into quarter-sized balls and chill.

Heat the oil in a saucepan over medium-high heat. Add the fish balls and brown on all sides. Lower the heat and cook for 3-4 minutes on each side. Let cool and serve.

7

LUMI

The elevator came to a smooth stop on the fifth floor, and a lead-footed Lumi dragged herself out into the chrome hallway. Jenny had told her to look for suite one.

The immense revolving door to suite one was labeled with a small, square silver plaque. With a shrug, Lumi pushed the revolving glass panel. Before she even saw another person, she heard the tapping of gel-lacquered fingernails on a desktop.

On the other side of the door, the owner of the nails came into view. She was fixated on her laptop screen and did not look up when Lumi entered. The woman was not unattractive, but Lumi wouldn't have called her beautiful either. She had golden skin and hawkish features that looked as if they had been filed to a point. Her honey-blond hair with black roots hung pin-straight down to the desk. Even her eye makeup was drawn into pointed lines at the corners of her eyes.

Standing in front of her desk, Lumi cleared her throat. "Hi," she began.

The receptionist jumped back, startled. She glanced up and down Lumi's figure, her eyes somewhat apprehensive until they completed their course, at which time they became pointed again. "Yes?" she asked.

Lumi regarded her with curiosity. She hoped that the woman didn't double as a security guard; with her attention level, aspiring miscreants would have no problem breaking in.

"Yes. I have an interview at noon with Julien Dax."

A look of recognition spread across the younger woman's face without belying any interest. "Have a seat, please. I'll let you know when Mr. Dax is ready," she said.

Lumi nodded and perched on one of the white leather modular mini-couches that lined the reception area. The secretary typed furiously on her laptop for a moment, and then they both sat in silence. Taking advantage of the downtime, Lumi began responding to Magda's and Brayden's email inquiries on how she had been holding up and updates on the Puggles' tour schedule, when the receptionist interrupted her to let her know Mr. Dax was ready and motioned toward the main office.

Lumi closed the office door behind herself and came face-to-face with the most strangely striking human she had ever met. He was at least a head taller than her, taller than she had remembered—but wait, he had been sitting. She froze before she could gain control of her reaction, and all she could do was watch as a smile of recognition and something else—amusement?—spread across the stranger's face.

"You!" he said.

"You," she groaned under her breath. Her reaction was not

lost on him, and as he watched her the corners of his mouth began to play upward.

"Please," he said gently, as if she were a startled deer and the slightest snap of a twig would send her barreling away, "have a seat."

Lumi gave him a curt nod and sat. She glanced around the office, aware she was being observed. The office was painted white, and it was spotless. If she had dropped an empanada on the floor, she would have had no qualms about picking it up and eating it, even after the five-second rule had elapsed. The furniture was minimalist, Zen, and it was all constructed from the same brushed metal, with square white leather cushions on the seats of the couch and chairs. She turned her gaze back to Julien. His eyes had not left her for a second.

And then they did, to peer down at her résumé before him. "So, Ms. Santana," he began, "what brings you here today?"

Lumi resisted the urge to roll her eyes. Wasn't the answer obvious?

"I'm applying for the job of sous chef, Mr. Dax," she said, looking down at the desk.

"Mm," he acknowledged. "But it says here that you were executive chef and owner at Caraluna in Inwood."

She glared at him. "Yep."

Julien studied her some more. "So, what happened? Burned the beef one time too many?"

Lumi felt bile rising in her throat. She cleared her throat. "Um, we closed in December and I need to get started somewhere as soon as possible," she said.

His thumb and forefinger caressed his square chin. The

same fishhook bracelet from the last time she had seen him glinted under the fluorescent office lighting.

"Well, I'm sorry to hear that," he said. "That you closed . . . not that you're looking to get started as soon as possible."

"I got that."

Julien leveled his gaze, his brow furrowing. "So, why DAX?" he asked.

Lumi shot him a look. "Do you always start with the easy questions?" she asked, a tiny, wry smile curving the corners of her lips.

Julien exhaled and sat back in his chair. "Sorry, I don't mean to grill you," he said with a grin.

"Ha-ha," she said. Lumi couldn't hold the eye roll any longer. Julien broke into a wide, unrestrained smile for the first time since she came in. She felt something do a flip in her belly.

"Please, go on," he said in a measured voice.

Lumi frowned. She hadn't thought of what her answer would be to this question if she were to be asked it in the interview. "Well, I can see you guys need a little color around here!" she joked.

Julien glanced around his office. "Not too much color, though," he replied. "I run a tight ship, Ms. Santana. We do traditional French fare with a little flair. But not too much flair."

He studied her reaction. Lumi smiled and nodded.

"And all recipes in the DAX kitchen must be memorized. Any chef who does not know the classics by heart does not belong here."

"That's fine," she said. She knew the classics by heart,

even if they bored her to death. "So, um, who's your chef de cuisine now? I mean, you must be busy managing this place."

"Oh," he said, straightening his posture. "It's still me."

"Right," Lumi answered.

"Yes," he added, "can't trust anyone with my baby . . . just yet."

His face shone with pride, and Lumi felt her stomach sink a little.

There was a moment of awkward silence as he looked at Lumi and she stared out the window.

"Okay! That's all," he said.

She gaped at him. "That's all?"

He nodded. "Yes, I've heard enough. Thank you," he said.

She pressed her lips together before her face could falter.

"Th-thank you," she said, and made a beeline for the door.

Lumi fluffed her scarf as she rode the elevator down to release the heat that was rising under her collar. *That's all?* What a waste of time. In all of her dreams and most carefully designed plans for Caraluna, there had never been a scene of her pounding the pavement after it had failed. If she had known Julien Dax was the man from the wedding, she never would have scheduled the interview. A surprise job interview with the seventh-grade teacher whose desk she'd glued a plastic spider to would have gone better.

Now what would she do? she pondered as she descended to the subway platform and rode the train uptown. There was always her habichuela stand, and she could send her résumé to every restaurant in the vicinity.

The train roared out from underground onto the rickety raised tracks, and a submissive *ding* sounded on her phone as service was restored. Her jaw fell open when she read the message.

MS. SANTANA. Please report for first day of work on Thursday, 2/1. Thank you, DAX Enterprises.

She stared at it as if it were written on self-destructing paper and would wisp into colorless smoke at any second.

8

JULIEN

Framed in the doorway of his office, Julien watched as Lumi headed for the elevator. She seemed to drift off, floating farther and farther away from him, until Esme, his secretary, cleared her throat loudly.

"How'd it go?" she asked.

He knew the polite thing would be to look at her as she spoke, but he was rooted in place, unable to turn away from the elevator. "Good," he said.

"Did you still want to grab a coffee?" she asked.

"Uh, you know what, Esme? I'm going to take my coffee at my desk so I can finish looking over these hiring papers," Julien said.

"S-sure," she replied, and went back to the typing at hand.

He went back in his office and sat, and the words on his computer screen blurred into a single swath of gray. He was going to need something stronger than coffee. Julien pushed his chair back and put his computer to sleep.

"Send all calls to voice mail, please," he said to Esme as

he walked out the door, and punched the elevator buttons as fast as he could. There was a little bar on Fiftieth Street where he could sit down for a quick drink . . . something to calm the faint thrumming in his veins and help him refocus.

A brisk walk brought him to the establishment, whose wrought-iron fence protected the café tables and chairs. He strode to the bar and ordered an old-fashioned, thanking the bartender with a nod and settling onto a barstool. He let out a slow exhale as his body relaxed into the seat.

Just as he was about to take a sip, a melodious voice sounded from behind him. "Julien! I didn't think I'd find you here," the voice said.

He groaned inwardly. He would recognize that voice anywhere. He was in the mood to be left alone, and there was no way the owner of that voice was leaving him alone.

"Hello, Shayla," he said as he forced himself to turn around.

A burgundy-haired woman with round glasses, a camel-colored coat, and a sparkling diamond ring stood before him. She smiled as they exchanged a quick air-kiss.

"Still drinking old-fashioneds, huh? How have you been?" she asked, her green eyes zeroing in on him.

"Quite well, thank you. And yourself?" he asked.

"Never better," she replied, brushing her bangs off her forehead with the hand that bore the dazzling gem.

"Congratulations," he said, the light refracting off the diamond catching his eye.

She giggled out loud as if she couldn't believe he noticed. "Oh, thank you, Julien! We met about eight months after you and I, you know, ended it, and we got married a year later. It's been three years now."

Julien stifled a yawn. "How wonderful. Happy for you, Shay."

She bowed her head in faux humility, and he knew what the next question would be.

"How about you?" she asked. "Still sowing your wild oats?"

He waved her off. "I was never sowing my wild oats, Shayla. I just—"

It was her turn to wave. "Yeah, I know. We don't need to have this conversation again. The first time was enough."

He took a swig of his drink.

"I just . . . hoped I would be the one to make you want to change that, Julien. But now I'm sure that that woman doesn't exist," she said.

Julien downed the remainder of the drink in one gulp. He saw no need to have the conversation again either.

"I'm sure you did. It was nice seeing you, Shayla," he said. "Give my regards to the lucky man." He set the glass down on the bar, and with a quick bow of his head in Shayla's direction, he hurried back onto Broadway.

9

LUMI

On Thursday of that week, Lumi stood before her mirror, tucking the stray hairs into the French braid she had styled her mane into to keep it out of her face. She liked the texture her tight curls gave the style, although she knew the crown would be mussed by her chef's hat.

Later that day, Lumi rang the bell at the service door of DAX. She had ridden up to the fifth floor in the service elevator, which was surprisingly spotless, considering the boxes of produce, fish, and meat that she was certain took the same elevator ride every day. After waiting for several moments, she was about to start knocking when the door opened and a round-faced smiling woman with an olive complexion and husky build stood before her. Lumi estimated that the woman was in her early fifties.

"Well, hello, Ms. Santana, and welcome to DAX! I'm Gloria. I'm the pastry chef here," she said in a hearty voice with a thick Brooklyn accent.

"Pleased to meet you, Gloria," she replied.

"I'll be helping you get set up. Julien has a molecular gastronomy conference in Long Island City tonight and will be in later. Shouldn't be hard—he mentioned you had your own restaurant before?"

Lumi winced and nodded. "Mm-hmm."

Gloria leaned forward as if she was about to comfort her with a hug, then seemed to think better of it and straightened up.

"Well! We'll have to get you a key card by the end of the day. Come, come," Gloria said, waving her toward a row of lockers just off the service entrance, her cropped platinum curls bouncing. "Here is yours," she said, pointing to the open locker in the row.

Lumi peeled off her purple peacoat and hung it inside. Then Gloria gestured for Lumi to follow her into the kitchen, and she did.

It was nothing like her cozy galley back at Caraluna. Just like Julien's office, it was painted white, and all the appliances were either white or brushed metal. There was a massive island in the middle of the kitchen with dozens of drawers and cabinets underneath, and it was flanked on both sides by two Sub-Zero refrigerators. Lumi's eyes followed the length of the space all the way down to the opposite end, where she could see the outline of a heavy oak door that looked to be a wine closet. She made a mental note to check it out later.

Gloria stopped in front of a metal chair next to the kitchen island, where a crisp white jacket and hat were waiting.

"These are for you, hon, and that's your workstation," she said, pointing to a corner of the island where a wooden cutting board and knife block sat.

"Thank you," Lumi said.

Gloria clasped her hands together in prayer position and nodded. "We aim to please here, Ms. Santana, that you will learn," she replied, widening her eyes and pursing her lips into a comical expression.

Lumi laughed, wondering what she meant by the face she made but not daring to ask. "Please, call me Iluminada. Or Lumi," she responded.

Gloria nodded as she pulled stitched sacks of flour out of the pantry for the phyllo dough and beignets. "Well, Lumi, I hope you will feel at home with us here at DAX. We are like a family . . . one with a grumpy father!" She laughed. "But don't let Julien scare you. His bark is all he has, no bite there . . . most of the time," she quickly added, no doubt realizing Lumi would have read the papers. "Anyway, behind all that there's a heart of golden butter," she said. She grinned as she completed her speech.

A heart of golden butter? Lumi thought. That sounded like a gateway to health problems.

Gloria began to measure the dry ingredients and Lumi felt her attention drift away. She could tell Gloria was friendly but not one for small talk. Just as well . . . neither was she.

Looking to get started, she glanced over the specials board for the night: phyllo duck, ratatouille, cucumber dill salad, and raspberry beignets with crème fraîche. She perused the kitchen island and found a deep earthenware dish, bringing it to the station that had been set up for her. She paced over to the refrigerator marked PRODUCE with cursive black letter magnets and pulled out the eggplant, zucchini, and other ingredients she would need to get started. She also found a round, crisp green apple. She picked it up and rolled it from right to left in her hand. It could add some contrast to the flavor profile.

This was the way Lumi cooked at Caraluna: she started out with a basic recipe in mind and added several new ingredients for an eclectic taste. At DAX, every chef cooked from memory too, so how could she be wrong for not following the recipe? For a moment, she wondered if it was the best idea. After all, DAX was much more staid. But then she shrugged. People were coming to DAX for a unique dining experience. If they wanted plain French cuisine with no pizzazz, they would have gone elsewhere. A little touch of tart would make their dinner more memorable, she was sure of it.

She laid the vegetables and apple on her wooden cutting board. First, she sliced the eggplant in thin rounds. Then the zucchini, onion, peppers, and, finally, the apple. She stood the slices up and packed the dish as full as she could.

The oven was warm and waiting. The phyllo duck that Gloria had prepared was already inside being broiled to golden crispness. Lumi popped the dish in the oven and set a small timer she found in one of the drawers below her workstation.

One by one, she peeled and sliced the cucumbers for the salad. She checked her watch: it was 4:30 P.M. The ratatouille would be ready just before 5:00. She turned back toward the produce refrigerator to get the dill, and as she was pulling out a bundle of sprigs, the kitchen door swung open again.

In walked a man with caramel-hued straight hair slicked back in a pompadour, bronze skin, and an expression of smug self-assurance. He was dressed in a black crewneck sweater and fitted pin-striped pants, and his fingernails were painted gunmetal gray.

"Richard!" Gloria boomed.

He crossed the kitchen in two strides, and they exchanged an air-kiss.

"Hello, beautiful," he said.

Gloria nudged him in the ribs and cocked her head in Lumi's direction.

"Oh!" he exclaimed. "And who is this angel?"

Lumi gave him a small wave from her workstation.

"Don't be shy, reina!" he said.

He walked over, taking her by the hand, raising her arm, and rotating his wrist as if to twirl her around. She followed through the turn, a giggle barely escaping her throat, feeling her face flush.

"Welcome to DAX!" he said, bowing from the waist. "I am Richard Olivares, sommelier, at your service."

Lumi curtsied in response to him. "Iluminada Santana, new sous chef here."

He smiled. "Oh! See, Gloria, she knows how to play the game!"

Gloria rolled her eyes good-naturedly.

"Ruben!" he called to a portly man with deep brown skin setting up the grill.

The man walked over and extended his hand. "Nice to meet you, ma'am. Ruben Carr here."

Lumi returned his smile. "Iluminada Santana."

"Iluminada Santana . . . Are you Dominican?" Richard asked.

"Yes."

"Wepa! We taking over this kitchen," Richard said with a little whoop of glee at the end. "I'll leave you two to continue getting ready. We're going to be great friends, angel, I can tell.

I'm going to take you to SoulCycle class with me. And just entre tu y yo, if you ever need a little sip on the job—"

"Richard! You lost your damn mind?" Gloria asked.

"What, sweetheart? You know it can get stressful here. Well, be back in a few! Gotta make my selection for the night before that ginger ogre gets here." And in a flash, he ducked into the wine closet, and Ruben returned to the grill.

Lumi giggled under her breath at Richard's comment and, dill in hand, wandered back to her workstation. At 4:45, Fallon, Heather, and Timothy, the three waiters working Thursday night, arrived, hung up their jackets, and prepared for a night on the dining floor. Their greetings to Lumi were brief but cordial.

At 4:50, the oven timer rang with a shrill ding. Lumi put on the purple silicone gloves she had stowed in her purse and pulled the baking dish out of the oven. She grinned to herself as she set the dish on a hot pad and resolved to set aside squares for Richard and Gloria, so that they could be the first to try her avant-garde version of the time-honored favorite.

At 5:00 P.M. sharp, she heard Timothy say that the main door had been opened, and they had already filled one of the tables. Lumi peered out the round kitchen window. The dining room was even bigger than the kitchen, extending back as far as she could see. The walls were painted a demure cream, and the round tables were all cherrywood with pristine white tablecloths and a tiny lamp in the center of each.

At the table, a gray-haired couple who looked to be in their late fifties took off their coats and pulled out their chairs. The man wore a sharp navy-blue suit with a tiny white handkerchief tucked into the breast pocket, and the lady, a black wool turtleneck dress. Lumi thought of her motley crew of patrons with their multicolored hair and fabulous nut necklaces, then brushed the thought away with a sigh.

"It's no use," she whispered to herself. "You're here now. Focus."

Lumi scurried back to her station before the couple could spot her peeking at them and saw that Gloria had removed the duck from the oven and left it to cool. It was time for her to prepare the plates.

She rustled through the knife rack for a chef's knife. Though there were more than twenty knives, she knew that just like at Caraluna, she would end up using the same two knives, the paring knife and the chef's knife, over and over.

Grabbing two oranges from the fruit bowl, she laid them next to her cutting board and sliced them into rounds to plate with the phyllo duck. As she was cutting, Heather popped back into the kitchen, a rectangular brushed metal clipboard in hand.

"Listen up!" she said. "We have one beet and goat cheese salad to start, one order of phyllo duck, and one ratatouille."

"I'll make the salad so that you can plate the entrées, Lumi," Gloria said, and Lumi nodded in silent agreement. Using a spatula, Lumi shoveled out a portion of ratatouille, draining the excess sauce, and lowered it onto one of DAX's shiny, bone-colored entrée plates. She topped the portion with a dollop of goat cheese and positioned the plate at the waiting table near the door, where it would be picked up once the salad was finished. She brushed the dill cuttings off her workstation and brought her dishes to the sink.

Although there were dishwashers on staff, she enjoyed washing her own dishes. The warm water sluiced over her hands and relaxed her. It helped focus her mind on the next task. As she washed, she allowed her thoughts to roam to what she would do after her shift. Inwood Hill Liquors would be closed by the time she reached home, unfortunately. But if she wasn't mistaken, she still had a bottle of shiraz in the refrigerator from last weekend. There had been a new Marvel movie that she wanted to watch too.

She was so engrossed in her plans that she didn't notice when Heather stopped right next to her.

"Um, Ms. Lumi," Heather began, and Lumi jumped.

"Jesus. I'm sorry, I didn't even see you there," Lumi said.

Heather held back a smirk, pushing her heavy brown bangs out of her eyes. "Well, the diner at table one has a complaint," she said.

Lumi stopped in her tracks. "A complaint?" she asked incredulously.

Heather nodded, her expression belying a touch of amusement. "Um, yeah . . . he says he found some . . . apple? In his ratatouille."

Lumi frowned. "Well, yes, I put some apple in there. But a complaint?"

Heather nodded again.

"Does he know that this is a three-star restaurant?" Lumi asked.

Heather cocked her head to one side. "Um . . . I'm assuming so," she said, drawing the words out.

Lumi glanced toward the kitchen window, baffled. "I'll go out and talk to him," she said.

"Um, wait, no, you, like, really shouldn't do that," Heather said.

Just then, the door swung open and in came Fallon, bearing the offending plate. The ratatouille was untouched, except for three limp slices of green apple that had been fished out with a fork and laid one alongside the other on the left side of the entrée. Lumi frowned again.

"Lumi," Fallon said in her clear, strong voice, "this diner needs a new serving of ratatouille with no apple, stat." She held out the plate to her.

Lumi laid it on the countertop, grabbed a clean plate, and portioned out a new serving, using a minuscule pair of tongs to pull out all the apple slices before tidying up the remaining vegetables.

"Okay." She sighed, passing the new plate to Heather. "Send him my apologies," she added, "with some raspberry beignets on the house."

Heather received the plate and trudged laconically to the dining floor. Fallon rushed out after her to receive the next set of diners who had walked in.

Lumi eyed her creation. She knew what she had to do to keep the night from becoming a repeat of the same unsavory scene. Using the tiny tongs, she riffled through the layered dish and pulled out every apple slice she could find, laying them on a paper towel, and when she had gone over it three times, she grabbed the paper towel by the four corners and upended it into the trash.

She returned to the sink and continued washing her dishes. For the first time since she arrived, it dawned on her that Julien had not shown up.

"Just as well," she muttered to herself. It would be better if he didn't know about the apple debacle. The claim he made in the interview had been proven: DAX was not a place for improvisation.

DAX RATATOUILLE
Makes 4 servings

2 onions
4 tomatoes
1 eggplant
2 zucchini
1 yellow squash
1 red bell pepper
2 tablespoons olive oil
2 cups tomato puree
salt, to taste
freshly ground black pepper, to taste

Preheat the oven to 375 degrees Fahrenheit.

Slice all the vegetables into thin rounds and sprinkle with salt and pepper. Drizzle the olive oil into the bottom of a 13"x9" baking dish. Pour in the tomato puree, and lay the vegetable slices overlapping one another to fill the dish. Bake for 45 minutes.

For Lumi's version, add 1 green apple, sliced identical to the vegetables.

10

LUMI

The morning sun shone bright, casting warm rays onto Lumi's pillow. She stretched and yawned as she glanced at the violet chrome alarm clock: 6:30 A.M., and she was free until 3:00 P.M., at which point she would have to hop on the subway toward DAX. She cringed, thinking of the night before. Hopefully the other employees would be kind enough not to inform Julien of the events of her first turn in the kitchen.

Her plan had been to sleep late. But it seemed that no matter how many glasses of wine she drank or how steely her resolve, her body was set to awaken at or before 6:30 A.M. She pulled on her gray yoga leggings and a fleece hoodie, tied on her sneakers, and bounded out the door, downstairs, and along West 218th Street toward Inwood Hill Park.

The muscles in her thighs cried out as she marched up the hill. They seemed to still be asleep and found this awakening none too pleasant. But the rest of her was luxuriating in the dawning sunshine and crisp breeze as she went down the other side of the hill and turned into the park. She set off on her favorite jogging path, the one that took her down to the Hudson River and wound back through the flower fields.

Inwood Hill Park was the only one in New York that she knew of where wild echinacea grew, even in the winter. She ran the whole path with steady energy, and when she came to the end, she stopped at a little patch to pick some echinacea for the vase in her kitchen and to maybe use for tea. She didn't know much about herbalism besides what herbs to use in the kitchen, but she enjoyed the scent of echinacea and the smooth taste of the tea. Anything it did for her immune system was a bonus.

She leaned in to smell the flowers, and the aroma pervaded all her senses, taking her back to the very first time she had smelled echinacea.

"This is where you wanted to take me?" Inés asked in disbelief.

Anahilda, Lumi's aunt and Inés's sister, looked her up and down and scoffed. "Like you've never been here before," she said with a snort.

The sisters and Lumi stood outside a green cottage with a glass storefront packed with gerbera daisies, pink peonies, and buttery-yellow sunflowers.

"Maybe so, but how is a florist going to counsel me on how to handle my daughter?" Inés asked.

Anahilda called out to a gray-haired man who was sawing a piece of wood on the curb, ignoring her sister's question. "Hola, Don Emilio!"

He waved back at the women, bestowing them with a brilliant smile.

"That's Doña Elia's husband," Anahilda said to Lumi, and then turned to face Inés. "Everyone knows that Doña Elia is as popular this side of Miami for her gift of vision and the botellas she prepares to heal the sick as she is for her flowers. Just follow me."

Inés rolled her eyes and rang the doorbell. While they waited, Lumi reached out to loosen one of the peeling leaves of paint from the wall until Inés halted her with a forbidding stare.

The door buzzed, and the women and Lumi stepped into a cavernous space filled with flowers of every kind. Light streamed in from the spaces where roses and hydrangeas did not block it and refracted off the glass and crystal vases, making some of the blooms look like disco balls.

Doña Elia was Cuban, and though they were not related, she and Inés bore a resemblance to each other. Like Inés, she was heavyset, with facial features that appeared to have been molded from thick clay. Her coarse curls, tinted copper, peeked out from the red paisley handkerchief she wore knotted on the right side of her forehead.

"Las hermanas Rosario!" she greeted them in a clear, confident tone, and pulled a lollipop out from a drawer in her desk for Lumi. She turned her gaze from sister to sister. "And where is my friend Mr. Teodosio today? Back from his trip to Santo Domingo?" she asked, studying Inés.

Inés stared at her through narrowed eyes. "Hmm?"

Anahilda shook her head vigorously. "It's been five years, Doña, since he . . . since 1988. Let's discuss it another time," she added, and Lumi could feel all three women look in her direction.

Doña Elia nodded. "What can I help you with today?" she asked.

Inés lowered her head and began to speak in a tone barely

above a whisper. "It's my daughter, Doña Elia. She doesn't want to eat anything I cook. And she says strange things about the food," Inés said.

The older woman glanced at Lumi sympathetically. "Strange how?" she asked.

"Well, for example, this morning she refused to eat her oatmeal because she said it tasted angry. There was nothing wrong with that oatmeal!" Inés said.

Doña Elia thought for a moment, then she picked up a small cylindrical glass vase with a cluster of feathery violet-tinged flowers resting in the water. She gestured for Lumi to place her hands on the vase.

Lumi followed Doña Elia's instruction and laid her small hands on either side of the glass. As she did, the smell of the flowers tickled her nose. She leaned in more and let it wash over her. Crisp, sweet, and almost papery. Clean. As she held the vase, Doña Elia studied the water, staring directly into the center of the glass.

Finally, she spoke, looking only at Inés. "The girl has a gift. Upon tasting food, she can discern the emotions of the person who cooked it at the time they made the food."

Inés stared at her dumbfounded, while Anahilda nodded enthusiastically.

"How is this possible?" Inés asked. "Nobody in our family has been able to do this before."

Doña Elia shrugged. "I don't know, the only thing I am sure of is that she has it." Her gaze grew stern. "You need to find a way to manage your thoughts. Either that, or your sister needs to start cooking for the child. Most importantly, don't think about *him* while you prepare her food. Your anger is making her sick, and that's why she hardly eats anymore, poor thing."

Inés winced at her words. Lumi let go of the vase and pressed her hands together, feeling her stomach sink. She had been telling her mother for years. Why did her mother have to hear it from someone else for it to become important to her?

"Take care of her," Doña Elia said, leaning forward to smooth Lumi's hair, "and if I were you, I would keep this a secret. I would never want to hear of this being used against her. And she must always guard what she eats. If she in any way does not trust someone, under no circumstances should she eat their cooking, no matter how slight the doubt of the person's intentions."

Doña Elia's sturdy fingers closed around the vase, and she held it out to Lumi.

"Here, m'ija. For you. These are called echinacea. A small recuerdo of this day," she said with a kindly smile.

"Thank you," Lumi said, taking the vase from her hand and clutching it tight to her chest.

Lumi exhaled deeply. She let the memory fade as she turned in the direction of home, bundle of echinacea flowers tied with a blade of grass in hand. She took the stairs two at a time and let herself into her apartment. She stuck the flowers in a small crystal vase and dropped in a slosh of water from the faucet. She glanced at her pantry and grabbed a bag of dry black beans from inside it. Using a knife, she slit the top of the bag and poured the beans into a round blue bowl, then covered them with cool water.

She hopped in the shower, soaked her curly hair in the

water, and washed it with her favorite gardenia-lime shampoo. She dried her hair with a fluffy towel and dressed in what would be least obtrusive under her chef's uniform later in the day: gray twill pants and a navy cotton sweater with tiny buttons on the cuff.

Back in her kitchen again, she drained the beans, replaced the water, and dumped the mixture into a pressure cooker, snapping the lid into place and turning the machine on. She pulled out her favorite cutting board. It was from the Metropolitan Museum of Art store and had a print of Matisse's *Dance* pressed securely between the glass panels.

From her herb bowl she retrieved a bulbous red onion, six cloves of garlic, and a sole, slightly wrinkled shallot that needed to be used as soon as possible. From her refrigerator, she pulled out a bundle of fresh green cilantro, two firm celery stalks, and a chunk of acorn squash. She diced them all into tiny squares in short order and hummed to herself as she heated up some safflower oil in her trusty KitchenAid saucepan.

She sat with herself for a moment to see what else she would want with these delectable beans. A peek into her refrigerator reminded her she had a red snapper she needed to use. A lightbulb went off in her head. She also had a fresh coconut that she had bought on a whim at Fairway the other day. Holding back no force, she smacked the coconut down on her kitchen floor between both hands, smirking to herself as it cracked in half. Sometimes she surprised herself with her own strength. It was something she had inherited from Inés, although Inés would have simply lopped off the top third of the coconut with the machete she kept under her bed.

Three hours later, Lumi sat at her kitchenette table, full

and satisfied, and she now had coconut fish, white rice, and beans for the next several days. Maybe she would even invite Rafelina and Jenny over for dinner tomorrow night, since she wasn't working at DAX. She washed her purple ceramic plate in the sink quickly, then headed to the bedroom to start getting ready for her second night at her new workplace.

When she arrived in the DAX kitchen, there was a note taped to her locker: MS. SANTANA, COME SEE ME IN MY OFFICE. The word "please" was scrawled onto the bottom right corner of the note, an obvious afterthought. Lumi frowned. So much for Julien not finding out. She took her chef's hat out, then gently put it back in its place. No need to get all suited up to see him.

She stepped into the office, and the first person she encountered was the secretary, the same woman who had been there when she came in for her interview. She stopped in front of the reception desk and was met by a razor-sharp stare complete with pointy winged eyeliner.

"Hi, there," Lumi said.

The receptionist remained silent.

"I'm Lumi. I didn't get your name the other day." Lumi held out her hand.

"It's Esme. Go on in."

Lumi let her hand drop to her side and continued past the reception desk.

Julien was seated at his desk, and in front of him was a porcelain dessert plate bearing a sizable slice of apple tarte tatin. His hair was combed back, and his face looked fresh, like he had just washed it before she came in, not like he had been standing over a hot stove. Lumi sat and looked straight at him, trying not to look at the plate. She knew that was what he wanted. He cleared his throat, and she could feel her annoyance growing. She exhaled soundlessly.

"Ms. Santana," he said in an even voice, "in my kitchen, this is where we keep our apples." He studied her face, and his expression was a mixture of annoyance and restrained curiosity. "We are clear, yes?"

Lumi bit her lip. None of the answers she could think of would help. "We are clear," she muttered. She stood up to leave and he started.

"Ms. Santana?"

She only half turned toward him, her eyes flashing. He hung on that last syllable, seemingly forgetting what he was going to say.

"Er, tonight is boeuf bourguignon. I will hope not to find a banana in there." The corners of his lips curved up.

Lumi stared him down for a split second, then turned on her heel and walked back to the kitchen, leaving him in his office.

Later that night, she thought back and it struck her that she had not seen an apple tarte tatin cooling on the pastry rack the previous night. Had he baked a tart to demonstrate to her the correct use for apples in his kitchen? Lumi groaned. What an irritating man. She thought of how she suddenly forgot her pithy answers in front of him and felt her face flush. So smug and self-satisfied. She would not be trying any of his cooking. No matter how great it was purported to be. With that infusion of arrogance, she was dead sure it would give her food poisoning at the very least.

LUMI'S COCONUT FISH (PESCADO CON COCO)

Serves 2

1 small onion, diced
3-4 cloves garlic, minced
$1/2$ cup cilantro, diced
1 teaspoon salt, plus more to taste
1 whole red snapper
2 tablespoons vegetable oil
12-ounce can coconut milk
2 tablespoons tomato paste

Combine the onion, garlic, cilantro, and salt. Make vertical cuts in the skin of the fish and stuff them with the onion mixture. Let marinate for 20-30 minutes.

Heat the oil in a pan on medium high. Cook the fish on each side for 2 minutes. Flip again and lower the heat to medium. Cook for 6-7 minutes on each side. Try to keep the fish from breaking into pieces. When both sides are fully cooked, add the coconut milk and tomato paste, and simmer until the sauce thickens, about 4 minutes.

11

JULIEN

Julien was still chuckling to himself as he walked down Broadway to Citarella. Bananas in the boeuf bourguignon. That was a good one, even for him. The look of surprise on her face was worth coming in early to bake.

"You're being an idiot, Dax," he said aloud to himself. It was imperative that he kept things strictly professional. He was resolute not to go down that road. He had worked too hard to build his business to put it in jeopardy over some schoolboy feelings.

The February wind whipped against his face, refreshing his senses as he walked. It reminded him of Montreal. Though it had been seventeen years since he left, he would always think of it as home.

He'd barely taken a breath since he left the office; he exhaled deeply and resolved to suspend judgment on his emotions.

Enjoying the brisk air, when he reached the Citarella storefront, he decided he wanted to keep walking. Multicolored displays and brilliant lights swirled on the periphery of his vision as he realized where he was going. Before he knew it, he was crossing Columbus Circle and turning into a treelined lane on the fringe of Central Park dotted with stone tables.

Most were empty, likely due to the cold, but near the end of the lane, Julien spotted three men chatting while two of them played a game of chess. The third man sat twiddling his bishops. He wore a red corduroy cap with a black peace sign pinned to the side to cover his gray curls.

"Hello, Rogelio."

"Dax, it's been a while." Rogelio nodded, and Julien took the seat across from him. Rogelio stood the pieces up that had been lying down, placed the bishops in their position, and gestured for Julien to begin.

There was no conversation, just the *clack-clack* sound of the chess pieces moving across the board. The sound brought him to a place beyond his thoughts, the closest to meditation he would ever get.

And then, because he never could meditate very long, his mind began to wander back to his restaurant and his sous chef in particular. Argh.

There were about four million women in New York, and 99.9 percent of them didn't work for him. *That* was the 99.9 percent he should be open to. He felt a tug in his chest, but he ignored it. Logic would have to prevail if he didn't want to complicate his life.

"Smart move, man," Rogelio said.

Julien gaped at him in shock. "Pardon?"

Rogelio gestured to the board. Julien had been so deep into his thoughts, he had castled his king and rook without noticing.

"Oh!"

The move wasn't smart enough. Rogelio needled his queen into the space next to Julien's king on the next move.

"Checkmate," he said in a near whisper, his eyes crinkling around the corners.

Julien gave a hearty laugh. "You can say it louder if you want. I'll still come back."

He folded a hundred-dollar bill into a tiny square and pressed it into Rogelio's palm.

"For coffee," he said before Rogelio could protest, and stood up to leave. He could hear the bill rustling in Rogelio's hand as he unfolded it.

"That's a couple of damn good coffees, Dax!" Rogelio called from behind him.

Julien grinned at him and began his walk back to Broadway.

12

LUMI

Lumi snatched her chef's hat and slammed her locker shut. When she turned around, she almost screamed. Richard was standing right in her face.

"Oh, Lumi," he gasped. "You're still here! I'm glad."

He pulled her into a quick hug. Lumi allowed him to hug her but shrunk back a bit.

"Yup," she answered, eyeing him quizzically.

Richard understood her meaning immediately. "I heard about yesterday's apple situation. Boss man must like ya. He has fired people for much less."

Lumi pursed her lips. It seemed odd. Gloria had told her that she had been working for Julien for thirteen years, and she thought that Ruben had said eight and Richard had said seven. So far it had appeared to her that he kept his employees on for a long time.

"Really?" she asked as Ruben entered the kitchen bearing a plate of marinated meats. He stopped to consider Lumi's question, holding one edge of the tray with his hands and resting the other edge on his rounded belly.

"Shit—*much* less," he said, chuckling heartily.

The door swung open and closed and a hush fell over the kitchen. Julien stood in the doorway, surveying his terrain. He brushed several locks of red hair back from his forehead and cast his clear brown eyes around. Richard nodded in his direction and escaped into the wine closet, and Ruben set to work on the tray of meats at his station, poking each cut with a toothpick to check for tenderness.

Julien did not acknowledge Lumi as he strode into the kitchen.

"Richard," he called in an even voice in the direction of the wine closet, "I will need a bottle of burgundy, 2009 or earlier, please."

He continued to the spice cabinet, casting a sideways glance at Lumi, who was laser-focused on dicing her celery. He grabbed the crystal door handle and pulled open the heavy oak door. He'd had the door specially installed to keep the spices fresh and to avoid having noxious metal odors interfere with their delicate flavors. "Dried bacon, dried bacon . . ." he muttered to himself as he riffled through the various pots, bags, and canisters.

He fell silent as he found the glass canister of dried bacon, sitting in the back corner of the condiments rack without a cap. He cleared his throat and the sound echoed through the kitchen, which had fallen silent as every soul present watched and waited. Then he pulled out the canister and slammed it down on the countertop with such force that Lumi was surprised that the glass didn't shatter.

Richard came out of the wine closet, bottle of 2009 burgundy in hand. He and Ruben exchanged glances. Julien looked from Richard to Ruben, his gaze coasting right over Lumi.

"Who . . . did . . . this?" he asked.

His jaw was hard, and Lumi could see a little muscle twitching in its square corner. She had a feeling that they both knew.

In walked Gloria, bearing a basket full of leafy Swiss chard, round juicy-looking beets, and oranges.

"Hello, Gloria," Julien greeted her calmly.

She smiled back, eyeing him with suspicion.

"Gloria," he asked, "would you happen to know who left my dried bacon open, lying in the back of the spice closet like garbage?" He leveled his gaze on her, and Gloria twisted her mouth.

"It was Heather," she confided, lowering her eyes conspiratorially.

Julien nodded slowly, leaning back against the marble counter. "Hmm," he said to himself.

When Heather walked through the kitchen door, she found Julien waiting and the entire staff looked away.

"Hello, Heather," he said.

Heather shifted from one foot to the other nervously. "What did I do?" she asked.

Julien regarded her. "Do you see this dried bacon?"

"Yes."

"This, Heather, is aged dried bacon that I brought back from Provence in the summer of 2013. This bacon is cured and produced from the pigs of Caille, who are raised eating only organic grass and organic lavender."

Heather stared at him blankly.

"This is not acceptable, Heather. Why would you leave this canister open?"

Heather glanced down at her feet. "Whatever, it's already dried anyway." She shrugged.

Julien cocked his head at her. All the other employees in the kitchen studiously focused on their stations, except Lumi, who watched intently. Julien's nostrils flared as he picked up his bacon jar once more.

"Yes, it is *dried*, but now it's *dry*. We're done here." He flung the jar into the trash can. "What a waste," he said, clucking his tongue and shaking his head.

Heather shrugged again and went to get her apron from her locker as Julien looked on in surprise.

"I don't think we are understanding each other. When I say we're done here, I mean you're done here. Ruben, please escort Heather out."

Heather gaped at him, not moving from where she stood.

"Esme will mail you your last check. I will be back, everyone . . . some pedestrian, mill-fed bacon from Citarella will just have to do." He sighed in dismay, and off he went to grab his coat.

Once he had left, Heather shuffled out the door. Richard and Ruben both nodded at Lumi.

"See?" they said, shaking their heads in unison.

Lumi let out a deep exhale and returned her focus to her station. She thought back to when Julien was chastising Heather. His steely gaze, his placid voice and how it contrasted with his angry words. She wanted to feel bad for Heather but didn't. The waitress had given her more than one eye roll since she'd walked into DAX. Still, she wasn't happy to see her lose her job.

She remembered what Richard had said. Putting apple in the ratatouille would seem to have been a worse trespass than leaving the bacon to dry. Although . . . that bacon probably cost Julien hundreds of dollars. She sighed to herself and decided not to think at all. The beef had not even been browned yet; there was no time to get lost in her own mind. She made a note to herself to analyze this inconsistency later, once she had made it through the night at DAX unscathed. She couldn't go on autopilot here as she did at Caraluna—that was now clear to her.

Gloria came up behind her. "Tea?" she asked. She held a steaming mug of hibiscus tea in her hand that she had boiled while the dismissal was going on.

Lumi smiled at her, her eyes crinkling at the corners. "Thank you," she said. She took the mug in both hands and sipped lightly. The smooth, slightly tangy flavor of the hibiscus washed over her tongue. At the same time, the tense crackling in her chest ebbed and faded away. She could sense the intention that Gloria had had to calm herself as she brewed the tea. Gloria beamed back at her, and they both returned to their stations.

"What fresh white hell is this?" Lumi said as she swept her gaze over Broadway.

She drew her arms around herself and hugged. It wasn't supposed to be snowing in March, right when she'd been looking forward to the first blooms. The crisp, clear crystals swirling through the air and coasting past the windows made spring flowers seem further away than ever. It had been a month since the ratatouille incident. Lumi had kept her head down, cooked what was on the menu, and kept her ideas to herself.

Julien cracked an amused grin. "Not a fan of the snow?"

"Lord, no."

"Why not? It's perfect for skiing, ice skating, hockey."

Lumi shivered. "I still haven't been able to understand why people would do any of those things of their own volition."

"They're fun. I, for one, quite enjoy the snow. My only concern today is that it could sabotage our pastry delivery. We're running low on cream and flour."

"Hmm." Lumi nodded with pursed lips and turned her attention to the sausage she was slicing for the cassoulet. "Pastry is the only thing being delivered today?" she asked.

"Yes. Pastry delivery is on Tuesdays."

"I didn't see any duck for the cassoulet."

"Ruben should have it."

"I saw you put tiramisu on the menu for tonight."

"Yes."

"Tiramisu's not French, it's Italian."

"I know. That's why I asked Gloria to bring the ladyfingers and mascarpone from Arthur Avenue."

Lumi scratched her head. Was that supposed to explain why they were having an Italian dessert special?

"I wanted to, you know . . . branch out a bit." He shifted from side to side.

"Aha. So making a Western European dessert at a Western European restaurant is branching out? Sure you're not living too dangerously?"

Julien clucked his tongue. "Tiramisu is southern Italian. I'd say it's more Mediterranean."

She restrained the urge to form the "W" of "whatever"

with her fingers and leaned against the cold metal of the work-station. "Will she even be able to get here with this snow?"

"She should be here any minute."

Tap, tap, tap. Lumi drummed her fingertips on the counter-top. One minute passed, then two. Julien himself was eyeing the clock.

"Did you call her?"

He grasped his phone and punched the buttons. "Gloria? . . . Yes . . . Oh, God, I am sorry to hear that . . . No, I agree, don't try to dig it out by yourself. Did you call for help? . . . Ah, okay. Please keep me posted . . . Bye."

He rested his forehead on the V between his thumb and forefinger for a moment.

"We'll just have to make crème brûlée again. Can you cover pastry today?" he asked.

"Fine. I'll get the cream. Oh, right . . . the dairy delivery."

Julien knitted his brow before flinging open the dairy re-frigerator. Interesting. He knew as well as she did that there wasn't enough cream in there.

"Indeed. Ruben, were there any drop-offs before we got here?"

Ruben shook his head. "Nothing, Chef. But you know who's not staying home in the snow, though? Diners. We have a line of five waiting for us to open," he said.

"Great. And we're going to make the dessert with . . . ?" Lumi asked.

"Nothing. I have no ladyfingers now. No heavy cream. No seasonal fruits . . . Tabarnak! All we have is this useless corn." He rolled his eyes heavenward, muttering curses under his breath.

Lumi stared at the corn for a moment, then jumped away from the workstation and snapped her fingers. "Ooh! I got it. Do you have any evaporated milk?"

"What? I was just joking about the corn. You can't possibly—"

"Oh, but I can. Do you have any lavender extract?"

"Of course," Julien said.

She laid the cobs of corn on her workstation and glided a knife down every surface until they were bare.

"So . . . corn bread? Raw corn . . . with sugar on top? I could see that being, er, refreshing."

Lumi side-eyed him. "Just watch."

She gathered the kernels and blended them with milk, cinnamon, lavender extract, and sugar. She reached under the station for a sieve. She strained the mixture into a pot as Julien watched, wordless. The swooshing circles of the wooden spoon inside the pot were mesmerizing to Julien.

"Preference on how to plate this?" she asked.

"I haven't quite decided yet, being that corn . . ." He took the spoon from her and let a few drops fall onto a smaller spoon to taste. "Wow." He rolled the dollop of pudding over the roof of his mouth with his tongue, flattening it into nothingness. "What's this called?"

"Majarete. I added the lavender as a personal touch."

He turned to Fallon and Timothy. "Just put it out as majarete, and if they ask what that is, say it's corn pudding. Or say it's sweet polenta mousse if you need to. We don't have to give any more details. And if they don't like it, they can pound sand. I mean, corn grits."

Fallon passed Lumi a plate of trimmed orchids, and Lumi prepared bowls of majarete with an orchid affixed to the side of each bowl. Doors opened, the prior courses were served, and then she passed them to Timothy and he began walking them out.

Five minutes later, he returned. "They love it," he said. "I need four more."

Lumi turned to Julien. "So, what were you saying about the corn?"

He opened his mouth, but no sound came out.

Lumi drew and quartered the grizzled strips of bacon, then diced them into minuscule morsels. She had been shocked when Julien announced that the kitchen would be offering maple bacon cheesecakes among the specials that night. It seemed the success of the previous week's majarete had inspired him to take a little more creative license with the desserts. Richard and Gloria had looked at him as if he had just announced he had contracted the Ebola virus.

Richard hummed to himself as he prepared the crust for the cheesecakes, and Lumi found the sound to be soothing. Gloria had roped him into helping her during his downtime, which he didn't seem to mind, as a friend. Lumi nabbed a little corner from one when he wasn't looking and tasted it. Richard believed in himself and was confident in his ability to step up to any task that presented itself. His cooking had a strengthening effect on her.

In the five weeks that she had been at DAX, she had begun to develop relationships that reminded her of the ones she'd had with her employees at Caraluna. She was happy that Magda, Brayden, and Giselle were doing well in their new jobs. But she missed the tang of Magda's lemonade, how drinking it spread liquid calm through her veins, and how Magda always seemed to set aside a serving of something soothing for Lumi when work got stressful. To her surprise, she missed Brayden lumbering around the kitchen too.

She imagined what it would be like to have them working alongside her at DAX. They were all neat, organized, and skilled. They probably would get along with Julien better than she did. A stray curl popped out from under the brim of her chef's hat, and she absentmindedly tucked it back in as she remembered the disastrous run-in she'd had with him the night before.

The previous evening, Lumi had arrived in the kitchen as usual. She was the first one there, which happened only when Richard had a party the night before or Gloria's grandkids had been visiting. She looked at the blackboard, and her shoulders sank just a little. Bouillabaisse.

Lumi had never been much of a fan of the spiced fish stew herself, so it was a challenge for her to cook it with the same enthusiasm she put into her other dishes. And since it was an entrée, it was left entirely to her. Once Julien had seen that her proficiency was at executive chef level, he had begun to leave her more and more of the main dishes.

Richard and Gloria mentioned that before Lumi worked there, someone named Simon had been the sous chef. What had happened to Simon? She couldn't help but wonder if his exit from DAX had gone the same as Heather's.

She reminded herself to focus and went back to preparing the bouillabaisse. It wasn't that Lumi found it hard to produce. On the contrary, her version had been complimented four Wednesdays in a row since she had started at DAX. Any dish that required a delicate balance of spices came naturally to her. It just wasn't a taste that appealed to her, unless it had copious amounts of hot sauce sprinkled over it, and in that case, it didn't taste like bouillabaisse anymore.

She didn't like eating lobster either, and she absolutely hated throwing live lobsters in boiling water, and of course, Julien insisted that a fine bouillabaisse was not complete without lobster. Searching for some inspiration, she perused the wine rack and pulled out a bottle of 2010 merlot. A fine year— 2010 was the year she had started culinary school. It wasn't like Julien would be using it anyway; he preferred to cook with wines that were aged ten years or older.

She opened the cupboard, poured herself a crystal goblet full, and took a swill. Now she would be more relaxed when the lobster delivery arrived. As if on cue, a burly deliveryman pushed through the kitchen door with a brown burlap sack in hand.

"Hello, miss," he greeted Lumi, "should I give these to you?"

Lumi eyed the bag in dismay. "Yes, that's fine."

She sighed as he held out a slip for her to sign. Lumi scribbled her signature and handed it back to him, thanking him under her breath as he left.

Once he was gone, Lumi stood in front of the bag, staring at it as she put on two silicone oven mitts and paced back and forth. Suddenly, the smooth outside of the bag started to ripple and rustle.

"Jesus Christ," she muttered as she walked to the other side of the kitchen.

She cast her eyes furtively around the room. Thankfully, the kitchen was still empty and there was no one to see her being such a baby. She willed herself with the most mettle she could muster to march back to those lobsters, pull them out of the bag, and toss them in the water and be done with it. Only when she went back to it, there was a lengthwise rip in the side of the bag.

"Ay, coño," she said. Her eyes darted wildly around the kitchen floor. Arming herself with a broom, she poked under cabinets, the oven, and the dishwasher. She checked under the refrigerator. Nothing. A sigh of relief escaped her. It appeared one of them had just ripped the bag, but none had escaped.

With the tips of her glove-sheathed fingers, inch by inch she tugged the bag over to the pot of boiling water, keeping it as far away from her body as possible. Using a spatula, she forced open the staples at the top of the bag and peered down. Ten spindly creatures were passively lying in wait, and she could swear they were staring back at her.

Making sure her gloves were on tight, she lifted one out with a pair of metal tongs. She glanced from the lobster to the water and back again. She turned to face the pot.

"I'm sorry, buddy," she whispered to the crustacean. "I hope there is some tasty algae waiting for you up in the big coral reef in the sky."

She took another deep breath and released the tongs. The lobster fell into the water with a sickening plop. She exhaled deeply. It had helped her to give it a little departing speech. She picked up the next one. It didn't squirm at all. Once again, she turned toward the pot. She looked at the lobster and did her best to send it loving end-of-life thoughts.

"I'm sorry, my friend," she began. "I hope that—" She was interrupted by a colossal laugh booming from the doorway.

She turned on her heel and threw Julien a sideways glance.

"You! How long were you standing there?" she asked.

Julien stepped forward. "Ms. Santana," he said, "in the fifteen years of Catholic school I endured, I never saw a priest quite like you."

Lumi rolled her eyes.

"Do you need an incense tower? I keep a spare in my office," he said, the lights in his eyes belying his amusement.

"I'm sure you do," Lumi shot back, returning to the task at hand. "Now if you'll excuse me, I have eight more lobsters who deserve their last rites."

Julien looked at her in surprise. "Oh. Well, then, be back in a bit," he said, and dashed off.

Lumi watched him go and then turned back to the lobsters. The interruption had scattered her focus. For the remaining lobsters, she gave each of them a quick "sorry" before she promptly dispatched them into the bubbling pot.

Soon her coworkers started filing in, and both Richard and Gloria greeted Lumi warmly before they assumed their stations. The lobsters finished boiling, and Lumi drained the water and fished them out with the tongs in preparation for shelling. She looked in the direction of Ruben's grill, which was still unmanned. There was no meat dish on the night's menu, so she hoped he would be free to help her shell the lobsters once he arrived.

But then a shrill scream came from inside the wine closet.

"Ooooommmmmmmiiiiigooooood, there's a monster in here!" Richard jumped out of the closet, clutching two bottles of cabernet. "Help!" he said.

Right behind him, a lobster scuttled out, its claws free and snapped in the air.

"Omigod, get it. *Get it!*"

Lumi gasped. She hadn't thought to check in the wine closet. Gloria grabbed the broom, but the creature evaded her and slipped under the kitchen island.

"Get it, Lumi," Richard said.

Lumi took the broom from Gloria and furtively poked under the island. "Get the tongs," she said.

Gloria thrust the tongs under the island and the lobster scurried out. All three of them jumped back as it ran out and quickly crawled to the opposite side of the kitchen.

"Damn it," Gloria cursed.

Just then, Esme appeared in the doorway. "What are you people making such a fuss about?" she asked. As she shoved the door toward the wall, the lobster ran out from behind it. "*Oh, shit!*" she yelled, and just as quickly ducked back into the hall.

"Where'd it go?" Lumi asked. She had lost track after the receptionist had opened the door. "Look under all the tables," she instructed the others.

There was the sound of heavy footsteps pacing down the hall. "I hope that's Ruben," Gloria said. "He'll catch this thing in no time."

Instead, Julien strode back into the kitchen. "Ms. Santana, I know you said no, but I brought the incense tower just in ca—what the hell is going on in here?" he asked as he surveyed his three cowering employees, all with mussed hair, crouching on the floor of the kitchen.

He thought for a second.

"Ms. Santana," he began, gently shaking his head. "You were trying to save one from its fate, weren't you?" He sighed in mock consternation.

Lumi felt her face flush. "I wasn't. It escaped," she said.

Julien raised an eyebrow. "Mm-hmm."

He held his hand out to Lumi for the broom and she passed it to him. With the tip of the broom, Julien nudged the lobster out from under the island, grabbed it by its tail with his bare hand, and, with a flick of his wrist, sent it sailing into the pot of water that Lumi had set to boil for the green beans, which were to be served with garlic sauce.

"All in a tizzy over a little lobster. And you call yourselves chefs," he said. He handed the broom back to Lumi. "Ms. Santana, can I trust that you can handle the rest of the night? Or should I be on hand in case any other dangerous creatures rear themselves from the recesses of this kitchen?" he asked, his eyes flashing devilishly.

Lumi crossed her arms. She felt her cheeks burning and hoped it did not show. "We'll be fine," she answered. "Goodbye."

Julien stared at her in pretend shock. "Being kicked out of my own kitchen, am I?" he said. "I won't be too far away, just in case."

He turned and sauntered out, and Lumi balled her hands into fists. She would be punching him in the face right now if she didn't clearly need this job.

As she shelled the lobsters, she began to ruminate to herself. She would talk to Jenny and thank her for her kindness but tell her this wasn't working out. She'd ask her to help her find something else. She would send her résumé all over New York City. She would take a job as a dishwasher, for God's sake, if it helped her get out of DAX sooner.

She twisted her mouth. Well, maybe not as a dishwasher. She still had student loans to pay from culinary school. She willed herself to take one deep breath and then another. She was no help to herself when she got frantic like this. She sighed and looked down at her cutting board. She had already shelled all the lobsters and had been so lost in thought that she hadn't even noticed.

She washed her hands and told Gloria she was going out to get some fresh air. Her prayers were answered when she walked to the elevator and didn't pass Julien in the hallway. She rode down to the ground floor and stepped out into the brisk March air. The early-evening breeze swirled over her face, quieted her mind, and brought her back to reality.

MAJARETE
Serves 4

4 cobs husked sweet corn
$1/2$ cup sugar, plus more to taste
$1^1/_2$ tablespoons cornstarch
$1/2$ teaspoon cinnamon powder
$1/4$ teaspoon salt
3 cups whole milk
$1/2$ cup water
2 cinnamon sticks
pinch of freshly grated nutmeg (optional)

Shuck the corn. Using a sharp knife, cut the kernels from the cob. Blend the corn kernels with the sugar, cornstarch, cinnamon powder, salt, milk, and water. Pass the mixture through a strainer (discard the solid parts). Pour the liquid into a 3-quart pot. Add the cinnamon sticks. Cook over medium heat, stirring constantly to avoid sticking. When the mixture thickens to the consistency of drinkable yogurt (approximately 15 minutes), remove from the heat. Stir in sugar to taste, if necessary.

Cool the pudding by placing the pot into another pot containing cold water, stirring to prevent a crust from forming.

To serve, pour into small bowls or ice cream glasses. Sprinkle with a small amount of nutmeg, if desired. If you prefer, chill before serving.

Recipe adapted from Clara Gonzalez and Ilana Benady's website, Dominican Cooking (dominicancooking.com).

BOUILLABAISSE WITH ROUILLE

FOR THE BOUILLABAISSE:
1 pound ripe tomatoes
3 tablespoons olive oil
1 large chopped onion
4 cloves garlic, crushed
2 tablespoons tomato paste
4 cups cold water
1 tablespoon anise-flavored liqueur
8 sprigs parsley
2 bay leaves
2 sprigs thyme
1 sprig fennel

1/4 teaspoon saffron threads

4 pounds fish heads and bones

1 lobster

4 potatoes, peeled and diced

3 pounds mixed fish steaks cut into large
   chunks

FOR THE ROUILLE:

3 baguette slices with the crusts removed,
   plus 12 more slices to serve

1 red pepper

3 cloves garlic, crushed

1 small red chili pepper, seeded and
   chopped

1 tablespoon fresh basil

1/3 cup olive oil

Cut an X in the bottom of each tomato and boil them
for 10 seconds. Remove from the boiling water, and
use the X to peel off the skin. Chop the tomatoes.

Heat the oil in a large saucepan over medium heat,
add the onion, and cook for 5 minutes without brown-
ing. Add the tomato, garlic, and tomato paste. Reduce
the heat and simmer for 5 minutes. Stir in the 4 cups of
water, then add the parsley, bay leaves, thyme, fennel, saffron, fish heads and bones, and lobster. Bring
to a boil, then reduce heat and simmer for 30 minutes.
Strain into a large saucepan, pressing the juices out
of the ingredients.

Reserve 1/4 cup stock. Add the anise-flavored liqueur to the saucepan and stir in extra tomato paste

if needed to thicken the sauce. Bring to a boil and add the potato. Reduce heat and simmer for 5 minutes.

Add the firmer-fleshed fish steak chunks and cook for 2-3 minutes, then add the thinner pieces of fish and cook for 5 minutes.

For the rouille, remove the crust from the bread and soak in cold water for 5 minutes. Meanwhile, grill the red pepper until the skin starts to blacken. Let it cool, and then peel off the skin. Squeeze the water out of the bread and place it in a food processor or blender with the peeled red pepper, chili, garlic, and basil. Blend, gradually adding the olive oil, until the mixture forms a smooth paste. Thin as necessary with the reserved stock. Serve with toasted bread.

Recipe adapted from The Essential Mediterranean Cookbook *(Bay Books, 2001).*

13

JULIEN

Julien returned to the office, still laughing, and sat down at his desk. When he reached for his keyboard, he was surprised to find a navy-blue gift box lying on top of it. He lifted the lid to find a gray checkered dress shirt. It was a 16.5-inch neck, 34-inch sleeve, his exact measurements.

He stared at the box for a moment before a thought lit up his face. Had Lumi given him a gift? He scrambled to shake the shirt out of the box in search of a card.

"Is it the right size?" Esme asked. She was standing in the doorway.

"Oh!" He started. "Esme, did you . . . get me this?"

She nodded. "You don't like it?"

"It's not that, it's . . . I can't accept this."

"Please accept it. How else can one day's salary last a lifetime?"

He stared at her. The words would not come. There was

an American Express commercial like that, wasn't there? His mind drew a blank.

"Esme, this has to be the last time. I can't accept gifts from you."

"No more gifts then. Got it." And just as quickly, she was gone.

What was it about this gesture? It wasn't exactly wrong . . . was it? It was just a shirt.

Julien picked up his phone to text his best friend, Patrick.

JULIEN: Pat, has your secretary ever gifted you a shirt?

Patrick responded a minute later.

PATRICK: My secretary is a 49-year-old man named Bonifacio Bartleby. No, Julien, Bonifacio has not given me a shirt. Did yours?

JULIEN: Mr. Bartleby's first name is Bonifacio?

PATRICK: Yes. Don't change the subject.

JULIEN: Yes, Esme gave me a shirt. It's my exact measurements and everything. Not too sure how she got them or even what to think.

PATRICK: Is she cute? Just kidding.

JULIEN: Not going there.

PATRICK: I'll take it if you don't want to wear it. Don't think too hard. See you Friday for brunch.

JULIEN: Yep, Friday.

Julien pressed the red button to end the call and lifted the navy-blue gift box off his keyboard, studying it. The question remained: Why would Esme give him this gift?

14

LUMI

If only Tia Anahilda could see this.

Tia wasn't a religious woman, but she had a habit of declaring "Dios bendiga" in a low voice every time she encountered a massive stockpile of food. In her view, dieting was a sin.

"Mientras que haya, se coma, m'ija! O-oh!" *While there is food, we will eat.* And today, there was an abundance of food piled up in the corner of the service elevator of DAX. Cardboard boxes held juicy crimson tomatoes, some of them bumpy and grooved, some perfectly round. Fronds of verdant lettuce still had snails stuck to several of their leaves.

The elevator began emitting a high-pitched beep as she surveyed the glorious produce.

"Is there a way to stop this thing?" She looked up and down the control panel. There had to be a pin she could push or pull, or something else she could do besides hold the door open and quickly haul out the food as the alarm bell blared on.

"Sure is," Ruben called out from the grill station. He hastened over, leaned in, and, with the push of a few buttons, locked the elevator in place and stopped the nerve-jangling beeping.

"Thanks."

"Were you planning to carry this all in yourself?" he asked.

Lumi nodded, and he lowered and shook his head as he grasped the first heavy crate and hoisted. They carried the crates to the center of the kitchen.

"Ooh! I'll grab that." Fallon dashed over and picked up several grocery bags.

With their help, the entire CSA delivery was sorted and stored in twenty minutes.

"Did you see this, Lumi?" Ruben handed her a slip of paper taped to the kitchen phone.

MS. SANTANA. THE CORN PUDDING WAS SUCH A SUCCESS THAT I'D LIKE YOU TO MAKE THE DESSERTS TONIGHT. WE DO FRUIT ON FRIDAY NIGHT. MAKE WHATEVER YOU WANT. JD

"Hon, you know Julien. Should we call and ask him what he wants?" Gloria asked.

"It said 'whatever you want.' I'm not asking what he wants."

A couple of empty cardboard boxes still lay in front of the produce refrigerator, and one of them had a sheen of light red juice hazing over the bottom. A small smile crept onto her lips.

"Gloria, is there an ice cream maker under your station?"

"That there is. Did you decide?" Gloria asked. Her gaze darted down to the juicy red produce now in Lumi's hand.

"You sure about that, Lumi?" she asked with a frown.

"Yep, I'm sure. Let me find out Mr. Three Stars doesn't know a tomato is a fruit. And if he doesn't, well, no one told him to say 'make whatever you want.'"

She put a small pot of water on the stove and stirred up a simple syrup while the tomatoes whirred around in the blender. Gloria watched from the pastry station as Lumi strained out the seeds and poured the liquid into the ice cream maker.

An hour later, Julien stepped in. Lumi was sitting in a chair, shucking green peas. He looked from her to the pastry station and back to her again.

"Hi. Did you get my note?"

"Yep."

"And?"

"Check the freezer."

He slid the freezer drawer open and peered down into it. "This looks good. Is it . . . what is this?"

"Tomato sorbet."

"Tomato?"

"The one and only."

"Oh, but . . ."

He glanced from the ice cream maker to Lumi, and she held his gaze, challenging him, daring him to say something. He stared back at her. Others turned and watched them. Heat crept up under Lumi's collar, but damned if she would be the first one to look away.

The corners of his mouth tilted and swayed in an awkward dance until they found their way back to neutral.

"Well done, Ms. Santana," he finally said, brushing imaginary dust off his sleeves and straightening his collar. "I'll be in my office if anyone needs me."

Her eyes followed him until he disappeared from view. Hmm. She had been expecting more fireworks. Though his words of praise confused her. She didn't expect the swell of pride that rose up at them either, and something about it bothered her. She shouldn't care. Caring wasn't in the one-year plan.

A month passed without much incident. Lumi cooked, Julien dropped in to check on things and left just as promptly, and everyone else went about their business.

One afternoon, Lumi got out of the elevator and was greeted by the curious sound of walnut shells being cracked from inside the kitchen. She found one redheaded man, sleeves rolled up exposing his freckled forearms, hovering over a bowl of walnuts, nutcracker in hand. A cursory glance around the kitchen revealed they were the only two there.

She let the door swing shut a little harder than usual, achieving the desired effect of startling him in the previously silent space.

"Oh, Ms. Santana," he said, welcoming her with a wave of his hand.

"Please, you can call me Lumi," she said, feeling somewhat relieved. She had been meaning to say that for a couple of weeks now.

His eyes followed her as she walked into the kitchen. "Okay . . . Lumi," he said, her name a caress on his lips.

She eyed the spread on the kitchen island.

"I felt like pan-seared foie gras with grilled figs today," he said in the form of an explanation. "I'll do the foie gras and you can grill the figs, please."

Their eyes met. Julien seemed to be in a more placid mood than usual. And he was here early.

She found she didn't have the energy to quibble with him over who was going to grill the figs. "That's fine," she said as she walked over to her locker, slipped out of her jacket and into her chef's coat. She swore she could feel his gaze moving over the curves of her body as she changed.

Julien had heated a bit of oil in a pan, and it was sizzling now. She watched as he lowered thick slices of foie gras into the scalding oil. As they cooked, the aroma of delectable, buttery duck fat filled the entire kitchen. Lumi felt her stomach rumble. As she prepared her station, she glanced at Julien while he flipped the slices in the pan in the calmest manner possible.

He was totally absorbed in his task, and for the first time, Lumi found herself unable to take her eyes off him. The sun had begun to set over midtown, and the beams of light from the window over the kitchen sink fell over his face and hair, making him look as if his hair were aflame. Even his long eyelashes glittered in the sun. She sensed him about to glance up and quickly moved to fetch the figs from the refrigerator.

Julien continued flipping over the slices and laid the finished ones on a large porcelain plate. She eyed the pan.

"Those look like they're getting a little toasty, don't you think?" she asked.

He shook his head.

"When do you stop?" Lumi asked.

"I stop when I'm jealous of the person who gets to eat them," he said, locking eyes with her.

She hugged herself, repressing a shudder. "Gotcha," she said.

"Would you like to try one?" he asked.

She froze. The truth was they smelled awfully good. "Um, no thanks. I've got to . . . the figs," she mumbled, clutching the package of figs.

He smiled an odd half-smile. "Er . . . Lumi?" he asked.

"Yes?"

"The grill's that way," he said, pointing at the opposite side of the kitchen.

She looked at where she had been going—in the direction of the wine closet. She swore under her breath. Why did she feel like she always ended up looking like an idiot in front of this man?

She muttered something about having known that and hastened toward the grill, which she fired up right away. To her surprise, he didn't laugh at her. He merely watched her stumble off with that same odd little half-smile.

Her coworkers arrived, and she knew she would soon need to hand over the grill to Ruben for whatever à la carte dishes he would need to prepare. She grilled the figs as quickly as she could and arranged them all on a long rectangular plate. She brought them over to the island where they would be plated with the foie gras.

As she laid the fig plate next to the foie gras plate, once again the delectable smell tickled her nose. She looked left and right. Julien was out in the dining room, and Ruben and Gloria were by the fridge. She had promised herself she wasn't going to try his cooking out of pure irritation. But her mouth was watering. How bad could it be? It's not like he would know, and she wouldn't have to compliment him if she didn't want to add to his already monstrous ego.

She just happened to have a fork in one of the pockets of her chef's jacket, and she surreptitiously pulled it out and speared the corner of a foie gras slice. She popped it into her mouth and tossed the fork in the sink before anyone could see her.

What she could not have been prepared for was the hum of electricity that she felt once she started to chew. It was a tingling that began in her mouth and spread to the roots of her hair. She shivered. Not knowing what else to do, she closed her eyes. There were the smooth flavors of the duck fat, the tasty, rocky grains of sea salt he had used. She rolled the salt around on the tip of her tongue. But there was also something else. An aftertaste of some sort . . . She tried and tried to put her finger on it but couldn't quite place it. It was herbal, astringent, aromatic.

Her mind flashed back to when she was eight years old and her mother had brought her to Doña Elia for a spiritual cleansing, after her mom had gotten them into a car accident by crashing into a driver who stopped short on I-95. The kindly elder had set some type of crusty-looking wands on fire and then waved them all around her head and limbs. They had a smell, those wands, and it was pungent and earthy, and the food Julien cooked tasted just like they smelled. How strange.

She mulled it over to herself. The oddest part of it all was that these foie gras didn't appear to have any herbs on them.

Julien's loud chuckle interrupted her thoughts as the door swung open.

"Yes, at the molecular gastronomy conference. See you,"

he called to someone behind him. He walked back over to the kitchen island, where Lumi was staring dumbly at the plates.

He picked up the plate of figs. "Well, thank you for grilling the figs," he said.

"Mm-hmm." She nodded, then shook her head abruptly and tried to look for something else, anything else, in the refrigerator. Julien looked after her, his expression puzzled.

LUMI'S TOMATO SORBET
Makes 1 pint sorbet

10 large tomatoes
$\frac{1}{2}$ cup sugar
Juice of 1 lemon, seeded
1 teaspoon salt
2 tablespoons ginger root, chopped
$\frac{1}{2}$ teaspoon ground cinnamon
$\frac{1}{4}$ teaspoon ground clove

Peel and chop the tomatoes. Combine all the ingredients in a large saucepan over medium heat for 30 minutes. Cool the mixture, then blend in a blender until smooth. Let it cool completely, then freeze in an ice cream maker. Remove the sorbet and place in a container (preferably one with a lid) and freeze for 2-4 hours before serving.

15

JULIEN

"It's all right, Berta," he called down the hall. "You can go home now."

Berta hastened to the kitchen and stopped in the doorway, bracing herself against the first of the Sub-Zero refrigerators.

"Are you sure, Mr. Dax?" she asked cautiously.

Julien wiped the sweat from his brow and leveled his gaze with hers. "Berta, I am certain. Take advantage of this time to drive up to City Island with Julio. April is the best time to go, before all the traffic starts."

It was only fair that after ten years in his employ, he knew what his housekeeper and her husband liked to do in their spare time.

Berta sighed. "Well then, Mr. Dax, I know I will find the kitchen more sparkling than I left it. See you tomorrow," she said. And with a wink, she was gone before he could change his mind.

Julien grinned to himself and walked over to the minibar. He poured a stream of bourbon into a highball glass and added some gargantuan chunks of ice. Berta had not been wrong. Clean he would. But he needed a minute to think first.

He felt himself, but not himself. He felt more alive, but also more anxious. And he couldn't deny for much longer that he felt like his blood was boiling every time that woman was around him. Letting logic prevail wasn't working out that well after all.

Whenever her hand brushed his when she reached for the paring knife, he felt fire. When she dashed by him in the kitchen and left behind a trail of the most sublime gardenia-lime perfume, he felt fire. He wanted to devour her, one inch of bare skin at a time. All roads to her were made of fire, and she wasn't interested in as much as a wisp of smoke from him.

"Damn it," he cursed under his breath. Maybe she was just another one. Oh, it would help so much to believe that. Another eye-on-the-prize girl that saw her time in his company as a stepping-stone to a richer future. The road to where he stood had been paved with them.

Even Shayla. In the three years they dated, there was sex but no intimacy, and it bothered him how little that had bothered her. She had been ready to move forward, get engaged, and sweep those issues under the handspun silk rug she'd picked out for their future home.

But there was something about the way Lumi looked at him, guarded yet wide open, so attuned to his overtures, that told him she was not just another one, that told him Lumi was nothing like Shayla.

It wasn't only her body, although he hungered for it. It was her very presence that unnerved him and made him forget everything that usually made him so unflappable. He knew other people probably would have used the term "pigheaded."

Julien exhaled deeply and strode over to the deep fountain-style sink, ignoring the Art of Shaving gift box he'd found on his desk the day before. He was going to have to have another talk with Esme, but for the moment, he was consumed by this newfound ache.

He wasn't used to being the only one. He had been in a couple serious relationships and a few less serious ones too . . . but Lumi hadn't shown any signs of interest in him, beyond having him move out of the way so she could reach the knives. He could tell that she thought he was a pompous ass. But that wasn't fair. She hadn't given him a chance to show her his softer side. How he would enjoy that if she did.

He stood back for a moment and scrutinized the tiles composing the backsplash behind the sink. Yes, they did need scrubbing. He knelt and opened the cabinet under the sink. There it was: his treasure trove of cleaning supplies. There was Pine-Sol and Fabuloso and his trusty standby, bleach. His mother had always said, "If it's not bleach, it's not clean."

He didn't know if he would go that far, but it did work quite well. It had earned its place as a mainstay in his arsenal, lifting the most resistant stains, the ones that had potential to mar his day. He took a microfiber cloth and sprayed a light dusting of Perfect Tile over all the tiles. Then, one by one, he began buffing them with the cloth, making sure to get in and scour the edges of the grout as well. He could almost feel his mother standing next to him as he worked.

She was the one who had taught him how to keep a kitchen clean, and some of his favorite memories were of telling her about his day as they scrubbed tiles. Little had she known how much her teachings would help him keep organized in his line of work.

The backsplash of Julien's fountain sink was white except for the occasional moonstone inlay, which caught the light and refracted it all over the kitchen. He stared at the iridescent pieces. He thought Lumi had a necklace that looked as if it were made of the same material. No, he was sure of it.

She had worn it to work two nights before. He had seen it just after she had removed her coat and before she put on her chef's jacket: a moonstone resting in the hollow of her throat. What would it be like if he were to stand beside her and slowly slide that moonstone out of the way to press his lips to that hollow? What would it be like to lay delicate kisses along the breadth of her collarbone? How would she respond? Would she push him away and tell him to stop, or would she throw her head back and wrap her arms around his neck, pulling him in for more? Hmm. If he did that in the kitchen, most probably the former, which is why he would never try.

He exhaled deeply, letting the tension ease out of his shoulders. He almost had to laugh at himself for turning into such a pantywaist. But he couldn't deny it. Something about her called unto the depths of his being. What would it be like to taste her mouth? Her succulent lips like mandarin segments. Her melodious voice hushed by the union of their feverish mouths. He wondered what it would be like to unite their bodies, minds, and souls in this most fervent dance. It would be unlike anything he had ever experienced before.

And that was what he wanted with her, and nothing less. To kiss her until she was dizzy, to love her with all the force of his fiery being. But she was still his sous chef.

"She will leave when she gets back on her feet," he said aloud, but no one was listening.

What would it be like to nuzzle her hair and trace the seashells of her ears with the tip of his tongue? He sighed. Logic had no place in his mind at the moment. Eventually, these thoughts would drive him crazy.

He wondered where he could run into her outside of the kitchen. Perhaps if she saw him elsewhere, she would be able to conceive of him as someone other than her employer. But he couldn't think of a single way to draw her out without it sounding like a date. He was starting to get on his own nerves, and he didn't have any answers. But even if they never went on a date, she needed to know there was more to him than foie gras and grill smoke.

16

LUMI

The second week of April brought longer hours of sunlight and, even better, fresh greens from farms upstate. The French Alliance was hosting its annual spring gala at DAX, and there was excitement in the air but also plenty of pressure. The staff knew that it was an honor for Julien's restaurant to be chosen, but they also knew he was on edge.

It was a Saturday night, and since Lumi hadn't worked on Saturdays since she started at DAX, she had forgotten to calculate that the A train was usually closed for construction north of 125th Street. She ended up having to take a shuttle bus, a regular bus, and the subway to get to work. Her usual forty-five-minute trip turned into a two-hour one, and by the time she popped into the kitchen an hour late, all the prep had been done.

All of her colleagues looked up as she swung through the door—except Julien. He was busy deboning a duck for the entrée, and he kept his gaze squarely focused on the task.

"Ms. Santana, nice of you to join us for the occasion," he said, his square jaw slightly clenched.

Lumi was taken aback. He hadn't called her Ms. Santana since last week when she had told him to call her Lumi, and she was surprised by how much it bothered her. She knew how important this event was to him.

"I'm sorry, Julien," she said, looking down. "The A train was not running and I texted you fro—"

"It's fine," he cut her off. "There is plenty of work that still needs to be done, so let's get going."

Gloria gave her a sympathetic glance, and Richard walked by and squeezed her arm. But before she could get to work, she had to fix her bra. It had ridden up while she was running for the subway.

The women's bathroom at DAX had two brushed chrome stalls. Lumi saw a pair of stilettos underneath one of them and instantly recognized their owner. There was only one staff member who spent all day seated.

She ducked into the other stall to fix her bra. Damn it. She wished her Crocs would've squeaked across the gleaming white tiles, as usual, so Esme would know she was being heard.

"Cristina—No, I didn't pick up the phone because I'm not busy, I picked up because you're my sister . . . Again?" Esme sighed. "How short are you on rent? . . . N-no way. Mami cannot go to the church about this." She paused to let Cristina speak. "I'll do it . . . The vacation? It doesn't matter. Tell Mami I got it and *not* to go to the church about this, 'kay? . . . Okay. See you later. You too. Bye."

Lumi tried to leave without making a sound, but her

Crocs squeaked across the tiles. Her hands flew to her hair, and she busied herself with arranging her curls in the bathroom mirror.

The metal door creaked open, and Esme stepped out. Her under-eye circles looked darker than usual, and her eyes were downcast.

A twinge twisted in Lumi's chest. The conversation was all too familiar. It reminded her of when she was a struggling culinary student, still not sure if she would even be able to get the loans she needed to start her business. Could Esme take on extra hours to offset the difference and not have to cancel her vacation? It may have been none of her business, but Esme was a hard worker. She was on time every day, and she stayed on top of all DAX's administrative needs. It was too bad for her to lose her vacation.

Esme stood at the sink next to Lumi, and their eyes met in the mirror. Lumi forced what she hoped was a sympathetic smile, and Esme held her gaze. She nodded curtly, and they washed their hands in silence. They exited the bathroom at the same time.

Back in front of the refrigerator, Lumi took out the eggs, mushrooms, and gruyère from the refrigerator for a soufflé. She had never made soufflé for a hundred people before, and her stomach tightened at the prospect. Soufflés were mercurial, and just a few strokes too many could make the difference between light, fluffy goodness and a rubbery mess.

She blocked out the rest of the kitchen as she diced, grated, and whipped. She ignored the dull hum in her mouth that begged for another taste of Julien's cooking. She worked as fast as she could. The canapé trays were already going out to the dining room, and the soufflés would need to be ready in about half an hour. She glanced at the clock and rubbed her temple.

Just then, a voice came from behind her, accompanied by the staccato click of stilettos on the floor tiles.

"Where's Julien?" Esme asked in her usual listless tone. Lumi looked around the kitchen to cover up her surprise. She had been so focused that she didn't notice he and most of the others had gone out to the dining room.

"Don't know." She shrugged.

Esme sighed impatiently and flipped her hair. Lumi chewed a corner of her lip, contemplating her. She thought they'd had a small human moment in the bathroom. Though Esme's tone made it seem like nothing had happened.

Esme pressed a sticky note with a phone message to the top of Lumi's workstation. "Well, I'll leave this for him, then," she said.

Lumi gingerly peeled it off and stuck it on the front of the refrigerator.

"So . . . what are you making?" Esme asked.

Lumi furrowed her brow. Esme had never hung around this much.

"Soufflé," she replied tersely.

Esme nodded, her face lighting up. "Oh! Do you know how he likes it?" she asked. "Because I do."

Lumi raised an eyebrow. "Um . . . these are not for Julien. They're . . . for . . . the . . . guests," she replied as slowly and deliberately as she could, hoping Esme would get the hint and leave her in peace.

Esme's nostrils flared. "Right," she said, turning toward the door.

"Lord, those heels!" Gloria leaned in to say once Esme was

out of earshot. "Doesn't look much like a pastor's daughter, does she?"

"Huh?"

"Her mother is the pastor of a church in Harlem," Gloria said. She gave Lumi a pat on the shoulder and then walked back to her pastry station.

Lumi thought back to the conversation she heard in the bathroom. And then she shrugged. She now had only twenty-five minutes to get the soufflés ready, since she had lost five talking nonsense with Esme.

"Lumi, are the soufflés ready?" Fallon called, poking her head inside the kitchen door.

"What? No! I just put them in."

"Shit! Give me something else to put on this table."

Lumi snapped back to the present and cast her gaze around frantically. "Where the hell are those salad greens?"

"They already went out and the guests already finished them," Fallon said, resting her hand on her hip.

"Shit, shit, shit. Here." She started slicing oranges as fast as she could. "Plate these and pass them out as a palate cleanser in the meantime."

"What? Those are for the duck, they're not supposed to be a palate cleanser."

"The guests don't know that, Fallon."

Before Lumi knew it, the soufflés were done and the wait-staff was sprinting them out to the tables. Julien had hired extra staff for the event, and she was glad he did because it allowed her to focus on the dishes. She baked a second and third duck and made more soufflés while Julien greeted the guests. As far as she heard, all the dishes got rave reviews, and she worked quickly to keep them coming out to the diners.

At the end of the night, Lumi was wiped. She let her body fold into one of the hard metal kitchen chairs and watched as Julien and the waitstaff wrapped up the dinner. Plate after plate rolled in on metal racks. They were all mostly cleaned, which was a good sign. It was evident to her that the evening had gone quite well. The staff seemed relaxed, and Julien was beaming.

He seemed to have forgotten all about the sour notes at the beginning of the night, until he surveyed the disarray of vegetable cuttings, knives, and plates that still festooned Lumi's counter. She caught his disapproving gaze sweeping across the mess and bit her lip. In the rush of the night, she hadn't had a chance to clean as she went.

She eased herself out of the chair and gathered the vegetable cuttings into a small pile. The waiters and dishwashers loaded the plates into the industrial dishwasher and swept the kitchen. Lumi was still sorting out her space.

Julien had draped his tall frame over the metal chair where Lumi had been sitting and watched as she discarded empty egg cartons, recycled empty glass bottles, and wiped down the counter, trying to make sense of the mess that had been made. Lumi felt his gaze burning her, and it rankled her nerves to think that he would stay behind to supervise her and make sure she cleaned her space well.

Finally, he spoke.

"I'm surprised. I know you went to the same school as I did, so I know you learned mise en place. 'Mise en place, mise en place.' My kitchen management teacher would always say that. Makes things a lot easier at the end of the night." He tsk-tsked under his breath. The playfulness of his tone was lost on her.

Lumi eyed him sideways.

"I'm sure this is not how you kept your kitchen at Caraluna," he added.

The mention of her defunct restaurant was enough to make her blood boil, and suddenly all the aggravation of the past several weeks came to a singular inflamed point.

"You know what, Julien," she snapped. She stood up and threw her dish towel on the floor. "I don't think this is working out."

His eyes had been on the unwashed cutting boards, and he turned his gaze squarely to her. In one step, he closed the distance between them and stood a few inches from her face.

"That's funny," he murmured, "I thought things were working out quite well." His eyes shone as he gazed into hers. "Besides, with your formidable talent, you certainly bring a ray of sunshine to my—to this kitchen."

Lumi pressed her lips together to keep her mouth from hanging open. A compliment? From him? Interesting. His proximity to her was making her skin tingle. The space between them buzzed, and they were both aware of any minuscule movements between them.

As she looked around the kitchen, she saw some of the dishwashers watching them, and she cringed. She quickly walked to her station, shoved the vegetable cuttings into a trash can and piled the dishes into the sink.

There was an abrupt slamming of the dining room door into its jamb, and she looked up to see a flash of straight honey-colored hair in the round window. *Esme?* She checked the wall clock. What would she be doing at DAX at 11:00 P.M.? No, it couldn't be her. She finished work at 7:00.

"I'm done," Lumi said, "and it's eleven, anyway. I have to go."

She ran for her coat, feeling eyes on her. She wanted to get out of the kitchen as fast as she could.

"Lumi, wait," Julien said.

She kept walking and he followed her to the elevator.

"Wait," he called.

"I can't," she replied, pressing the elevator button as fast as she could. "I need to get home."

"At least let me order you an Uber," he said, pulling his phone out of his pocket.

"I'm okay. I can—"

"Can what?" he asked, his eyes thoughtful. "Take a plane, train, and automobile to get home?"

She glanced up at him. He had read her text after all. She sighed. He was right. She watched as he ordered an Uber for her, feeling chagrined but also secretly glad to not have to take the subway, bus, and shuttle home.

Later that night, safely ensconced in her bath, Lumi thought back to her close encounter with Julien and her entire body shivered. Her ears rang as she recalled his words. The memory of the electrified space between them brought chills up and down her spine.

She hadn't expected that at all. This was the man who had made her feel furious, and ashamed, and a million other things. And, if she admitted to herself, intrigued. But she worked for him, and that in itself was challenge enough. It could only lead to disaster.

What would Inés say if she thought Lumi was cozying up to her boss?

Lumi thought back to when she was a child. There was a neighbor in Miami who asked Inés and Anahilda if she could have a job at their salon. The woman was looking to make ends meet after being dismissed from her position as a secretary at a Miami Beach law office.

Lumi didn't understand all of their conversation, but she heard something about the lawyer's wife discovering jewelry hidden away in her husband's briefcase. "Only cueros sleep with the boss," Inés had muttered under her breath to Anahilda when the woman had gotten up to use the restroom. Nevertheless, they had given the woman a job washing hair. At Salon AnaInés, there was no danger of the woman sleeping with the boss.

Lumi sighed. She twisted the knob of the tap to increase the flow of hot water down into the bath and hoped the warmth would help ease her nerves. Just when she felt her shoulders easing down a bit, another thought popped into her head. Her eyes opened abruptly. What was the deal with Esme?

That woman was rude and seemed so possessive of Julien for no apparent reason. Julien didn't seem interested in her in the slightest. When she walked into a room he reacted like a pigeon had flown onto a park bench. Lumi wondered why she acted like Julien belonged to her. And why was she still hanging around at the end of the night?

An acidic feeling gnawed at and twisted her stomach. She reached for her glass of cabernet and downed a healthy gulp, telling herself that she was imagining it all. And besides, there was no reason to worry about any of this, anyway. The thought felt strangely comforting.

"This should be an easy night," Gloria said, "since there's not that much for us to do. Not much we *can* do," she mused, glancing down at the glossy black flyer in her hand.

SUSHIYA AT DAX! FRENCH-JAPANESE FUSION
SUSHI-MAKING COURSE—ONE NIGHT ONLY! $200
PER PERSON. INCLUDES MATERIALS, INSTRUC-
TION, AND ONE GLASS OF WINE PER PARTICIPANT.
BE THERE OR BE A SQUARE ROLL.

"Julien must have written that," Lumi said, wincing at the corny tagline.

In the dining room, the instructor rolled out bamboo mats and stocked the tables with sheets of nori and jars of pickled carrots. The staff had laid out a long table on the opposite side of the room, across from the main entrance, and had pushed all the round dining tables closer to form a half-circle facing the table.

"Can we at least watch?" Ruben asked, leaning his hefty frame against the doorway, his eyes clearly on the tall, dark-haired woman teaching the class.

"Yes. Well, Ruben, I'm going to need you to grill some chicken for the sushi, please," Julien said as he strode into the kitchen with baskets of nori. "After you're done, you are welcome to participate in the workshop, as are you all."

His gaze connected with Lumi's, his eyes twinkling. The tiny hairs running down her spine stood to attention. What was happening to her?

"Chicken for sushi? Okay, whatever you say, boss," Ruben said, scratching his head.

Lumi had already prepared her contribution to the evening, roasted red pepper mayo. She was free to take off and spend the night catching up on *The Crown*. But her body had other ideas. She found herself an observer as she marched through the dining room doors and claimed an empty seat at the round table closest to the left-hand side of the long workshop table. Nine participants had arrived and were busy getting comfortable at some of the other tables.

Her seat was far away from Julien's table, and she hoped she would be able to concentrate and enjoy the opportunity to do something creative at DAX. Julien was sitting to the right of the workshop table, his attention focused on the workshop teacher, who introduced herself as Mariko Takata. Her long black hair had been pulled into a French twist that tucked neatly into the back of her sushi chef's hat, and her rosy cheeks were smattered with freckles.

Gloria came into the dining area, leading an elderly man with a bow tie and walking stick. "This is my friend, Mr. Ronin," she said. "He has limited vision. Can we get a front seat for him?"

Julien jumped out of his seat. "Here, take mine," he said, and pulled out a chair for Mr. Ronin. When the elderly man was comfortably seated, Julien moved his materials from his table and walked over to Lumi's, pulling out the chair next to hers.

She racked her brain for something to say before an uncomfortable silence could set in. "I thought fusion wasn't your thing," she said.

"It's not," Julien answered. "Ms. Takata contacted me to rent the dining room for her workshop. She brought most of her own supplies."

"Ahh, so that's why we don't have to cook almost anything," she said.

"Yes."

"Are you . . . friends?" she asked.

Julien paused and turned his head toward her. "Colleagues," he said. "Why do you ask?"

"Just wondering," she said quickly, and grabbed some nori sheets to start smoothing over her mat.

Right as Ms. Takata began the class, Esme snuck through the door and made a beeline for Julien and Lumi's table. She pulled up a chair next to Julien and plopped her square black notepad on the table. Lumi and Julien turned to look at her.

"Oh, Esme. I didn't expect you to be at work so late," Julien said.

She flipped her honey-colored hair over her shoulder. "I came to take notes for you," Esme said.

"On the sushi workshop?" His furrowed brow belied his confusion.

"You . . . don't need any notes for this?"

"No, no thank you. That won't be necessary."

Lumi crinkled the ends of her nori sheet between her fingers as she listened.

"Oh . . . my mistake. See you tomorrow morning then." Esme stood up and hastened away just as quickly as she came, leaving the black notepad behind.

Lumi met Julien's gaze, and they both shrugged.

"That was weird," Lumi said.

"Indeed."

"Do you think she'll be needing this?" Lumi asked, pointing to the notepad.

Julien frowned. "I'll put it back in the supply closet before I go."

"Have you ever made sushi before?" she asked him, eager to change the subject.

"I took a class like this one a few years back, but it's been a while," he said. "You?"

She nodded. "At my restaurant, we did a sushi night about

once a month. Instead of fish, we would use fried cheese, fried salami, ripe plantain . . . and lots of fresh avocado."

"Yum," he said, licking his lower lip. Her eyes followed the movement of his tongue until it slipped back into his mouth. She shivered again. He didn't seem to notice, as he took a few nori sheets for himself.

They added rice and small strips of fish to the nori sheets from the trays Ms. Takata passed around. They also took goat cheese and julienned escargot, a treat for the more daring of the bunch. In the middle of their rolling, Julien suddenly jumped up from his chair.

"I almost forgot my sauce! Be right back," he said.

He returned with a porcelain bowl and ladle. Lumi concentrated on her own roll, but when he placed it on the table, she had to look. A smooth, rich green sauce with golden flecks filled the vessel.

"Would you like some?" he asked.

Lumi shook her head.

Julien studied her for a split second, then shrugged and poured the sauce over his sushi roll liberally. It spilled down the sides, wetting the bamboo mat with earthy green matter.

As Lumi looked up from the table for a moment, she saw Gloria approaching.

"Er, Julien, we can't find the second serving of fish," she said, biting her lip.

"Are you serious? I have to do everything around here," he said as he followed Gloria to the kitchen. Once Julien was gone, Lumi stared at his mysterious green sauce. Were those golden flecks pine nuts? She glanced around her, hoping no one would notice her sneaking a taste.

She nicked a piece of sushi off his mat with her chopsticks

and brought it to her lips. The surge of electric energy swept through her body, as her face flushed and her scalp and hands tingled. And just as the first time she tasted Julien's cooking, it had a taste that she then recognized as sage.

The golden flecks were indeed pine nuts, and they exploded beneath the crush of her teeth with a satisfying, oily pop. Her mouth was on fire, and at the same time, there was a cooling note in this sauce.

"Hmm," Julien said as he sat down and regarded his mat.

Lumi focused on filling a new roll with studious attention. When Julien averted his gaze, she asked, "What's in that sauce, anyway? Looks like some kind of pesto."

"Ah, this. Yes, it's a mint pesto. Very simple. Mint, basil, olive oil, and roasted pine nuts. Are you sure you don't want to try it?" he asked.

"Thanks, I'm good," she said.

With that, she focused on her sushi rolling for the rest of the workshop. When it was over, the participants thanked them and left merrily with their take-home boxes. Lumi helped put the tables and chairs back in their proper places and packed the mats for Ms. Tanaka. Back in the kitchen, Julien, Gloria, and Ruben were storing the leftover food.

"So, who's staying to help clean up?" Julien asked.

Lumi knew she could, but just then, a current rippled through her, reminding her of those few pleasurable bites she had taken earlier. And that was how she knew she had to leave as soon as possible.

"Sorry, I have plans!" she said. Lumi grabbed her jacket from her locker and double-stepped it out of the kitchen. Her only regret of the night was that she did not have a chance to roll a piece of sauce-covered sushi into a napkin and stick it in her pocket for later. But she could live with that. There were worse regrets to be had.

MUSHROOM AND GRUYÈRE SOUFFLÉS
Serves 3 (2 soufflés per person)

2 ½ tablespoons butter
²/₃ cup mushrooms, sliced
²/₃ cup whole milk
2 eggs, separated
2 tablespoons all-purpose flour
²/₃ cup gruyère, grated
¼ teaspoon salt
¼ teaspoon black pepper

Preheat the oven to 400 degrees Fahrenheit. Grease 2 ramekins with a dab of butter. Heat 2 tablespoons of the butter in a saucepan and sauté the mushrooms for about 2 minutes. In a small bowl, whisk together the milk and egg yolks, and add the salt and black pepper. Add the flour and the remaining tablespoon of butter and whisk continuously. Pour the mixture into the pan with the mushrooms and continue to whisk. Add the gruyère and stir until it melts. Fold the egg whites into the mixture, pour the batter into the ramekins, and bake until risen and lightly browned, between 15 and 20 minutes.

17

LUMI

Lumi stood in front of her full-length mirror, scrutinizing her appearance. She had decided on wearing a forest-green sleeveless brocade dress that hit just above the knee and a pair of platform heels she hadn't worn since the grand opening of Caraluna. It was the night of Rafelina's office's spring fling, and Lumi was going as her date since Rafelina's husband, Anthony, would be working his shift as a police officer in Alphabet City.

Lumi wasn't one for high heels and disliked the idea of contorting her feet into torturous positions, but the party was at the Museum of Modern Art, so it had to be dressy. Besides, if Rafelina wore her usual five-inch stilettos, Lumi would end up looking like a willowy dwarf at her side.

She tucked a pair of foldable ballet flats into her purse for later and returned to the mirror to weave her curls into a French braid, fastening it into a low bun at the bottom. She added a pair of crystal chandelier earrings and brushed a few strokes of mascara onto her lashes. Once she was dressed, she hobbled down the stairs and hailed a cab on the corner of 218th Street near her apartment.

She dozed off on the way down the West Side Highway, and before she knew it, the cab was pulling up to the curb of Fifty-Fourth Street and Rafelina was opening the car door.

"Come on, Lu," she said, blowing a quick air-kiss next to Lumi's cheek, "the open bar is only till twelve."

Lumi looked Rafelina up and down. Sure enough, she was decked out in sky-high fuchsia stilettos and wore a bottom-hugging black dress—of which there was much to hug—with a silver zipper down the back. Rafelina had also flat-ironed her jet-black waves into submission.

"Preciosa, mi amorch," Lumi said, and Rafelina smiled.

The vast entrance hall of the museum was filled with throngs of well-dressed people, which didn't surprise Lumi in the slightest, since Prestone Capital, the hedge fund Rafelina worked for, had a staff of about five hundred. Rafelina guided her through the crowd, air-kissing people she knew in the crowd as she walked. Lumi smiled at Rafelina's coworkers but didn't stop to converse. Instead, she followed Rafelina out into the tastefully manicured sculpture garden.

Lumi thanked God that she had brought her jacket. On that April night, the bone-crushing chill of winter had faded, but the air was still breezy enough to make an evening outside in a sleeveless dress uncomfortable.

The garden had been decorated with iridescent bulbs, which cast a psychedelic glow over the famed sculptures and greenery. Small rectangular tables bearing flutes of champagne had been interspersed along the cemented paths, and wait-resses dressed entirely in gold lamé were making their rounds through the garden offering glasses of rosé from circular enameled trays.

Lumi plucked a glass from one of the waitresses' tray, took a sip, and sighed deeply. It was nice to be served for a change, instead of worrying about dishes not being done on time, or who had found an apple in their dinner, or whether the soufflé had congealed into an inedible piece of rubber. She inhaled the fresh night air deeply. Although MoMA was only ten blocks from DAX, she felt a world away.

Lumi was busy enjoying the tango-electronic music that was playing in the background when she scanned the crowd and saw him standing near a potted palm on the opposite side of the courtyard. The red stubble and freckles on his face caught her eye. She inhaled deeply again, this time for a different reason, and when she let out the breath, Rafelina turned to her.

"What is it?" she asked.

"It's him," Lumi said, gesturing through the palm fronds. "That's Julien."

A hushed gasp escaped Rafelina's lips. "*That's* Julien? Damn, girl!"

Lumi barely heard her as Julien stepped into full view, his brown eyes finding hers. A faint electrical undercurrent hummed through the air. People were talking and waving hands all around them, but to her it was all white noise. It was just him and her in the courtyard, and none of the normal restrictions of the workplace. The night suddenly felt dangerous.

She was compelled to look away. Before she could turn around, she smelled his woodsy cologne. She glanced at Rafelina, who was no help at all, as she was busy ogling Julien, a goofy grin plastered on her face. When Lumi looked up, he was standing right in front of her.

She looked straight at him, feeling a flutter in her chest as she took in his stubbled face. He was dressed in a navy dress shirt with the sleeves rolled up, as usual, and dark gray slacks. Even in the nippy April night, he still managed to exude warmth.

"Julien," she said. "Fancy running into you here."

He broke out into a beaming smile. "Can't go anywhere these days without seeing you, Ms. Santana," he said, then winked at Rafelina.

"Julien, this is my good friend *Mrs.* Rafelina Acosta. Rafelina, this . . . is Julien Dax." She decided not to add any further detail about who he was, and he didn't say otherwise.

Rafelina took Julien's hand and shook it briefly. "A pleasure, Mr. Dax," she purred. "Sooo, what brings you to Prestone Capital's spring party?"

Julien barely heard her. He was staring at Lumi, studying the way she shifted her weight from one foot to the other, admiring the way her favorite moonstone necklace lay in the delicate hollow of her throat. Lumi raised her eyebrows in his direction.

"Soooo, Julien, what brings you here?" she said, mimicking Rafelina's comical tone.

Julien met her eyes. "My sister," he said.

"You have a sister?" she asked in surprise.

"That's what my parents have been telling me all this time," he said, grinning.

Lumi followed his gaze across the room, her eyes landing

on a portly strawberry blonde with a self-assured air who was gazing back at them.

"Come, let me introduce you," he said.

Lumi and Rafelina exchanged glances, falling in step behind Julien as they followed him around the perimeter of the garden.

"That's the HR director of the company," Rafelina whispered to Lumi as they trailed behind him.

"Hello!" the young woman greeted them jovially.

"Lumi, Rafelina, this is my sister, Rochelle Dax. Rochelle, this is Lumi Santana, accomplished chef, and her friend Mrs. Rafelina Acosta."

Rochelle smiled. She gave Julien a questioning look, and he nodded almost imperceptibly. "Oh!" Rochelle gushed, clasping Lumi's hand. "It's so lovely to meet you."

Rochelle was wearing an olive-green cocktail dress with chunky asymmetrical rhinestones around the collar. Her nails were painted a demure shell pink, and her hazel eyes were perfectly lined with black liquid liner.

Lumi returned her handshake, looking between brother and sister to see if there would be any more surreptitious communication. They were now both focused on her.

"So, what brings you to our little office party?" Rochelle asked.

Lumi nodded toward Rafelina. "Rafelina is an accountant at the firm."

"Oh, of course," Rochelle said, smiling. "You were on the tax panel last week at the presidents' meeting."

Rafelina nodded and straightened her posture. There was an awkward moment of silence as Rochelle looked at Julien,

Julien at Lumi, and Lumi at Rafelina, all with varying degrees of expectation.

Finally, Rafelina said, "Well! We're going to finish checking out the sculpture garden . . . as well as the bar. Great meeting you both."

She grabbed Lumi's arm, and Lumi turned and gave a little wave to Rochelle and stumbled behind her friend.

"Don't start gossiping about them, they can still hear you," Lumi hissed.

Rafelina laughed under her breath. "Did you know he had a sister?"

"No," Lumi said. "We don't talk about anything in the kitchen."

"Nothing?" Rafelina asked incredulously.

"Not really, no," Lumi said.

"Mm-hmm," Rafelina said. She managed to remain silent for nearly five seconds before blurting out, "Girl . . . you trippin'," and shaking her head.

Lumi looked at her through narrowed eyes. "What do you mean?"

Rafelina puckered her lips and used them to point in Julien's direction. "He is . . . wow. That man has, like, animal magnetism or whatever that shit is called."

Lumi sighed. It was even more apparent to her at this party with the way he looked in the moonlight, the way he downed a shot of something with some compatriots and threw his head back and laughed heartily.

There was a gaggle of women now standing around him and Rochelle. Lumi made a disgusted face.

When they got to the bar, Lumi realized that the open bar

Rafelina had promised proved to be a figment of her imagination. After paying seventeen dollars for a mojito, Rafelina was ready to go home. "I could have sworn they said *open* bar," she muttered under her breath, stirring the mint leaves at the bottom of her glass with a tiny swizzle stick. Lumi had stuck to a single glass of wine, not feeling the desire to drink more. She didn't mind at all when Rafelina announced she was ready to leave.

Back in the sculpture garden, they looked around to see if they spotted Julien or Rochelle. When they saw neither, they dragged their pained feet out onto the museum's front steps to wait for the Uber they'd ordered. As they stood there, they felt a breeze whip through their hair when the door opened behind them.

"Leaving so soon?" Julien said softly.

Lumi nodded.

"That's too bad," he said, "I was just going to grab some dinner. Do you want to come with me?" he asked Lumi, his eyes hopeful.

Lumi bit her lip. "I need to make sure Rafelina gets home okay," she said, resting her hand on her friend's arm.

Rafelina shook her head vehemently. "No way, go ahead. I'll take the Uber back home."

Lumi studied her friend. "Are you sure?"

"Yes!" Rafelina responded emphatically, waving her off with both hands. "Anthony should be home by the time I get there, anyway."

Lumi breathed a little sigh of relief. She felt better about sending Rafelina home alone if Anthony would be there. "Okay . . . thanks," Lumi said.

Rafelina looked mystified, as though she expected Lumi to protest. She looked from Julien to Lumi as the Uber arrived. "All righty," she said. "I'll text you when I get in. Bye then."

She hopped into the car and pulled the door closed behind her.

18

LUMI

Lumi and Julien were silent for several minutes before Julien spoke.

"There's a Jamaican place downtown I've been wanting to try. Shall we?" he asked, holding out his hand. Lumi studied it but didn't move to grab it. Julien stuffed it into his pocket.

"You're telling me you eat something else besides French food?" she asked in mock surprise.

Julien laughed. "Of course I do. DAX is my job, but it's not my life."

"Really?" she asked in disbelief.

"There's a lot you don't know about me," he said, studying her face. "So . . . what do you say?"

"I don't know," she said. "I try not to eat out too much. It can be emotionally draining for me." She realized how odd that sounded after she said it out loud.

"Oh, I know exactly what you mean," he said. "Some of these chefs make you want to cry when you see how sloppy they are."

Lumi laughed out loud. "Yeah . . . something like that."

"Well, while we decide, why don't we start walking to the subway?" he asked.

"You take the subway?"

"Christ, Ms. Santana, what do you think I am?"

Lumi looked at him coyly. "Are you sure you want me to answer that?"

"Hmm, maybe not." He smiled wryly and held out his arm in the direction they would be going.

They ambled down the street and turned onto Fifth Avenue.

"Wait," she said. "I'm definitely going to need these."

She opened her bag and pulled out the flats, shucking off the platform heels to slip them on. He offered his hand to steady her, and she took it. Then she tucked the heels into her bag, pushing them down as far as they would go.

They looked down Fifth Avenue and searched the street corners for the green light that signaled there was a subway station nearby. There wasn't one in sight. "Let's walk to Fifty-Third and Seventh and take the train from there," he suggested, and she nodded in agreement.

They walked on.

"So, is it just you and your sister?" she asked.

Julien shook his head. In the light that streamed from the streetlamps, his hair reflected bright orange. "No, my brother, Christophe, is the oldest," he said. "He stayed in Montreal."

"Oh. Montreal? That's where you're from?"

Julien nodded.

"Did you play ice hockey growing up?"

"Of course."

She laughed at his blunt response. "Sorry. Not to change the subject from your brother."

"Yes, no worries. He was the one to assume the mantle of the family business. My father would have preferred me to . . . In fact, he's never gotten over it."

"Even after seeing how successful you have been?"

"Yep. To him, culinary is not a 'real' profession. To him, I'm a fool for leaving his business behind."

"Oh? And what's his business?" she asked.

"Finance. He finances start-up companies, buys and sells, blah blah blah."

"Well, that sounds dreadful," she said. Her heart fluttered when he responded with a dazzling smile. "I think you made the right choice."

"Do you?" he asked, his eyes earnest.

"Yes." She nodded emphatically. "When I see you working at DAX, it's clear that you are pursuing your passion."

"Well, yes," he replied. "Ever since I was young, it was clear to me I'd need to pursue my passion to be happy."

"So how did you get into cooking?"

"My siblings and I would spend the summers at my grand-mère's place in rural Quebec. She taught all of us how to cook. Christophe didn't care for it, but Rochelle is an excellent cook—probably better than me—but she listened to my father and found her way into finance. As for me, once I started I didn't want to stop. My father and I fought about my path constantly. When he said he was going to call all his friends in Montreal to make sure no one would finance my venture, I left for New York."

"Wow. And you made it."

He nodded. "Yes. Not an easy endeavor, but I accomplished what I set out to do."

She wanted to say, *Good for you for following your dreams*, but the words wouldn't come. Instead, she looked at her watch. It was 12:30 in the morning.

"Are you sure this place will be open this late?" she asked.

Julien thought about it for a minute. "I think so," he said. "It is New York, after all."

They entered the subway at Forty-Ninth Street and Seventh Avenue and boarded the N train moments after they descended to the platform.

They traveled along in silence for fifteen minutes, sitting side by side on the subway bench. Every time the train lurched, the movement threw Lumi against Julien's side. After the second time, she decided not to slide away, feeling her willowy arm pressed against his muscular one.

It felt surreal to ride in a subway car with Julien after midnight, their arms pressed together in this way. It was new for her to feel safe in a man's presence. With Colton, she had always suspected that if they were to get mugged, she would be the one fighting off the attackers while he hid behind a tree.

The subway came to a stop at Eighth Street. Julien took her hand and she followed, walking quickly to keep up with his long strides.

"West, we should walk west. East is where I would walk if I were going to play chess," Julien said.

"You play chess?"

"I like to, when I have the chance. You can imagine how often that is," he said, grinning.

They stopped in front of a cavernous restaurant named

Miz Suzie's Island Spice, whose awning had been fashioned into a faux thatched-roof hut.

Julien held the door open for Lumi and they stepped into the restaurant. The space was decorated with strings of multi-colored lights and potted palms similar to the ones at MoMA. A boisterous dance-hall beat played in the background.

An amicable-looking woman with coffee-colored skin ushered them to a corner table. Julien pulled out Lumi's chair for her and then scooted it back in after she sat. There was an aroma of coconut and rum in the air.

"Is someone drinking coconut rum, or do they just spray that around?" Julien wondered aloud.

Lumi shrugged. "If that's a spray, I want it for my apartment," she replied.

A tall waiter with tortoiseshell glasses greeted them and asked for their drink order.

"I'll have a rum and Coke," Lumi said, inspired by the aroma in the air.

"Make that two," Julien added.

He leaned back in his chair, which was upholstered with a palm-tree print linen fabric. He had loosened the first couple buttons on his shirt, and Lumi could see a smattering of red chest hair peeking out. His face looked relaxed, and his eyes were twinkling. Lumi would have never thought so, but Julien seemed to blend right in with the environment. She smiled.

Julien cocked his head, gazing at her with curiosity.

"You're so different here than you are at DAX," she blurted out.

He smiled widely. "I suppose I am. For me, the best part is that for the first time I get to sit down at a table with you," he said.

Lumi glanced down at the salt and pepper shakers. Was it really so wrong for her to be out with him, getting some fresh air and good food?

He reached across the table and grabbed her hand. "This seems like as good a time as any to tell you that I don't know what it is, but you *do* something to me," he murmured, his voice low enough for only her to hear.

She swallowed, taken aback. Had he been reading her mind? He studied Lumi's eyes, her expression, her body language, and whatever he saw in her did not deter him from speaking the rest of his mind.

"Whatever it is, I've never felt like this about anyone before, crazy as that may sound when you're talking about thirty-eight years of life." He paused, his amber eyes fully focused on her brown ones. "And I have to know if you feel it too. Lumi, we're far away from DAX. What do you say we just forget about the restaurant and be ourselves for one night? If it doesn't work out, we don't have to ever talk about this again."

That didn't sound unreasonable. One night without so many rules. If she was being honest with herself, he did do something to her too. No one else's cooking had the same surge of electricity as his did. She had never tasted sage in someone's dish and still wasn't sure what it meant. If this thing did end up working, what would that mean for them? She decided to shelve the issue until another time and nodded at him in agreement.

The waiter returned with their rum and Cokes and asked if they were ready to order.

"I'll have the coconut shrimp and rice with peas," Lumi said, not having looked at the menu.

Julien nodded. "Mmm, sounds good. I'll have the oxtail."

They fell into a lull once more. Livelier music started to play and Lumi heard some cheers and whoops from behind her. She glanced over her shoulder and saw that there was a tiny dance floor in the back of the restaurant.

She turned back to Julien. "Do you dance?" she asked.

"No, not at all," he said, grinning.

"Too bad."

The waiter came back, bearing their steaming plates. They ate and Lumi was relieved to find that whoever had cooked had been in a jovial mood. She blessed him or her silently. Julien seemed to be enjoying the food too, and he offered her some fleshy discs of oxtail to try. He also speared a shrimp off her plate.

When the meal was done, the waiter came around once more and asked if they would like anything else.

"I'll have an espresso and the dessert menu, please," Lumi said, and Julien contorted his features into a playfully shocked expression.

"An espresso at one thirty A.M.?" he exclaimed.

She shrugged. "In my family, there's no set time for drinking coffee," she said simply.

Julien focused on her more acutely. "Lumi, where *is* your family from?" he asked.

Someone in the kitchen had adorned her plate with an edible orchid, and she picked it up and examined it in the candlelight. "My mother is from the Dominican Republic, and my father is, or was too."

"Is, or was?"

She looked down at the flower. "We don't know his whereabouts. He left my mother when I was one and a half years old," she said.

Julien placed his hand on her forearm as he took in this new information. "I'm sorry to hear that. It must have been very hard for your mother."

"Well . . . what can I say? To my mother, good men are like ghosts: everyone swears they're out there, but nobody can substantiate having encountered one. So, who knows . . ." She tore the corner of a leaf off the orchid and squeezed it between her thumb and index finger until she extracted some juice.

"And you, what do you think?" he asked.

Lumi let out a long exhale. "I don't know," she said, "I've never been much of a ghost hunter."

Suddenly, she didn't feel like dessert anymore. The mechanics of chewing felt crude, and she was aware of how intensely Julien was watching her.

"Anyway, that's enough about me," she said. "Why don't we get the check and walk a bit?"

Julien seemed pleased by this suggestion and signaled for the check. Lumi was itching to stand up. She was overcome by the urge to stretch her legs . . . and the feeling that she had said too much. She hadn't planned on talking about her family life with him, but there was something disarming about having him listen attentively to her every word.

It felt good to be outside in the fresh air. It had gotten colder since they were last outside, and between the espresso filtering into her bloodstream and the brisk night air, Lumi felt revived.

They had walked several blocks when they stopped on the corner to wait for the light to change. Julien turned toward Lumi and took her hands in his, looking deep into her eyes.

"You're quiet all of a sudden," he said.

Lumi turned away. "I talked way too much in there," she said.

Julien shook his head. "I don't think you talked too much at all." He paused. "Ms. Santana, can I kiss you?"

She nodded, and he pulled her close to him and touched his lips to hers. The kiss was sweet, but there was a jagged edge of hunger. She felt a faint churning in the pit of her belly, gradually growing stronger as he slid his hands down her waist, pulling her even closer to him.

She thought of what he said at dinner. *Just for one night, forget about all the rules*, she told herself. Their tongues twisted together, and he caught her lower lip between his teeth, giving it a playful little nibble. She could feel his smile against her lips. He pressed her body flush against his.

A low whistle came from behind them: "Woohoo, get a room." A pack of frat boys who looked like they had just stumbled out of one party passed by looking for the next. Lumi pulled away from Julien, remembering herself and that they were, in fact, in the middle of Avenue A.

She looked up at Julien, and his eyes were burning with desire. "Do you want to . . . go somewhere?" he asked, his voice thick and gravelly.

Across the street, Lumi eyed a shrouded storefront with an eerie green light glowing around the edges of the curtain.

"Absinthe NYC . . . what's that?" she asked. She knew that a bar wasn't what he had in mind, but she didn't feel quite ready to go somewhere more private. Once they were alone she wasn't sure she would be able to convince herself that being with him was a bad idea.

Julien studied the storefront. "Looks like a bar to me," he said.

"Right, I got that," she said, "but do they actually serve absinthe in there?"

Julien shrugged. "Only one way to find out," he said, as they walked over to the door. He pushed back the curtain and ushered Lumi inside. The entire bar was lit with eerie green lights that formed a chartreuse-colored halo over the top fringe of the window curtains. The lounge area was scattered with small triangular tables, almost all of them taken by men and women who nursed mysterious, colorful drinks. Cacophonous jazz music blared over the stereo, combining percussive drumbeats with dainty trumpet solos that made an almost comical contrast.

Julien leaned over the top of the bar, keeping Lumi close at his side.

"Good evening, sir, do you in fact serve absinthe in this fine establishment?" he asked.

The bartender rolled his eyes. "Yeah," he answered in a flat voice.

"We'll take two shots of your finest absinthe, then," he said, picking up a tiny info card that rested on the bar top.

ABSINTHE—FAMED LIBATION FROM THE 1800S, MUSE TO MANY ARTISTS AND WRITERS, CREDITED WITH INSPIRING SOME OF THE GREAT WORKS OF THE BELLE EPOQUE, ALONG WITH MAKING SOME OF ITS PROPONENTS GO MAD.

"Well, there's a recommendation," he said, chuckling.

He held out his hand and helped Lumi climb up onto one of the barstools. The bartender passed them their shots over the bar, and they each took one in hand. Julien examined the bright green liquid, turning the shot glass this way and that. He looked at Lumi with a raised eyebrow. "Are we really doing this?"

She laughed. "Yes!" she answered, as they clinked glasses and downed the shots as fast as possible. Her throat burned as the absinthe slid down, but she forced herself to swallow it in one gulp. Julien shook his head like a dog shaking off water.

"Christ. That tastes like it's from the 1800s," he said. He laughed loudly, then turned to Lumi. "Are you okay?" he asked. "Do you want any water?"

Lumi shook her head sweetly. "I'm fine."

Just then, the bartender drummed on the bar top to get their attention. "Hey, sorry, but I'll need you guys to move to one of the tables," he said. "We have a jazz band playing an after-hours set in ten minutes, and they're going to be setting up in front of the bar."

Julien and Lumi exchanged glances.

"I love jazz," Lumi said.

They took a seat at one of the tables lining the wall opposite the bar and fell into a comfortable silence as the sounds of laughing, singing, shouts, and clinking glasses swirled around them.

After a while, Lumi started to grow a little warmer and more fluid. She got an uneasy feeling that they were being watched. She looked around the room and met the eyes of a pale, heavyset man with wild curly hair and a flushed face. He was watching them intently.

Lumi leaned into Julien. "Do you know him?"

She gestured with her chin in the direction of the watcher. Julien rubbed his eyes and looked toward where she had pointed.

"Who is that?" Lumi whispered, her eyes not leaving Julien's face.

Julien groaned. "That's Verdi, the owner of Maison Neuf.

It's only a block away from here. I should have known he would be lurking around. He's a nineteenth-century liqueur connoisseur," he muttered, absentmindedly running his free hand through his hair.

"What's your deal with him?" she asked.

He made no attempt to conceal his irritation. "He had dinner at DAX one night and since then has claimed that I stole his boeuf bourguignon recipe." He sighed and rolled his eyes.

"But the recipes you use are the most standard versions of the classics," she said.

"Exactly! It's nonsense. He's a petty man who is envious of my business and knows he'll never have as steady clientele as I have in midtown."

When she looked up, she saw Verdi waddling over to where they sat. "Wait. Why is he coming over here?" she asked.

"Well, that's another thing about Verdi," Julien said. "When he's drunk, he likes to argue."

Lumi's eyes widened. "Great. And will you—"

"No," Julien interjected. "I will not fight him. He can say or do whatever he wants. I'm not getting you in the middle of that. Whatever he tries, we will just ignore him and continue enjoying our night."

Lumi paused to think this over for a moment. "Should we leave?"

"Absolutely not. I will not give him the pleasure of having any power over me . . . or you."

She rested her chin in her palm. "All right, then," she said, though she was sure that leaving was still a better idea.

Verdi stopped right in front of their table. He grabbed the back of a chair and began to pull it over. Julien shot him a forbidding stare, and he stopped in his tracks.

"Look who decided to come downtown. Slumming today, Dax?" asked Verdi. "Or did you just decide to swoop in and see what other recipes you can steal?"

Julien looked at him in disgust. "When are you going to stop spreading lies?" he asked him.

Verdi furrowed his brow and narrowed his eyes. "No one else puts tarragon and mushrooms in their boeuf!" he said, slapping his thigh for emphasis.

Julien yawned. "That's nonsense," he replied. "My grandmother put tarragon and mushrooms in her boeuf bourguignon all through my childhood in Quebec. Now, can you please leave us alone?"

Verdi glared at him and then leered at Lumi. "You just wait until I copyright my recipe, Dax. Then you'll have to send me a check every time you sell that dish," he said.

"No problem, Verdi. I'll send you the dirty plates as payment," Julien said.

Verdi turned on his heel, his beady eyes menacingly illuminated in the green-lit room, and walked back to his table.

Julien let out an exasperated sigh and turned to Lumi, running his hand down the length of her arm. "Sorry about that," he murmured. "Let's not let that idiot ruin our night."

She nodded uneasily and leaned into him, letting him wrap his arm around her. She tried not to look toward Verdi as he glowered at her from his table near the entrance, but the feeling of his eyes seemed inescapable. She squirmed in her seat. Julien noticed.

"You know what, on second thought, there are so many other places we can go that won't make you uncomfortable. Let's get the hell out of here."

They stood up and headed to the door. Julien strode right

past Verdi, stepping in front of Lumi to open the door for her. She thought they had cleared him until she heard Verdi's chair squeak out from under him.

"Hey, Dax," he shouted, "you can pay me back for the recipe whenever you want. And while you're at it, why don't you throw in your little Cuban chick as interest? Then we'll call it even."

Lumi cringed as she heard the words and squeezed her eyes shut. When she opened them, Julien had already moved in on Verdi. She heard a sickening crack as his fist connected with the rival chef's jaw. It was an unyielding curveball of a punch, and that combined with however many drinks Verdi had had that night knocked him clean off his feet. He flailed and stumbled backward, tripping over a chair and falling flat on his posterior.

"Damn, Julien," he sputtered, shaking his head and rubbing his sore jaw.

Julien glared at him. "I can't imagine what else you would have expected, friend," he said. "I mean Verdi. 'Friend' is clearly not the fitting term here. And she's not a chick, she's a woman and chef, and a better chef than you." The sleeve on the arm he had punched Verdi with had rolled down, and he ceremoniously rolled it back up, turning toward the door.

"W-wait," sputtered Verdi. "Isn't anyone going to take a video of this?" he asked, casting his gaze around wildly.

"Oh, is that what you were hoping for, to get me some bad press?" Julien glanced around the bar, where the other patrons had gone back to nursing their drinks. "That doesn't seem to have panned out for you. Enjoy the rest of your night," he said, and they exited the bar.

Julien exhaled once they had taken a few steps away from

the bar. He stopped to lean over and rest his hands on his knees. Once he caught his breath, he straightened up and touched his hand to Lumi's chin.

"This wasn't exactly what I had in mind for a nightcap," he said.

Lumi allowed her eyes to drift down to his hand and let his soft touch against her face calm her. She was unsure what to say. And what did Verdi mean by calling it even? She made a mental note to ask him another time, when he wasn't coming down from having punched someone in the face.

"It wasn't what I had in mind either, but . . . thank you," she said softly. "You know what? It's three A.M. I should head home."

"Hey. I feel bad ending the night on this note. Why don't you come back with me to the kitchen and I'll make you dessert?"

Lumi hated that the mention of the word "dessert" sounded so enticing. It sounded pretty intriguing, though . . . her and Julien alone in the kitchen (she liked how he referred to his restaurant simply as "the kitchen"). She looked at him and felt a twinge deep in her belly. Her proximity to him, the lingering feeling of his lips on hers and of his hair in her hands, the smell of his cologne . . . was a fun fantasy that came alive in her imagination. But that's all it was. Tomorrow night, and the night after that, they would be back to work as though nothing happened. It would *have* to be like nothing happened for it not to be awkward in the workplace.

She gently shook her head. "That sounds nice, Julien, but I should really get home."

His shoulders drooped a bit, and he nodded. "Okay, then. I'll order you a car."

When the car pulled up, she gave him a quick peck on the side of his mouth and jumped in. When she glanced back quickly to wave goodbye, the look in his eyes was pure flame.

LUMI'S MIDNIGHT ESPRESSO
Serves 2

$^3/_4$ cup water
$^1/_2$ cup ground coffee (NOT instant)

Fill the bottom of an old-fashioned espresso maker with the water. Drop the metal filter in place and add the coffee grounds. Screw on the lid and place on the stove on high heat. When the coffee is heard bubbling up, remove from the flame immediately and serve in demitasse cups.

For best results, wait until after dark.

19

LUMI

The next day turned out to be sunny, and yet Lumi could think of no better place to spend the morning than in her bathtub. She sighed contentedly as she sank in and thought back to last night. She let out a long, deep breath as she remembered the events: the museum party, sitting on the subway with Julien, his wide smile and hearty laugh, the feel of his hair as she twisted it between her fingers, the flush of his freckled skin when they had stumbled out of Absinthe. The feel of his strong arm around her shoulders, spiriting her away from the chaos. His broad, wide shoulders.

She shivered as she thought about him and his body. She leaned her head back and let her hand slip between her legs. She knew her own body and what would quickly bring her pleasure. As she caressed that spot, she thought of Julien. What would it be like to feel his bare skin against hers? How would it be to feel him inside her? She could practically hear his deep, ragged breathing against her ear. She bit her lip as she felt the familiar but welcome swell and rode the spiking waves until she found her release.

As she drifted into a pleasant and relaxed space, she had to admit that as much as she loved her own touch, it was the thought of Julien that had ignited her desire. She thought back to the hunger she felt in his kiss, tempting her, tantalizing her, and suddenly it felt silly for her to keep fighting this growing urge.

She thought about the next time she would see him. It wouldn't be tonight, since she had the day off. But what if it was? What would happen if she were to show up after closing time when he was the only one left?

It would be clear that she was only there for one thing.

She willed herself to stand up, shaking droplets onto the floor and disturbing the tranquil surface of the bath. Something had been awoken in her, and suddenly she was less concerned by what people would think and where their relationship would lead. There was something sparking between them, and maybe she should let it run its course naturally. Then they would be able to work together normally without this incandescent whatever-it-was constantly being a distraction. At least that was what she told herself as she rummaged through her closet to choose an outfit for her nighttime trip.

20

JULIEN

Julien awoke with a start and glanced at the clock. It was 7:00 A.M. He had slept for only three hours, yet he felt wide awake. He got up and paced around his apartment, stared out the window as he watched the cars go by. He scrutinized the kitchen, tile by tile. They were all white and sparkling.

"Damn," he muttered under his breath. He needed something to do to distract himself from this flame of passion that was consuming him.

Frustrated, he headed toward the shower. He peeled off the boxers he had slept in. He twisted the knob to turn the showerhead on, and as he waited for the warm water to flow, his thoughts drifted back to last night. To Lumi. Hearing her name on his lips thrilled his heart, and he whispered it to himself and felt the hairs stand up on his arms.

The smart thing to do would be to take a step back before this went any further, but at the same time he knew this was more than just a crush. He thought back to their kiss last night, and his mouth burned with desire as he recalled the taste of her lips, juicy as raspberries. He ached to drink of them.

And then that imbecile Verdi had come around and ruined everything. He could feel his fist closing reflexively as he recalled Verdi's comments. How dare he say anything about the woman who ignited his being in this way. Verdi was lucky to have escaped with all his limbs intact.

He recalled the feel of her body pressed against his and he suddenly couldn't stand still another second.

He took hold of himself and began to stroke. He was starting to recall the feel of her pert breasts pressing against his chest when the doorbell rang. He tried to ignore it, but it rang a second time. He cursed under his breath as he stepped out of the bathroom, wrapped a towel around his midsection, and strode to the door. He peered out the peephole, sighing under his breath.

"Berta, what are you doing here this early?" he asked.

The housekeeper stared at him, confused. He was usually happy when she came early.

"I came at seven thirty today, Mr. Dax, so I can be leaving early. Little Julito has his first softball game of the season," she explained.

He nodded his head in a hurry. "Okay. Great. Thank you," he replied, and ducked back into the master bedroom, shut the door behind him, and climbed back in the still-running shower. The appearance of his housekeeper had somewhat doused his passion, but he still felt like he was about to burst.

Touching himself again, he guided his thoughts back to Lumi and her body. He thought about the times that he snuck glances at her in the kitchen, as he admired the way the smallness of her waist gave way to the swell of her hips. The flush of her face as she worked made him wonder what she would look like if she was flushed by a different kind of exertion. He was starting to feel his climax coming on when the phone rang. He ignored it until the phone rang louder and louder.

"Fuck," he muttered under his breath, abandoning his pursuit. He threw on a towel and stepped out to grab his phone.

"Dax here," he said in a thick, woolly voice.

"Julien, are you still in bed?" said a man's voice on the other side of the call.

"No, Patrick," Julien grumbled. "What's going on?"

There was a moment of silence.

"Julien . . . our breakfast plans . . ."

Julien stared at the phone blankly for a moment and then slapped his forehead. He had forgotten all about their Friday breakfast. "Shit. What time did we say?" he asked.

"Julien! Eight o'clock at Brasserie Cognac," Patrick said, his voice strained.

Julien glanced at the clock and groaned. "Calm down, Patrick," he said. "I'll be there in twenty minutes." He hung up without saying another word and thought for a moment. It was no use. Now Patrick was waiting for him. He turned up the water as hot as it would go and quickly lathered and showered.

He threw on a loose pair of cargo pants and a white T-shirt and dashed out the door. Brasserie Cognac was on Fifty-Sixth Street and Broadway, just a few blocks from Julien's apartment, which overlooked Columbus Circle. He walked down Broadway until the latticed sidewalk tables and his irritated friend and former next-door neighbor came into view.

Patrick focused on his tiny demitasse cup and swirled the espresso he had left at the bottom so that he didn't have to make eye contact with Julien as he approached. He pulled at his short locks as though they had suddenly become too tight for his scalp.

"Morning!" Julien said, pulling up a chair.

Patrick looked from Julien to his watch and grimaced. Julien noticed that Patrick was practically wearing his shoulders as earrings. As Julien sat, they lowered one centimeter at a time.

"I can't believe you forgot our breakfast plans," Patrick said.

"I'm sorry. I had a long night."

Patrick raised an eyebrow. "Well, it's been a while since I had a long night," he said. "Everything good at the kitchen?"

"Y-yes, yes, all good," Julien answered. "How is Wall Street treating you?"

Patrick shrugged. "Oh, you know. Same old."

"And how's the new apartment?"

"Eh. Water Street is not Columbus Circle. But you can't beat the five-minute morning commute," Patrick said.

"Sure."

A waitress passed and he ordered a plate of steak and eggs with a double espresso. Patrick stuck to his coffee.

"You're not eating anything?" Julien asked.

Patrick shook his head. "Nah, I lost my appetite." There was a pause. "So I started renovations this past week on the investment house on University Avenue in the Bronx," Patrick said.

"That's great. I'll have to get some investment pointers from you some other time."

Patrick furrowed his brow. "Why some other time? We're here now."

Julien's gaze was fixed east, in the direction of the Museum of Modern Art. "Mm-hmm," Julien replied.

Patrick cleared his throat. "*Anyway*. I need your help choosing the kitchen appliances. I'm thinking whether I should put in a basic stove and a better-quality fridge, or vice versa."

Someone passed by wearing a strong infusion of gardenia perfume. Julien breathed deeply and his senses went reeling. A moment passed and Julien still hadn't answered Patrick.

Patrick's frown deepened. "Or I could just light the kitchen on fire and see how that goes," he said.

"Yeah, mm-hmm. Sounds good," Julien said, looking for the source of that perfume.

"Julien!" Patrick said.

"What is it?" Julien asked, irked by Patrick's tone.

Patrick leveled his gaze on him as the waitress placed Julien's plate before him. "I just said I could light the kitchen on fire. And you said yes."

Julien's face was a mask of horror. "What? Why the hell would you do that?"

Patrick hung his face in his hands. "Julien . . . man. What is going on with you? You haven't heard a word I said since you got here."

Julien rubbed his eyes, inhaling the aroma of the grilled steak and runny eggs. "Ah, just need some protein, perhaps," he said, biting into the croissant that came with his breakfast.

Patrick stared at him. "Yup, croissants are world renowned for their protein content," he said, sighing to himself. "You've met a woman, haven't you?"

Julien's gaze flew to Patrick's face. "How did you know?"

Patrick rolled his eyes. "Come on. Spill it."

"Remember I told you I was getting a new sous chef?"

Patrick nodded. "She's the woman?"

"Yes."

"Hmm."

"What's hmm?"

"Nothing, just . . . be careful there."

"I will. Thanks, Mom." Another pause.

"All righty. Good talk," Patrick said, and finished the last sip of his espresso. "I'm going to head to Home Depot, then, and start choosing my paint colors." He dropped a few crumpled bills on the table for his coffee.

Julien looked at him as if he had just dropped a dead fish on the table but didn't bother to argue. "See you, Pat," Julien replied, and drank his remaining espresso in one long swig. He was going to be at the kitchen until ten that night since Lumi was off . . . at least in theory. He had already decided to close early if the night was slow and catch up on his rest.

He scanned his surroundings one last time to see if he could determine where that gardenia perfume was wafting from. He didn't see anything or anyone in sight, but it made him feel like Lumi was an April breeze away.

21

LUMI

The brass teakettle whistled, jolting Lumi to attention. The night had turned blustery, so she decided to make herself a hot toddy to warm up and bolster her courage before setting out on her late-night trip to DAX. She painstakingly applied her black eyeliner after the pressed powder and added mascara and rose-colored lipstick to finish the look. It was the most makeup she had worn in a while.

She shimmied into the tightest dark wash jeans she owned and pulled on a thin mauve silk blouse. She left her curly hair cascading back. Amethyst chandelier earrings swung from her earlobes. A quick glance at her watch told her that she had exactly forty-five minutes to jet down to DAX. If her calculations were correct, Julien would be closing up around that time and there would only be a few employees left at the restaurant.

The subway ride down was a blur. Her heart pounded in her chest as she thought about how unlike her this plan was. Before she knew it, the train had stopped at Forty-Second

Street and she skipped up the stairs to street level. When she checked the screen of her phone, it was 9:45 P.M.

She used her key card to open the service entrance door and rode the elevator to the fifth floor, walking out into the eerily quiet hallway. The lights in the restaurant were already dim. Lumi stopped, looking from left to right. Where was everyone? She felt her stomach sink into her pelvic floor.

The entire floor was deathly silent. She tried the restaurant doors, but they had already been locked. She stood in front of them, and as she saw her reflection in the glass of the doors, tears of shame welled up in the corners of her eyes.

"Stupid, stupid, stupid," she muttered to herself. She pulled her earrings out and stuffed them into her jeans pocket. She couldn't help but look at herself in the reflective doors once more and felt bile rising in her throat. She wiped her eyes with the sleeve of her blouse, dragging streaks of black mascara across her cheeks like war paint, not even noticing soft footsteps in the hall behind her.

22

JULIEN

Julien stepped into the hallway to find this beautiful spectacle muttering to herself. He had no idea what Lumi was doing outside the door of DAX at nearly 10:00 P.M. on her day off, but he was more interested in the why. They were alone in the building, which proved the perfect time for him to make things right with her.

He approached her from behind, and it was impossible for him to ignore her alluring curves in such tight jeans. She was lost in thought and had not heard him leave his office. He cleared his throat, wishing to subtly alert her to his presence. Still, she jumped, whirling around toward him. Their eyes met, and he could see that she had been crying. Mascara was streaked across her cheeks.

"Lumi," he whispered. "What are you doing here?" He touched his hand to her shoulder.

She looked up at him. "Where is everyone?" she said.

"I closed early," he answered, "at nine. It was a quiet night." He grabbed her hand, threaded his fingers through hers, and thought back to his original question. "What are you doing here?"

She gazed up at him, and the thousand things she wanted to say to him made her incapable of speaking at all.

Julien saw that Lumi was conflicted. "Come, let's go in the restaurant for a bit," he said, reaching one arm around her to unlock the door.

23

LUMI

Lumi and Julien stumbled into the kitchen as Julien opened the door. She thought of what to say to explain her strange behavior.

Julien leaned back against the center kitchen island, focused on her expression. She looked up at the skylights and bit her lip. The scenario that she had thought of in her head was not going according to plan. "I—I don't know what to say," she managed, shaking her head sheepishly as she stared off toward the dining room.

"Then show me," he said. His eyes burned with desire.

"Sh-show you?" she asked.

Julien nodded wordlessly, not taking his eyes off her.

Her heart seized within her chest. If they decided to do this, it would be the point of no return. She took a deep breath. The same energy that had spirited her to this very kitchen in a haze would also be her parachute.

She reached out to Julien and took hold of his shirt collar, pulling him in for a passionate kiss. Once their lips touched, he lost all pretense of calm composure. He swooped her up onto the island so she faced him and his lips trailed down from her mouth to the hollow of her neck, and bit her softly, sending shudders through her entire body.

She wrapped her arms around his shoulders, and when he let go and pulled back, she leaned in, kissing his neck in turn. He pulled away from her again.

"Mmm, don't do that, love," he whispered hoarsely, "I'll lose it too quickly." And then his attention was back on her. He gently bit, kissed, and sucked on her tender skin. A low moan escaped Lumi's lips, and she was surprised to hear it, but at the same time was helpless to contain it.

In her excitement, her breasts swelled, and she gasped as Julien slid his lips down the front of her chest, unbuttoning her blouse as he went. She was impressed by how he managed to do all this in one deft move and was temporarily distracted by that thought until he unhooked her bra and fixed his mouth to her nipple, causing her entire body to arch back in pleasure and her mind to abandon all other concerns.

He coursed his other hand up the plane of her belly and firmly encircled one of her breasts, gently kneading it as he tended to the other. As if they had a mind of their own, her legs came up and wrapped themselves around Julien's hips, interlocking behind his back. She could feel him briefly smile against her breast. He rose to kiss her mouth, and she could swear she felt his lips tremble as they met hers.

He pulled back from the kiss and began a trail down her belly. When he got to the waist of her jeans, he looked into her eyes as he unbuttoned them and then slowly peeled them off, followed by the burgundy lace thong. His arms slid around her waist to pull her closer to him, and he flashed her a beaming smile before he leaned down to nip at the fullness of her thighs. He bestowed little bites on the tender skin, making inroads toward her core, teasing her. He gazed up at her, a look of feigned innocence on his face and a devilish glint in his eyes. Then he ran his tongue between the folds of her sex, and she felt her breath seize in her lungs. He continued this languorous motion, slowly and deliberately.

There came a moment when she could no longer bear it, and she pulled on Julien's shoulders, begging him with her body. He broke away and grabbed the metal chair that rested next to the island, where he had thrown their discarded clothes. There was a crinkle of aluminum foil as he fished a condom out of his wallet. "Got it," said Lumi, and she ripped it open and rolled it on. He sat down on the chair and, with one arm around her waist, brought her down to him. Slowly, steadily, he plunged inside her.

He sucked in a sharp breath as he felt her warmth and wetness envelop him. She sighed as she felt him filling her entirely. They stayed like this, motionless for a moment, until Julien leaned forward, buried his face in her neck, and slowly began to move. He edged out of her and she felt bereft of him until he slid back in, giving her that delicious fullness again.

It was so much easier for her to move since she was on top of him, and she found herself helping him, grinding her hips against him, raising them up and then dropping the full weight of her pelvis on his. He groaned every time she did this, leaned back in the chair, and let her control the pace.

Somewhere between the flumes of sheer fire that filled the space between them, she lost track of where her skin ended and his began.

His name began to form on her lips, but at that moment he

thrust deep into her, deeper than before, and the only sound that came out of her was a primal moan as her orgasm spread through every fiber of her body. Julien, who had been on the verge of climax, lifted her up onto the island and pulled her even closer to him. Seeing that she had found her release, he allowed his own to engulf him.

Once they had both orgasmed, it occurred to Lumi that they hadn't said a single word to each other since they first groped against the kitchen island.

Lumi gazed out the immense kitchen window and watched as dawn marbled the sky. The kitchen island had become a make-shift bed, and Julien's shoulder was her pillow. She stifled a yawn. She was unsure exactly what time it was. Morning was about to find them entwined on the countertop, and somehow this did not bother her at all.

She shifted her weight to her side so she could look at him. After the third time they had coupled, he'd said he was just going to close his eyes for one minute and had drifted off to sleep, hugging her close to his chest. The slope of her shoulder held an imprint of the fishhook from his bracelet.

Awake now that light was starting to stream into the kitchen, Lumi studied Julien's features. She admired the way the light danced off the tips of the orange lashes that fringed his eyes. Who was this man who drove her wild? She thought back to how he seemed to enjoy her arousal, how pleased he looked when her face was contorted in pleasure. She had never experienced that with anyone.

She was surprised by how sweet he was with her. How he held her in his arms as if she were porcelain. At the same time, he treated her as though she could hold her own. She thought back to his words when he had punched Verdi at the absinthe bar. *She's not a chick, she's a woman and a chef, and a better chef than you.*

Seeing him this peaceful and vulnerable, she couldn't help but admit that she felt something for him. She reached out to trace the outline of his jaw with her fingertips. Julien stirred, stretching his body. He caught her hand in his and kissed the back of it. She closed her eyes, savoring this feeling. When she opened them, his amber ones stared sleepily back at her.

"Lumi," he whispered. "Hey. Would you like some breakfast?"

He yawned and stretched his muscled form.

"Breakfast sounds pretty good," she said over the rumble of her stomach.

"Well, then . . . first order of business: wipe this countertop down with bleach," he said, laughing.

He tightened his arms around her and pressed a gentle kiss to her forehead, then jumped down from the island. He held his arms out to help her down. He pulled on his green plaid boxers and jeans, and Lumi reached for her bra and panties.

Then he walked toward the closet for cleaning supplies. He cleaned the counter quickly and walked to the refrigerator. He took out a carton of brown eggs and milk and grabbed flour, onions, some potatoes, and olive oil from the pantry.

Lumi sat in the metal chair, her eyes following his movements around the kitchen. Two months ago, she had sworn to herself she wouldn't taste his cooking, and now here she was, watching him cook breakfast for her shirtless. She sighed to herself, bemused. Life sure had a lot of unexpected twists and turns.

He glanced up at her and blew her a kiss, causing her to

break out in a fit of giggles. "Can I help you with anything?" she asked.

He shook his head. "No, just sit there and watch me, looking achingly beautiful."

She pouted playfully. "'Sit still, look pretty' has never been my strong suit," she said.

Julien grinned. "You're on your feet all day. Learn to let someone else do something for you for a change."

She looked out the large window. The sun was high in the sky now. "You're killing my buzz, man," she joked, and he shook his head and waved the eggbeater at her.

"Sh-sh-sh, never mind that," he said. "We'll talk later."

In what seemed like the blink of an eye, Julien had set eggs Benedict, shredded hash browns, prosciutto, and fresh-brewed coffee upon the counter.

Seated and excited, Lumi raised the first forkful to her mouth and savored the simple flavors. The eggs were warm, runny, and delicious. She felt that now-familiar electric buzz emanating through her body from the first bite. And once more, she tasted that savory, pungent note of sage.

She had to ask him.

"Julien," she began, her voice casual, "can I ask you something?"

"Of course," he said, turning toward her as he poured hollandaise over his eggs.

She knew it was a strange question. "Did you . . . did you put sage in the eggs?"

He shook his head gently, his face amused. "No, love. Do they taste like sage to you?"

She was unsure if he would think her totally crazy for saying yes. "Um, just a little," she said.

"Mmm," he remarked as he chewed, clearly blissed out. "Is that a good thing?"

She eyed him coyly. "Yes . . . yes, it is. They're excellent. Everything is. Thank you," she said.

"You don't have to thank me," he answered. "I wouldn't let you go home on an empty stomach. Not after a night like that."

They laughed together and fell into an easy silence as they ate and sipped their coffee.

Then the kitchen door slammed open, the metal door banging loudly against the frame. They both looked up.

"Oh!" Julien said. "Is it nine o'clock already?"

Esme stared back at them haughtily, raising a hand to rest on her hip. "It's eight actually. I came in to organize the corporate files. Looks like the early bird got the worm today," she said.

Julien stopped drinking his coffee and shot Esme a frigid gaze. "Kindly return to the files, then," he said, "and I expect your discretion about the rest of this."

Esme glowered at them both before she slammed the door shut behind her. Lumi stared in the direction of the door, her mind slowly putting the pieces together. She turned back toward Julien.

"Julien, I have to know . . . Are you sleeping with her?" she asked.

Julien shook his head. "No, I'm not."

She eyed the door, still settling in its hinges. "Have you slept with her?"

He shook his head again. "No, of course not."

Lumi rested her chin in her palm. "I see."

They sat in silence, no longer eating their breakfast.

"Why is that an 'of course not'?"

Julien cocked his head. "What do you mean? She's my secretary."

Lumi stared down at her plate. "And I'm your sous chef," she said quietly.

Julien furrowed his brow and reached for her hand. "Lumi. What you and I shared last night was completely . . . sacred to me. If it didn't happen here, it could have happened somewhere else. It has nothing to do with where we are and everything to do with how we connect. I do believe that assumption to be a little unreasonable."

"Oh, you think I'm unreasonable?"

"I didn't say *you* were unreasonable, I said *that* was unreasonable."

Lumi slowly drew her hand back, and Julien watched her cautiously. A stupid grin spread across his face before he thought better of it and checked himself.

"Are you . . . jealous?" he asked.

She narrowed her eyes at him and recoiled. "No, I'm not jealous," she snapped. "You sure look pleased by that idea, though."

Julien broke out into that goofy grin again.

"You know what, Julien, you are so selfish," she said, crossing her arms. "That's just one of the many reasons I don't like you."

Julien's eyes widened, though there was still mirth behind them, which made her want to slap it out of him. To his credit, he managed to keep a straight face.

"You . . . don't like me," he said.

She shook her head vehemently, her eyes defiant.

"Well. There were a few moments there where I could have sworn you liked me. At least a little bit," he said.

She squinted at him through her still-narrowed eyes and took a deep breath. "You know what, Julien. I think this was a mistake. A huge mistake," she said.

"Lumi," he began, "I'm sorry, but I can't bring myself to regret it. In fact, I'm not sorry at all. I feel connected to you, and after last night, I felt that connection deepen. Don't you feel it too?"

She closed her eyes and took a deep breath. There was no way for her to say yes to that, because if she did, what she was about to do wouldn't make any sense, even to herself.

"No," she said, biting her lip. "I don't."

She glanced toward the kitchen window to avoid the pained look on his face.

"It was a mistake, and one I'm certain cannot be undone. I'll be here tonight for the Atlantic Records dinner party. I'm not leaving Gloria, Ruben, and Richard hanging. But after tonight, Julien, I'm done," she said.

He looked at her in shock. "Done . . . here?" he asked.

She could hear the slightest waver in his voice. It made her feel sick to her stomach, but it was too late. She couldn't trust him anymore. And besides, it would be better this way. Easier to move on and focus on what she needed to: her next venture. She nodded emphatically.

"Even if you don't want to work here, can I still see you?" he asked.

"That would defeat the purpose of quitting," she said, as she snatched her clothes off the metal chair. She pulled them on angrily.

"Lumi, but we were just . . . getting to know each other better," he said. "Why don't you take a few days away from here, if that's what you need? I think you are taking this the wrong way."

"No, I'm pretty sure it's the right way," she said as she stepped into her boots. "Thanks for breakfast," she added. She walked quickly out the door, shut it behind her, and didn't look back.

24

JULIEN

Julien heaved a sigh and sank into the metal chair. Then just as suddenly, he jumped up as if he had sat on a cactus. That chair was the last place he wanted to be. It only reminded him of how sour things had gone.

He took the dishes and hastily dropped them in the main kitchen sink and headed off to his office. He clenched his fists involuntarily. Argh, why did Esme have to show up at the worst possible time?

When he got to the office, he found a flat package wrapped in butcher paper with a note written in red ink on magenta printer paper stuck to the top. THIS SEEMS AS GOOD A TIME AS ANY TO GIVE YOU THIS. ESME. He peeled back the paper to find a framed photo collage . . . of himself.

There were magazine and newspaper clippings from the *New York Post* and *Food and Wine*. There was a printed screenshot of the *BuzzFeed* Tasty video he did, demonstrating how to make cherry clafoutis. That video was from a year ago. How long had she been putting this together?

That was it. He crumpled the note into a haphazard ball and tossed it in the trash. He had to have a talk with Esme. The gifts had to stop. The other ones had been mildly inappropriate, but this was borderline creepy.

Esme was out, so the conversation would have to wait. And what to do about Lumi? He needed a distraction. He reclined in his desk chair and made paper airplanes out of Post-it notes and sent them sailing across his desk. He watched one little structure as it coasted through the air, picked up momentum, and then finally took a nosedive and scraped across the plastic keyboard before it came to a complete stop on the edge of the computer. He sighed.

There was probably nothing he could do to change Lumi's mind. He could still try, though. No matter what the outcome, trying would be better than not doing anything at all and just sitting back to watch her leave.

What if he cooked something for her? Not a full meal, but an artful, well-made dish or pastry to say what he wanted to say in words. He jumped out of his chair and ran to the kitchen.

25

JULIEN

Julien stood with his back resting against the cold stove. He was still avoiding the kitchen island. He riffled through his memory, thinking of what he could make to please her and soften her stubborn resolve against him. Something that mimicked the succulent taste of her skin . . . "Stop it," he told himself aloud.

Rose crème brûlée came to mind, but no. He wanted something more *her*, something that would show her he had been paying attention all along. He surveyed the pantry and refrigerator once more and found a bar of guava paste, fresh ricotta, and Meyer lemon cookies—perfect for a crust.

He crumbled the cookies between his thick fingers. Then he melted some butter in a small cast-iron saucepan and poured it over the pulverized crumbs. His freckled skin flushed pink as he stood over the rosy cubes of guava boiling in an inch of water, stirring with deep intention. Next, he mixed the soft cream cheese and sugar for the cheesecakes. He was about to grate in some lime zest when Esme stormed into the kitchen.

"Julien, you have an urgent call on line one," she said.

He glanced at the phone mounted on the kitchen wall.

"Damn it, this phone is out of order," he said. He narrowed his eyes at Esme. "You and I need to talk. Meantime, do me a favor, please? Can you stir this mixture while I take the call in my office?"

He saw her eyes flit from the saucepan and back to his face. A scowl crossed her expression and then faded just as fast.

"Of course," she said, holding out her hand for the stirring spoon.

"Dax speaking."

"Hello, son."

"Lucien."

Lucien cleared his throat. "How about a little more respect for your papa?"

Julien rolled his eyes. "I haven't called you papa since Maman died. If you'd have been paying attention, you'd have known that."

"Oh, but I am, son, much more than you think."

"Why did you call?"

"Some of the bonds we opened for you have matured."

"Your fresh-out-of-college girlfriend knows what bonds are? I'm shocked."

"Christine and I. You know I meant your mother."

"Ah."

"I can give you the paperwork. When are you coming to Paris?"

"Never," he lied. "When are you coming to New York?"

"To see Rochelle, perhaps." Leave it to Lucien to come to New York to see only one of his two children.

"You can email me the info and I'll do it."

"J-just take care of it. For once," Lucien stuttered.

"Bye, Lucien." Julien hung up.

After the call had been resolved, Julien walked back into the kitchen and found Esme stirring at a furious clip. She was muttering something under her breath, and though Julien couldn't make out the exact words, it sounded like she was angry.

"Ahem, Esme, I'm back," he said.

She jolted, as if startled from a reverie, and all but tossed him the spoon before retreating from the kitchen.

Not having any time to waste, he shrugged and returned to the task. He took out a tray of dessert shell molds from the cabinet next to the oven and pressed in the crumble crust, then surveyed the cheesecake mixture in comparison to the number of pastry shells and quickly mixed up a second batch of cream cheese filling. He spooned the mixture into the molds. In went the tray to the already scorching oven, and he sat down to think in the chair he had dragged in from his office into the kitchen.

With nothing to do besides wait for the pastries to bake, his mind raced over every detail of the past twenty-four hours. It had been two nights since he had slept more than three hours at a time. He wanted to fix that, but for the moment there was no time, not while his relationship with Lumi hung in the balance.

He felt a sinking in his chest as he thought back to the moment she told him she would be leaving. It was the first time he could remember letting anyone win an argument. And what had happened to her to make her so distrustful? He thought back to the story about her father leaving and frowned. Was it that? Was there another man in her past who had hurt her? He gritted his teeth at the thought.

Julien was not one to be readily given to fear. But he did feel an icy gale in his heart when he thought that she could be serious about not coming back and not wanting to see him again.

And then he smiled, recalling how much she'd resembled a pouty little girl when she told him she didn't like him. He had to laugh despite himself. Then his good humor soured when he remembered her reaction. Had he really been such an ass for being amused by her adorable contradictions? Couldn't she just admit that she was falling in love with him too? If only she could have seen herself the previous night. The look in her eyes when he'd told her to show him what she meant was not one he would ever forget.

The oven timer gave a tinny ring, and he marveled over how fast half an hour had passed. "I hope you guys can help," he said, hoisting the tray out of the oven and placing it on a cooling rack. Carefully, he topped each pastry with a heaping drizzle of guava preserve and a few diced chunks of the paste, and affixed a sprig of mint to every other one. He pulled a blank piece of paper from the miscellaneous drawer in the kitchen island.

FOR LUMI. ALL OTHERS: TOUCH THESE AND DIE, he wrote in big block letters, and gleefully affixed the note to the base of the cooling rack with a piece of tape. Then he pulled out another piece of paper—this time for a more personal note.

26

LUMI

When Lumi stepped out of the subway on Saturday afternoon, she found the sky had taken on an olive-greenish cast. She shuddered. She hadn't seen skies that color since Miami. Could there be a hurricane coming? In April, in New York, it seemed unlikely. Against all logic, she kind of hoped there was. It would give her the perfect excuse as to why she wasn't coming in to work until she felt like telling her coworkers the truth about what had happened.

Yes, once she got just a little more space and a little more closure, she would call Richard, Gloria, and Ruben from the comfort of her own home and let them know it wasn't just the hurricane—she was gone for good. She would explain it all to them, they would make plans to go out for drinks and a raucous night, and all would be well. They would understand, she was sure of it.

She arrived at 108 West Forty-Second Street and rode the elevator to the fifth floor. She was early, and that was precisely her plan: to finish her share of the cooking and leave before anyone else arrived. She went to the uniform closet and reached for her white coat, wrinkling her nose as she pulled it close. It absolutely stunk of fish. She grimaced. Someone must have left the door to the uniform closet open while they were braising a cod fillet.

There was no time to launder it. She started to tug it on anyway and took it off just as quickly when she felt her stomach turning. There was no way she was going to be able to wear it for three hours. She tossed it on top of the uniform hamper and paced over to the menu board to see what they would be serving for the Atlantic Records annual spring soiree. Her brown eyes scanned the listings. Marinated filet mignon, coq au vin in tiny phyllo dough cups, savory onion beignets, garlic asparagus, and poached pears in wine sauce.

It was an easy menu, and Lumi began by dicing the onions for the beignets. She would marinate the filet mignon, fry the beignets, and cook the coq au vin.

Ruben had once told her Julien hated balsamic vinegar in marinade. She remembered this fact as she doused the filet in a liberal stream and then poured on a little extra just in case.

She cringed. Just one night ago, things had been different . . . but that was before she found out that he was who she thought he was from the beginning. It stung to think that in all the moments she felt like there was something special growing between them, she was just being played.

On the other hand, she didn't know for a fact that he had slept with any other employees. And there had been many moments where he seemed to be saying that he felt there was something special between them.

She thought of his words to her at Miz Suzie's Island Spice, his sweet eyes pleading with her to be open to what she felt for one night. She closed her eyes and breathed deep and recalled his state of Zen as he woke up and found her at his side. She felt the tightness that had been holding her insides captive since she stormed out of the kitchen soften.

She took another deep breath and slapped her forehead. "Stupid," she muttered to herself. Shame stung at her cheeks as it became clear to her how much she had overreacted. "I need to tell him," she whispered, smoothing a stray curl away from her face. Hopefully it was not too late. It couldn't be. It had only been half a day. She would go to him and they would talk, and she would tell him she was sorry for assuming. As much as he incensed her at times, she wasn't ready to let go of her feelings for him.

Suddenly, Lumi felt annoyed with herself. "Focus, focus," she said, tapping her cheeks, bringing her attention back to the tasks at hand. She looked down at her station and began to mix the flour, eggs, water, and scallions for the beignets. Her legs felt strangely leaden as she walked to the stove to heat up the oil. She willed them to walk anyway.

She shaped the dough in small balls and dropped them into the shimmering oil. As she waited for them to be done on the first side, she turned absentmindedly toward the cooling rack and spotted a tray of pastries that she hadn't noticed there before. As she crossed the space, she saw that they were miniature cheesecakes—for her, apparently, according to the sign warning all others off.

They had a lovely crimson marbling on top. Some of the cheesecakes had sprigs of mint atop them and some did not. There was also a crisp piece of white paper folded under the tray. She teased it out and recognized Julien's block lettering right away.

LUMI,

YOU HAVE SWEETENED MY DAYS IN
WAYS YOU CANNOT EVEN IMAGINE.

PLEASE FORGIVE ME.

AND PLEASE STAY.

JD

Her heart fluttered in her chest, and she hated herself for reacting that way. The distrust in men she had been taught by Inés had come out when she had least expected or needed it. She skipped across the aisle and turned over the beignets, then was back contemplating the cheesecakes. Her chest swelled with emotion as she picked one up and bit into it.

As she did, she nearly choked. Beyond the creamy cheese and cookie crust it tasted exactly like the hair relaxer she had stuck her tongue in as a child in Inés's salon. There were strong notes of ammonia and alcohol, and in her solar plexus she felt a roiling, a flaring of rage and something that felt as if it were grabbing her by the throat. She heaved as if to vomit, but nothing came up. The blood drained from her face and her mind stalled on one thought: Had he . . . *poisoned* her? She couldn't believe it. She grabbed another pastry off the plate and bit it to be sure. To her shock, it tasted of paradise, of ambrosia, of sage, and it started a thrumming electricity that coursed through her body and made her heart soar.

But the first pastry was already working its way through

body, and when these two flows of energy met, it produced a clash that rattled her, and she felt herself seizing and suddenly losing control of her limbs. She stumbled away from the kitchen island, but before she could reach for water, her legs gave out from under her, causing her to free-fall forward and hit the handle of the wok, flipping it up onto her.

Her lips moved to form an O and emitted a cry that disturbed no sound waves. She contracted into herself as the scalding oil washed over her face, chest, and hands. Blindly, she stumbled, looking for something, anything, to grab on to, her skin crawling and the burn raging all across it. Without seeing what was in front of her, she hit her head and sank to the floor. The open burner continued to shoot flames toward the ceiling, and the skillet lay on the floor at an angle with her body.

27

JÚLIEN

Julien strolled up to 108 West Forty-Second, and he couldn't help feeling a little proud of himself for paying such close attention. Lumi, strong and independent as she was, was a conflict avoider. If his calculations were correct, he would find her in the kitchen, doing her part so she could leave before anyone else arrived.

He knew she would be angry to see him there, now that he had figured her out. The thought made him smile softly to himself as he punched the elevator button. It would make her angry, but he hoped in a more secret, inner place that she would be pleased. Given that it was three in the afternoon, maybe she hadn't sampled his little gift yet. He would offer her one himself, with espresso on the side. If she could just sit with him, have a little guava and a little espresso, hopefully she would let her guard down a bit and listen to reason.

But when he swung open the kitchen door, all thoughts of guava and espresso quickly evaporated. Lumi lay on the floor, unconscious while the stove shot flames and the wok lay on the floor next to her. As he got closer, he could see that her face, chest, and hands were engine red and blistering.

"Lumi? Lumi!" He shook her shoulders to no avail.

His heart threatened to explode in his chest. While his mind shouted a thousand things at once, his arms acted of their own accord. They slipped beneath her limp body and lifted her up. He rested her head against his chest, careful not to touch her singed cheek to the fabric of his shirt. His head darted from left to right. It was fruitless to yell for somebody to call 911. He knew good and well that they were the only two people on the fifth floor.

He could not hesitate at a time like this. Still holding her close, he lunged toward the stove, flicked off the burner, and then barreled down the stairs.

"Ambulance! Somebody call an ambulance!" he yelled as they broke out onto the street. Startled passersby stared at him, and their faces all blurred together in front of him.

"Mr. Dax?"

His eyes zeroed in on the face of the afternoon doorman. "Billy! Please, please call 911 now."

He leaned against the building's entrance, shifting from one foot to the other in the quest to find the angle that held her head upright but didn't let her face loll against his shirt. She didn't stir, but he felt the hammering of her heart through the arm pressed against her back.

"Keep breathing just like that, love," he whispered, and he repeated it to her until the red lights and sirens broke through the blur and jerked to a stop before them.

MINI GUAVA CHEESECAKES
Makes 18 mini-cheesecakes

$1/2$ cup butter

2 cups graham cracker crumbs

24 ounces cream cheese

$1/2$ pound ricotta

$3/4$ cup granulated sugar

2 eggs

1 teaspoon vanilla extract

juice of $1/2$ lime

1 pound guava paste

Preheat the oven to 350 degrees Fahrenheit. Melt the butter and mix with the graham cracker crumbs in a small bowl. Press the graham cracker mixture into the bottoms of lined muffin tins to form the cheesecake shells. Bake the shells for 5-7 minutes or until lightly browned.

In a large bowl, mix the cream cheese, ricotta, sugar, eggs, vanilla, and lime juice. Spoon the batter into the cheesecake shells and bake for 30 minutes. Meanwhile, dice the guava paste and melt on the stovetop on low-medium heat. Pour over the cheesecakes. Let cool for 10-15 minutes at room temperature and then refrigerate until chilled.

Best served without bad juju.

28

LUMI

In the hospital bed, she faded from light to dark and back again, her mind taking a much-needed vacation. In the absence of her usual spool of anxious thought, she floated back to a vague memory of a taste from so long ago that it felt like an imprint on her tongue. There was vanilla, honeysuckle, the promise of forever love. The first taste.

Drifting in the lucid stream of memory, she found herself at the first and last slumber party she ever hosted. It was a sweltering ninety-eight-degree Saturday in Little Havana, and she had invited her three closest friends from seventh grade over. Amid tubs of Turkey Hill ice cream, the girls watched *Dirty Dancing*, oohing and aahing over Baby's retro outfits and Johnny's biceps. All of them wanted to practice the lift, so they turned on the ceiling fan and pranced in front of the TV, high on sugar, and looking like four raccoons until Inés had lumbered over, bottle of Bacardi in hand, and blocked the screen with her fleshy form.

"I just want you girls to know that all of this is make-believe," she had said in a tone that still rang in Lumi's ears twenty years later. "This is nonsense." She raked her gaze over the confounded young faces. "In real life, Baby would have been pregnant by now, and Johnny would've been hightailing it to the border. Keep your eyes open, girls, and don't believe everything songs and movies tell you about love. Love—"

Lumi was startled by an insistent hand shaking her unburned shoulder.

"Jesús Santísimo . . ." Inés whispered to herself.

The first thing Lumi saw when she peeked through her weighted lids was her reflection mirrored in her mother's sunglass lenses. Her eyes were swollen nearly shut, and almost her entire face, chest, and arms were covered in gauzy white bandages, including the patches along her hairline where the hair had been singed off. The nurses had pulled her hair up and away from her face and tied it in a loose bun with the ends out; she resembled an obscene pineapple.

Lumi winced. As much as she knew she was supposed to appreciate the gesture of Inés flying up from Miami to be with her, she would have preferred to be alone. It would have been so much easier to convince the nurses to just keep feeding morphine into her IV nonstop until she went home. Under Inés's watchful eye, every pill and drip they gave her would be measured. She was none too sad to discover that the bandages wrapped tight to her lips relieved her from the expectation of upholding conversation.

The worst part was seeing how the nurses, and now her mother, looked at her. Like she was a thing to be pitied. Like they were three steps away from crying at her funeral. It was too much for her.

Inés sat down in the chair next to Lumi's bed, and for a while neither spoke. Finally, Inés cleared her throat.

"You're lucky it wasn't worse," she said, and Lumi squeezed her eyes shut as if that would help drown out the rest of Inés's speech. Thankfully, that was all she said. Inés leaned back in the chair and frowned as she surveyed the plastic tubing coming off the beeping machine behind Lumi's bed that connected the IV to the underside of her arm.

"I got here this morning," Inés said. "I got the call yesterday. The nurses were calling your emergency contacts." She paused and then let out a long, heavy breath. "Ay, m'ija, sometimes I fear that I have failed you."

Did her mother imagine that Lumi's business and now her health had failed because she didn't learn her mother's lessons well enough? The thought gave her a twinge sharp enough to supersede the painkillers, and she shook her head from left to right as firmly as she could without agonizing her wounds. Inés watched her, and her eyes grew glassy with moisture before she turned away toward the street-facing window.

Lumi groaned and leaned back against the foam mattress, which a thoughtful nurse had propped into an upright position so that she could watch TV and gaze despondently out the window.

"Do you want anything?" Inés asked, the tone of her voice softer than before.

Lumi was about to answer her when the blond nurse popped her head back in the doorway. "Ms. Santana, there's a Mr. Dax here to see you," she chirped.

Lumi's head shot up and she began to shake her head vehemently, but it was too late. The nurse had retreated, and in walked the man she least wanted to see this side of the universe.

His eyes were underlined by dark circles, and a carpeting of reddish stubble covered his cheeks and chin. She squeezed her eyes shut again as if by doing so she could make him go away.

When she opened them, he was still there, eyes trained on her. She stared tersely at the gray plastic tray table attached to her bed until Inés broke the silence.

"I'm Inés Rosario. Are you a . . . friend of my daughter's?" she asked, gaze focused on him expectantly. Lumi heard her brief pause and knew Inés was wondering if she had slept with him. She sighed under her bandages.

Julien's eyes widened for a second before he regained his good posture and polite expression. "You're Lumi's mother. I'm Julien Dax. It's a great pleasure, ma'am," he said, stepping to the side of the bed to shake her hand. "I only wish we were meeting under more, uh, pleasant circumstances," he added, letting out a heavy sigh.

It occurred to Lumi that he hadn't answered the question.

"Lumi," he murmured, reaching out to stroke the fabric of the blanket alongside her hand. He leaned toward her, his broad shoulders curving slightly.

Lumi pretended she hadn't heard him. Suddenly, not being able to move her mouth was not beneficial anymore. She wished she had a pen and paper to write GO TO HELL with, imitating his blocky letters. In the back of her mind, she knew she was being cruel, but she was unable to stop herself.

She still didn't understand what had happened when she had tried his cakes. Again, her mind turned to poison. The first bite had tasted like ammonia and death, and the second one had tasted like everything she'd ever wanted. What did that mean? And if he wanted to poison her, why didn't he make them all the same way?

She reminded herself that he didn't know about her gift, and as far as she knew she hadn't presented any symptoms besides the burns now emblazoned across her upper body. The cakes had been poisonous only on an energetic level. But why only some of them? Was he angry with her for leaving him when he started making them and in a better mood by the time he was done? She started to raise her hands to hang her head in them and stopped when the skin pulled sharply. The relentless thoughts were too much for her while she was in pain. She shifted her body slightly so she could stare toward the door in hopes that would give him some indication of what she wanted from him. When he didn't move, not noticing her change of direction, she gathered her strength and moved her hand away from his on the blanket. She ignored the shadow of pain that crossed his face, keeping her eyes trained on the door.

"Lumi," he whispered. She knew he wouldn't try to take her hand or put it back next to his.

Inés's curiosity over the nature of their relationship was slowly morphing into concern. "Sir, why don't you come back another time, in a few weeks perhaps, when my daughter is better and will be able to talk to you," she suggested in a polite but pointed tone.

Julien's expression remained gracious, but there was iron behind it. "I can't," he said simply, not taking his eyes off Lumi. "I can't leave you."

She drew her hands to her chest as if to hug herself and winced as the skin tugged and a small corner began to tear at her elbow just under the bandages. What she wanted least was to cry, and she needed not to for the sake of her face, but she couldn't help it. She could feel more tiny rips at the corners of her eyes and across her cheeks as she grimaced in an effort to hold back the tears that struggled to rush forth.

A trickle of blood escaped from under the bandages and oozed over her lip, and she wiped it away with her bandaged arm. Watching her, Julien's face was stricken.

"Just let me stay with you, let me help you get better."

"Mr. Dax, this is a bad time," Inés said. "Please, please leave."

Julien shook his head, looking from Inés to Lumi. As Lumi saw his resolve, she couldn't contain it anymore, and the sobs began to pour out, racking her upper body. Her skin cracked as it was pulled and distorted by the movements made by her cries, and the bandages began to soak through with blood.

"Look what you're doing to her," Inés cried. "Get out now!"

The blond nurse popped her head in, hearing the commotion, and gasped when she saw Lumi's bandages. "Oh, my Lord," she said. "Sir, I'm sorry, but you need to leave right now."

"But, miss, you know I—"

"Please wait outside then. Please don't make me call security."

"Security?" He balked, and Lumi heard that telltale tone in his voice.

She looked at him, and she hoped he could see her eyes through the bandages. She caught his gaze, and for a moment she let go of her rage and beseeched him with her eyes to leave. *Just go,* she thought as loud as she could, as if that would help him hear her.

He stopped insisting, a barreling train colliding with a mountain of powdery snow, soothed by having gotten at least something from her. He stilled himself, remembering where he was.

"You all have a good day," he snapped, and the words rang hollow to all four people in the room.

She closed her eyes, and when she opened them once more it was just her, Inés, and the nurse, pulling out a roll of fresh gauze.

29

JULIEN

For the first time since its inception, DAX was closed on a Sunday. Julien contacted the kitchen employees the previous day, informing them of the events and instructing them to stay home Sunday until further notice. The Atlantic Records party had gone on without him. He had requested Gloria set aside the tray of cheesecakes until he could examine it.

He stood in the kitchen, hair ruffled by the wind, having walked there directly from the hospital. His legs ached from spending hours folded into the metal chair outside Lumi's room while she slept.

He had a strong inclination to buy a few bottles of bourbon and go on a little bender until she was released. But he knew he wouldn't. He needed to know that he could be there for Lumi the moment she changed her mind. And he needed to figure out what had happened.

He paced to the refrigerator and pulled out the tray. There were eighteen cheesecakes, including the two Lumi had bitten from, which he had instructed Gloria to save as well. Lumi was unconscious when he found her, and she had been burned . . . but second-degree burns were not likely to render someone unconscious. It was almost as if she had tasted the cheesecakes, fainted, and *then* hit the wok on the way down.

Julien grabbed a knife from the wooden block and cut a piece from both of the pastries Lumi had bitten. He raised each to his lips and chewed, waiting for something to happen. Nothing. No retching. No dizziness. They didn't even taste different. He thought back to that morning, and every ingredient he had used was at peak freshness. Hell, the pastries had been in the refrigerator for over a day and they still tasted fresh.

He sighed. How could he help Lumi if he had no idea what had hurt her? For the moment, he didn't have any answers, and that was an uncomfortable place for him to be.

30

LUMI

To Lumi's relief, Julien did not return to her bedside during the week she stayed at the hospital. The hours of solitude stretched over the loom of her memory, and she found herself filling them with images of the best moments at Caraluna. Removing fish from sheaves of paper, scaling them as she hummed a tune. Peeling orange carrots and green plantains. Her arm muscles tingled, letting her know they remembered these things too.

After three days home from the hospital, the doorbell rang late one afternoon while she was sitting on her burgundy velour couch. She had been surfing Netflix, her unburned hand glued to the remote, anything to keep her mind off Julien's face when she asked him to go. It kept haunting her.

Her phone had pinged, alerting her to a new text.

GLORIA LA MUJER MARAVILLA: Miss you + pls let me know if you need anything. Get well soon. <3

She had held the phone over her heart and squeezed, and then the sound of the doorbell made her jump.

"That better not be him," she muttered under her breath, though she already knew it was him. It had to be. Inés had gone home yesterday, Jenny had been there just this morning to check on her, and Rafelina was in Punta Cana for the week. She wondered if her coworkers from DAX besides Gloria had heard about the incident. They must have by now.

The peal of the bell was followed by an insistent knock. If she just pretended she wasn't home and didn't answer, would he go away? She didn't have any desire for him to see her looking like a mummy, much less to feel pitied by him. And there were still a thousand questions in her mind about why one of his pastries had tasted like the most burning hate and the other had tasted like an orgasmic out-of-body-experience.

She sighed and willed herself up off the couch and to the door, peering through the peephole. There was no one there. She tried to see as far as she could to the left and right, though it was hard to see much through the tiny glass circle.

As she continued watching, he came into view, climbing back up the stairs with a nondescript bottle in hand and a long-leaved aloe plant. Lumi sighed. She suddenly felt the need to look away from the peephole. It felt uncomfortable to be watching him when he didn't know he was being watched. He rang the doorbell again, this time pressing it down for a longer stretch.

She rested her hand on the knob. "Lumi," he said, as if he could feel that she was now present and listening. She still could not talk adequately, as the scabs around her lips and across her cheeks had started to harden. To speak would be to stretch and crack them open again. She had had enough of that already. She thought for a moment, then fetched a seashell-print notepad and pen that she kept by the phone.

GO AWAY, she wrote on a square of paper, and slipped it under the door. She could hear his fingers grasp the sheet from the floor.

On the other side of the door, he snorted. "Lumi, don't be ridiculous." And then in a softer tone: "I need to see you."

She stared at the notepad, wincing as a single tear welled up and fell from her eye.

I'M NOT MUCH TO SEE RIGHT NOW, she wrote in block letters. She had never been one to write in block letters before Julien.

He sighed on the other side of the door as he read the missive. "Lumi, I *need* to see you," he repeated, and there was a strain in his voice that brought his face in the hospital back into full focus in her memory. She hesitated with her hand on the lock for a moment before she undid it and cracked open the door just a bit.

He edged his shoulder into the crack in the door first, then squeezed his entire body in before she had a chance to change her mind and close the door on him. He held the massive plant easily in one arm, its leaves brushing across the front of his wool jacket. There was a strained expression on his face when he stepped in, and she saw it ebb and fade away as he held her in his sights.

"Oh, Lumi." He sighed, locking eyes with her. The shadows on his face were still there. He looked like he had not gotten much sleep since the hospital. She stared back at him through her bandages, petulant. He took her bad hand and, light as a butterfly, planted a kiss over the bandages. She looked away toward the window. She jotted something down in the notepad again and passed it to him as his eyes followed her every movement.

"'Nothing to talk about,'" he read aloud, sounding out every syllable. She could see him flinch just a fraction, but then something changed and his countenance became neutral again.

"Well, that's fine," he said matter-of-factly, "because I'm not here to talk with you anyway."

Her eyebrows raised, straining under the gauze.

"I'm here to do this," he said, and casting his sights around, he found the kitchen and effortlessly produced a gleaming chef's knife from the wooden block on Lumi's counter. He sliced a leaf off the plant, then led Lumi to her couch as if the layout of her apartment was familiar to him.

He caught her less burned hand and, using a small cotton pad, spread a delicate layer of aloe over the smallest burns she had there. She began to pull her hand back, but the feel of the cooling gel soothing the burn took her by surprise. She breathed in sharply. The smallest ones were the most painful, since the larger, deeper ones were mostly numb.

Seeing that she did not fight him, he gently laid that hand to rest on her lap and moved to her right hand. Without looking, he ran his fingers along the underside of her arm until he found the tiny metal hook that held the bandages together and released it. Grabbing hold of the loose end, he unwound the gauze, layer by layer, until her skin was exposed.

The swirls where the oil had fallen still pronounced themselves in an angry red, and each one was marked by a ridge of blisters. Lumi studied his face as he took in the sight. His expression was laser-focused on squeezing just the right amount of gel out of the leaf, which he then dabbed on and around each blister and rise of the burn.

She let out a deep sigh as she allowed him to minister to her. Though the question of what had happened with the cakes still burned in her mind, it was hard to feel the tenderness that radiated from his hand and believe that he had intended to hurt her. She still wanted to find out what happened, but for the moment, she let his soothing touch wash over her and gently ease the agony of the last ten days.

When he had thoroughly covered the burns of her hands and arms, he moved to her chest. Gingerly, he loosened the adhesive around the edge of the square bandage that covered the grisly maroon semicircle where the wok had flipped up onto her. He winced when he beheld it, but did not stop what he was doing.

Again he squeezed the aloe leaf between his freckled fingers until it oozed transparent gel. He caught the gel with a cotton pad and gently spread it over the crest and edges of the burn. He leaned in closer to reach the one on her chest, and she breathed him in, a touch of woodsy cologne mixing with the scent of the aloe.

When he finished there, his hand floated up to the bandages of her face.

"Don't," she whispered.

His eyes met hers, and they stared at each other for an infinite moment, a tender contest of wills. He opened his mouth to say something but thought better of it.

"Okay, love. No problem. I'll be back again at the same time tomorrow, then." He planted another feather kiss, this time on her unscathed hand, which sent shivers up her arm. She squeezed her eyes shut in response to the sensation, and when she opened them, Julien was already out the door. The aloe plant sat making itself comfortable on her side table.

31

JULIEN

Julien stared out the window of the cab and watched the sunlit waters of the Hudson flow by. Yesterday had been good. She hadn't been able to talk to him, but she had opened the door. She had written him notes. She had let him put aloe on her burns. It was progress.

It felt funny to him, this caretaking, like it was the first time using a muscle he had always had but had never exercised. He had always been a selfish bastard—his father had told him more than once, and Julien hadn't ever had the disposition to correct him. But now it seemed he was self-correcting. And that suited him just fine.

The cab pulled to a stop in front of Lumi's apartment building, and Julien ironed the bills over his knee before handing them to the driver. With a nod of thanks, he stepped out, slammed the door shut, and strode toward the prewar building. The buzzer was out of order, so he simply pushed the metal door open and began his ascent to her fifth-floor walk-up.

The staircase was overlaid with a sort of mosaic tile he

was certain had gone out of fashion about a century ago. He reached out for the banister and just as quickly recoiled his hand when he saw that it was coated with a fine patina of dust.

"Yikes," he muttered under his breath, absentmindedly dusting his fingers off on the hem of his gray wool jacket.

When he reached the fifth floor, he leaned on Lumi's lavender door and knocked briskly. When there was silence, he brought his ear closer and listened for any noises. Nothing. And then suddenly the doorknob twisted, and since he had been leaning on the door, he stumbled in.

A pair of almond-shaped brown eyes peeked out at him between gauzy off-white folds.

"Hey, Lu," he said, trying to look around and not focus his gaze on her bandages for too long. He had bestowed a new nickname upon her, and so far she didn't seem to mind. "I told you you're not getting rid of me too easily," he added, cracking a grin.

Her eyes followed him, her words didn't.

He shifted his weight from one foot to the other, unable to relax into the silence. "How often do your hallways get cleaned, once a year?" he asked.

She cut her eyes at him, pulling out the square notepad. *EYE ROLL*, she wrote in thick block letters, handing it to him with a sullen stare.

He chuckled to himself and turned on his heel toward the kitchen, scanning the countertop for any hints as to her state of mind.

There were three boxes of Rice Chex and one box of powdered milk, lined up one after the other. Next to them there was a blender, its lid ajar, filled with a grainy beige substance.

"What the hell is this?" he said. He grabbed a spoon that

lay on the counter and dipped it in, pulling out a rounded spoonful that didn't slosh off as quickly as he would have expected.

He raised it to his lips and tasted, his brow wrinkling as he found that the mixture lacked any discernible flavor. Then he pivoted back to the cereal boxes again. Lumi stood in the doorway, staring at the orchids and balloons she had brought home from the hospital, which now sat on her kitchen island.

"Lumi, are you . . . *eating* this processed muck?" he gasped.

She didn't meet his gaze, only nodded her head once, so quickly that he could have missed it had he not been studying her intently.

His face grew somber "What are you doing, trying to kill yourself?" he asked.

She shrugged and lowered her gaze to the floor.

He walked over to her and took her by the shoulders. He wanted to squeeze but he didn't. When she refused to look at him, he sighed and turned to the couch. Lying on top of her sherpa throw was a glossy blue paperback: *Wills and Testaments for Dummies*.

"Holy shit, Lumi, you're not going to die from this!" he exclaimed, snatching up the book and sending it flying across the room. She had followed him into the living room and was perched on the arm of the couch, her gaze fixed on a tiny rip in the fabric from which a tendril of cotton protruded like a baby's first curl.

"Are you figuring out who to leave your purple kitchen set to, or what? I don't get it."

She glared at him, still silent. He stared back, until he saw a drop of moisture soaking into the bandage below her eye. Right then, he had to look away. He let himself sink into the couch and racked his brain for helpful words, but they evaded him.

"Lu . . ." he began with another exhale. He reached out from where he sat to touch her knee. "It's terrible, I know. But you can't start feeling bad for yourself. If you start feeling bad for yourself, you're done."

She crossed her least burned arm over her chest and let the badly burned one dangle at her side.

"Let me make you something," he offered, his eyes pleading.

She shook her head and, after thinking for a moment, extracted the notepad and pen once more.

I WANT TO TASTE AS LITTLE AS POSSIBLE. YOU WOULDN'T UNDERSTAND, she wrote.

He examined the square of paper until the letters went out of focus and all he saw before him was a blur of purple ink.

"Well, at least let me get you a smoothie," he said.

She shook her head again.

"A bland one," he added.

She shifted her eyes from left to right, hesitating.

"Be right back," he said, snapping his fingers and dashing out the door before she could say no.

Julien walked a block, then two.

"Come on," he muttered. "There has to be a juice bar somewhere in this neighborhood."

He walked down two more blocks and was about to give up before he spotted a black chalkboard with a drawing of a glass filled with whole strawberries on the sidewalk.

"Hello, good juice people of Inwood," he called, flashing a megawatt smile as he sailed through the door.

Ten minutes later, he was bounding up the stairs of Lumi's building two at a time, his hand numb from holding the large

Pineapple-Strawberry Surprise he had hunted down for her. He popped in through the door he had left ajar and handed it to her. She shrugged but took it from him, inserted a straw into the cup, and took a sip. Even though she still had her bandages on, he could see her face smoothing out beneath them as she sipped. And slowly, the swaths of skin that were visible began to take on a warmer, rosier tone.

"See, Lu? Isn't that better? Stay on the side of the living. We need you here," he said with a grin as he plucked the aloe plant off the round table. When she was done, he applied the aloe gel just as he had the day before, and he noticed that she squirmed less than she had the previous day. When he finished, she sat on the couch, staring at him. "What is it, Lumi?" he asked.

She pulled out the notepad, but instead of writing him a message, she traced the edges of the pad with her finger. Finally, she scribbled one word: THANKS.

He pressed a kiss to the top of her forehead. "Don't mention it, love. I'll be back at the same time tomorrow," he said, and with that, he was gone.

32

LUMI

Lumi stretched out on the couch and laid a magazine in her lap. She was up to the advice columns when the doorbell rang. Did Julien forget something? She scanned the living room and came up empty. The doorbell rang again, and she pushed off the couch and trudged to the door.

She stepped up on her tiptoes and her lips tugged against the bandages; she couldn't help smiling when she saw Gloria there.

"Hey, honey," Gloria said in a soft tone. She laid her hands on either side of Lumi's shoulders and gave her a barely there squeeze. Lumi's heart swelled within her chest.

Lumi scrambled for her notepad, but Gloria waved her to the couch.

"Don't trouble yourself, hon. No need to talk, unless you want to, and no need to entertain me. I'm here for what you need. And . . . to bring you this."

She heaved a paper bag onto Lumi's kitchen counter and began to unpack it. There were five large Tupperware containers, along with plastic cylinders filled with minestrone soup.

Lumi took up her notepad despite Gloria's insistence that she rest.

GLORIA . . . THERE'S FOOD FOR A WEEK IN HERE!

Gloria smiled. "I hope so, honey. Unless you are eating too little, which from the looks of ya is possible."

She unpacked a Tupperware container of eggplant parmesan and, using a plate from Lumi's cupboard and a spatula, cut and plated a saucy serving.

"I was going to make you sfogliatelle, but I figured with the flakiness . . . the bandages . . . you know."

Lumi shook her head. YOU ALREADY DID SO MUCH, she wrote, and passed the pad to Gloria, then quickly snatched it back, scribbled something, and passed it to her again.

THANK YOU ♡.

Gloria answered with a smile and wiped a bit of mist from the corners of her eyes. "It's nothing, Lumi. I'm just glad you're okay, honey."

Lumi nodded and gave Gloria's hand a quick squeeze.

Gloria's eyes alighted on the aloe plant, the boxes of Rice Chex, and the smoothie cup, but if she thought anything of it, she didn't mention it to Lumi.

To her surprise, Lumi's stomach started rumbling about an hour after Gloria left. The Rice Chex pinged against the glass of the blender as she filled it to the one-cup line and poured in a stream of water, followed by a handful of powdered milk. The mixture had been helping her feed herself without tasting, but this time a wave of nausea rankled her belly. *Ugh, what am I doing?* she thought. Gloria's eggplant parmesan had to be a better move.

Julien had a point: it was unclear which one was more

depressing, her meal or her reading material. She shoved the blender into the fridge to be dealt with later and chucked the will-writing guide into the trash. For however long she would be home, she would need things around that gave her something to look forward to.

She retrieved the plate that Gloria had made for her and, ever so slowly, peeled back the bandages that went over her lips. The first forkful of eggplant parmesan felt strange and textured after so many days drinking smoothies and eating mush. As she took a second forkful, she felt something like butterflies caressing her chest and expanding it at the same time. Gloria had prayed for her as she cooked this meal. To feel it in her cooking made her grateful all over again for Gloria's visit.

She looked forward to seeing Gloria again soon, and Julien would be back tomorrow too.

But there was something else that wanted to be let out, to be seen by her—something she had been thinking about since that night. She sat down on the couch with her seashell-print notepad in hand, pen in other, motionless for a long time.

Then, as if self-directed, her hand began to sketch. The burned skin tugged as she gripped the pen, but she didn't stop, just pressed a little lighter. Lines became squares, one, two, three, until they no longer fit on the small notepad. She got a bigger one and started all over. There would be a vegetable station, meat station, fish station, and separate refrigerators. There would be a wooden stand holding circular baskets full of plantains, yuca, and West Indies squash. And it would be in Inwood.

She lit a short, stubby candle for intention and retrieved a pack of colored pencils from her desk. One by one, she colored in the burgundy of the gleaming wine bottles, the tawny orange of the squash, the glittering silver of the fish scales. She stared at her drawing. Lumi leaned back into the couch, resting the eraser end of the silvery-gray pencil against her lip. She could do a bakery window to start, like she had wanted to at Caraluna. She could do a set menu, like at DAX. As much as she liked inventing one every day, what she had observed was that diners wanted to know what to expect. She would need a marketing plan. Word of mouth wasn't enough for a restaurateur who wanted to reach past her neighborhood to bring people to it.

Social media wasn't her thing, and she didn't have any personal accounts, but she would have to make some for her new place. And then she would need a way to get her food in front of people. Oh! There was that summer event at Lincoln Center she had considered doing two years ago when she first opened Caraluna.

That would give her a table, a platform, and a way to meet people and connect, all while they sampled her new offerings. LINCOLN CENTER, she scribbled around the margins of the drawing. And—she never imagined she'd be saying this—she might even consider doing some French-Dominican fusion. Just not bouillabaisse. Never bouillabaisse.

LUMI'S RICE CHEX SMOOTHIE

1 cup Rice Chex cereal
$^2/_3$ cup powdered milk
1 cup water

Preparation instructions: Don't.

33

JULIEN

Julien bounded up the steps of the walk-up building, buzzing with energy. It was nearly sunset, and he was right on time, just like he had promised the day before. He was keeping his word. He couldn't wait to see her. As he climbed the steps it occurred to him that below the burns on her chest the rest of her body had been unaffected. He could probably make love to her if they were very careful . . . She was still hurting, though, and he knew that. He knew it was probably the last thing on her mind.

He took it as a good sign that it was on his mind, though. It meant things were slowly going back to the way they were before. For the past week, he could think of little else except how well she had been healing. Gloria and Ruben had been left in charge of the kitchen, as he had not been able to focus or contain himself there for more than five minutes.

He stood in front of her door and raised his hand to ring the bell. He pressed down the shiny black button and waited.

There was no answer. He rang again and again. Julien frowned. It was the same time as the day before. She had to be home.

What if she had decided again that she didn't want to see him? He groaned under his breath. The least she could do, then, was slip a note under the door.

"Lumi?" he called, loud enough for her to hear if she was in fact in the living room. There was only silence. He rang again. That was strange. Knowing her, she would have gotten annoyed with all this ringing by now and would have at least put a note under the door telling him to shut up.

His stomach lurched in a sickening twist as a new thought came to mind. What if she couldn't hear him? His chest grew cold as he recalled the moment he had found her, unconscious on the kitchen floor. What if she had passed out? He began pounding on the creaky purple wooden door. Lumi had painted it purple herself, because the rest of the doors on her floor looked like they hadn't been painted since the building was constructed in 1898.

There still was no answer. His heart racing, he banged on the door louder, faster, harder.

"I swear to God, I will break this door down," he said, and just when he raised his fist to punch the door once more, it retreated from its frame, and his own momentum sent him stumbling into the apartment.

Lumi's look of consternation was clearly visible through the strips of gauze that circled her eyes. "Are you *trying* to get my neighbors to call the cops?" she asked. "Or were you just going to break down the door? I mean, seriously—What? Why are you looking at me like that?"

Julien cracked a wide smile, regaining his composure and

his breath. Even with the bandages, she was adorable to him when she was irritated.

"You're talking," he gasped, oblivious to everything else she had said.

She was standing in front of him with a towel tightly wrapped around her body, though her arms, shoulders, and legs were dry.

"I'm sorry," he said sheepishly, leading himself to the couch and taking a seat. He continued to hold her gaze. "It's just that . . . when you didn't answer, I imagined the worst."

She still looked annoyed, but he could see the edges of her face relaxing. She padded lightly to the couch and sat facing him.

Her skin looked a little brighter than the previous day, and she moved with more bounce in her step. He couldn't help but think that the aloe and his tender care had helped. He inhaled deeply, his breathing mostly back to normal by then. Reaching for her unburned hand, he looked into her eyes.

"I can't compare my experience to what this has been like for you . . . and would never try. But you have to know that it hasn't been easy for me either. When I found you that way, on the floor . . . my God." He sighed. "I thought I was going to have a heart attack." He winced at the thought. He stroked her unscathed hand in his.

His eyes traveled up her arm, taking in her naked shoulders and the graceful curves of her exposed neck. The springs of the couch squeaked as she shifted away from him uncomfortably.

"What is it?" he asked.

She stared hard at a warp in the wood on her living room floor. "Don't look at me like that," she whispered back, "not when I'm like this."

He frowned. "Lumi, if you think I want you any less than I did before," he responded softly, "you are quite wrong."

She looked glumly at the floor, and he had an idea. He reached across the space that separated them and smoothed his fingers around the edges of the bandages on her face.

"You do know you can't leave these on forever, right?"

"I—I'm not ready," she said.

Julien zeroed in on the bandages, scrutinizing them. "The edges are lifting up. If you let these burns get some air and let me put some aloe on them, it could help them start drying out more."

She gazed into his eyes and he could see the fear there, openly exposed. It made him want to wrap his arms around her, but instead, he lifted his fingers to loosen the edges of the bandage that covered her right cheek.

"You're beautiful, you will always be beautiful to me, Lu," he whispered, hoping to keep her distracted as he peeled them off as fast and gently as he could. He saw her cringe as she felt the hundreds of tiny gauze threads lifting off her skin, and for the first time in two weeks, the spring breeze, which filtered through her living room window, tickled her cheek.

He examined the angry red splotches and swirls. They spread from her temple to the corner of her mouth on the right side of her face. The edges of her lips on the same side were hardened and encrusted with dried blood. He quickly grabbed a knife from the kitchen, cut a leaf, and squeezed out some gel to apply with the greatest delicacy to her face. She held still as he finished dabbing on the gel.

"See, that wasn't terrible, ma poulette," he said.

"Poulette . . . as in hen?"

"Yep."

"I'm not your hen, Julien."

"Sure are."

"People don't poison their hens."

He sighed. "We need to talk about that."

Lumi's gazed flitted back to the floor. "I've already talked way more than I planned to today."

He pursed his lips. "Fair enough," he answered, and he saw the look of surprise on her face when she saw he wasn't going to argue. She stood up then.

"I'm just going to go put some clothes on," she announced, pacing toward the back hallway.

"On my account?" he asked, eyebrows raised in mock surprise.

She narrowed her eyes at him, although he could see the left corner of her mouth curving into a smile. "I'll be right back," she answered, and she was off.

Without her in front of him to capture his attention, he looked down and noticed that his knuckles were bleeding from his earlier endeavors. Sure enough, when Lumi returned, dressed in a sleeveless blue cotton dress, she brought ice, more cotton, and some alcohol. She offered them to him without a word.

"I don't have to go back to the kitchen tonight. What do you want to do?" he asked softly.

Lumi sighed. "I'm really tired. I was going to take a nap."

"I'll take a nap with you."

She studied him, leaning her head to one side. "I'm serious, you know. Just sleeping."

He flattened one hand and raised the other one as if he were swearing on a Bible. "You have my word."

Before she could add anything else, he had taken off his shoes, arranged them neatly on the floor, and stretched out, encompassing the full length of the couch. He opened his arms to her, an infectious grin playing on his face.

She sat down on the edge of the couch, testing the waters. She inched down vertebra by vertebra, until she was lying parallel to him. He slid his arms under her and pulled her close, her back pressed along the length of his body.

"Are you sure you're going to be able to sleep like this?" she asked.

"Yes, I'll be running a reel of the senior nuns from grade school in my head until I lose consciousness," he said. He felt her torso muscles contract to suppress a giggle.

He dared to plant a soft kiss on her neck, wanting to do more but remembering his promise to her. The warmth of her body pressed against him had a calming effect, and contrary to what he thought, he soon slipped into a restful sleep, the first one he had had for weeks.

34

LUMI

When Lumi's eyes opened three hours later, night had blackened the apartment. The first sight she saw in front of her were Julien's fingers interlaced with hers, blood crusted on his knuckles. She felt a pang of remorse as she stirred against Julien's chest. He responded by nuzzling her neck and sliding his hand to hug the curve of her hip.

"What time is it, love?" he asked in a woolly voice.

"It must be about eight o'clock," she answered, yawning. "We slept for a while."

They lay in silence for a stretch.

"Do you want to go for a walk?" Julien asked.

Between the hospital and her home stay, she had been indoors for two weeks.

She bit the unscathed side of her lip. "It's probably a good idea to get out before I start getting cabin fever. Will people look at me like a freak, though, if I put my bandages on?"

"You forget what city we're in. There's a man on my block who goes for a nightly stroll in his Wonder Woman costume.

Usually around the time I'm getting home. Nobody looks at him twice. Very nice man, in fact," he mused aloud.

Lumi laughed, and then she stopped in her tracks. "Oh, my God, I don't even know where you live," she said, clapping her hand to her mouth lightly.

Julien shrugged. "Columbus Circle" was his blunt response.

"Not too bad, Mr. Dax," she teased.

"It's not a big deal. Bought that because it was close to the kitchen more than anything."

She leaned her head back into his chest and allowed herself to enjoy the warmth that emanated from that little cavern between his neck and shoulder.

"Do you want to come see it?" he asked.

Her head snapped up. "Now?"

"Sure, now is as good as any other time, as long as you feel like it," he said.

She laughed. "Um . . . okay. Why not. Let me just put my bandages back on."

He sat upright, fully awake. "Or you could just let your face get some air."

She rolled her eyes good-naturedly but decided not to look for the bandages. Instead, she grabbed her jacket and pulled on some combat boots, and off they went down the stairs and out of the building.

They walked the two blocks to the A train station and hopped on the downtown train that would take them directly to Columbus Circle. As they passed the throngs of people and took seats on the train, nobody seemed to give her a second look. It occurred to her that they were all too preoccupied with their own hardships to be concerned with hers.

Julien's building was directly across the street from the

subway station, on the corner of Fifty-Ninth and Broadway. She took in the sight of the statuesque fountain and sculptures at the entrance to Central Park, and her gaze lingered there until he gently led her to his building.

He pressed a button on the elevator, and she watched him curiously as he followed the ascent of the elevator on the dashboard. With a ding, the elevator stopped on the nineteenth floor. She inhaled sharply as he unlocked the brushed chrome door and an immense white panorama revealed itself before her eyes. Almost everything in the apartment was white, except for the silver and brushed metal accents.

She let out a low whistle. "Um, this is no normal New York apartment. This place is amazing . . . Understatement of the year award goes to Mr. Julien Dax."

His eyes darted to the floor. "It *is* just a place. I . . ." Julien glanced up, beaming at her. "What can I get you, Lu?" he asked.

"I wouldn't mind a good cup of coffee if you've got one," she replied.

"Right! Right. Coffee. Why didn't I think of that?" he said, eyeing the futuristic-looking silver wall clock in the kitchen. He stuck his tongue out at her from the corner of his mouth. "We can also get sushi if you like. I know you're not into the idea of me cooking. Although . . . now that I mentioned it, I sent the pastries to the lab last week, to see what could have harmed you, Lumi. And I just got the report back today." He pulled his phone out of his pocket and flipped through emails. "See?" he said, holding it out. "They couldn't find anything."

Lumi shook her head, her expression sorrowful. "It wouldn't show up there."

He cocked his head to the side and inched closer to her. "What do you mean?"

She heaved a long sigh. "There's something you don't know about me, Julien. You couldn't have known, really. I've never told anyone before."

He inclined his ear toward her.

"You'll probably think I'm crazy," she said, biting her lip.

He grinned at her and drew her closer, putting his arm around her shoulders. "Whatever it is, you can tell me, Lu. There's nothing you could say that would change the way I feel about you."

"It's pretty . . . different, though, and I'm not quite sure how to explain it in a way that makes sense. Like I said, I've never done it before."

He angled himself toward her and said, "Just say it however it comes out."

She studied the pattern of the shiny silver buttons nailed into the arm of the couch. "Have you ever heard of people who can pick up an object and know who it belongs to or what they did that day, things like that?"

He shook his head. "I mean, I've heard of psychics before, reading tarot cards and the like, but that specifically? No."

"Right. You know what, let's just have the coffee. We can talk about this some other time."

"No, no! I'd really like to know. Take your time," he said.

Among the thoughts swirling around her mind was the realization that she didn't have to tell him, she didn't have to do this. Even so, she turned to face him. "Well, I've had this ability . . . since I was a child. To know what someone was feeling by tasting their cooking," she said.

Julien's eyes grew wide, but the rest of his face remained unchanged. "Go on."

"No, that's it. I taste someone's food, and I instantly know whatever that person was feeling when they cooked it, you know. Whether people are aware of it or not, they actually transfer that energy into the food. And by eating it, I transfer that energy into me. With just one bite, I'll know if they were happy, sad, angry, disappointed, any emotion really."

"Wow," he said.

"Do you think that's crazy?" she asked, wrinkling her nose.

"No. I mean, I believe you, although at the same time I just . . . don't understand how that's possible. I mean, where does that information come from?"

Lumi shrugged. "It has its source, you know? It comes from the same place as sunlight, or strangers who show up to help just as your tire went flat."

"You mean, like . . . God?" he asked, a slightly horrified look on his face.

"I don't know," she said. "I don't know what to call it. For most of us who went to Catholic school, God was the old man with the beard hoarding lightning bolts to strike down masturbators. That doesn't work for me. That, to me, is not God."

Julien rolled his eyes. "Yep. I got enough of that in Catholic school to last me the rest of my life. I'm good in the God department."

They fell into silence for a moment.

"So . . . how does it work?" Julien asked.

She thought for a minute. "Do you have anything here that was cooked by someone else?" she asked.

Julien thought over the contents of his refrigerator. "Mm-hmm." He went to the fridge, pulled out a plate, and came back with a slice of pear tarte tatin. He gave her a fork and she cut off a piece of the front. She tasted the tiny tip using the unburned corner of her mouth.

She paused a moment as she evaluated her bite. "This person was in a hurry. Possibly wanted to get home . . . end of the day, perhaps? There's also a motherly kind of affection and concern here . . . Was this made by your mother?" she asked.

He shook his head, his eyes crinkling at the corners. "Oh, my God, that's incredible! It was made by my housekeeper, Berta. She is a motherly sort, and she made that before she left today, so yes, she would have been in a hurry to get home to her family."

She gave him a small smile.

"Is there any time this ability comes in handy? I'm sure there are a lot of instances, but I imagine, something like saving someone's life or—some other important thing must have come into play at one time or another?" he asked.

Colton was the first person to come to mind. She thought of what to say and decided to leave out the time she felt a rush of pride, cheering Colton on at one of his poetry slams. She would also leave out the gold ring he had proposed to her with. And the angle of the ballerina's legs around Colton's waist when she walked in on them.

She cleared her throat. "Well, it did help me catch my ex-fiancé cheating."

"What?" he asked in a whisper, though they were sitting close in a quiet room.

Lumi took a deep breath and nodded. "He would cook dinner for me nightly, and about two weeks after we got engaged, every single thing he prepared made me nauseated. It didn't make any sense because it was all fresh, high-quality food. But it dawned on me that it could be something emotional. One day I came home early on purpose and found him in bed with someone else." It was interesting to her how she could fit the end of a two-year relationship and engagement into a neat little package.

Julien reached for her hand and squeezed her brown one in his freckled pink one. "I'm so sorry you had to go through that," he said.

She squeezed back and they sat in silence for a long while.

"I have to tell you, I think if I had that ability, the last thing I would ever do is become a chef."

She sighed ruefully. "It's exhausting sometimes. But it helps me feel connected to other people. I'm not naturally social and it's easy for me to feel like I'm all alone in my little bubble. And other times . . . like with you . . . it gives me a glimpse of another side of the person that perhaps I would never have seen."

"With me? What did you learn about me from trying my cooking?" he asked.

Her throat grew thick. "That you were . . . different than what I had initially thought about you."

A smile spread slowly across his lips. "It's a damn shame I can't kiss you for another week."

Her laugh came out as a surprised giggle. "A week? What, did you ask the doctor or something?"

He nodded playfully. "We had a little chat."

"Of course you did," she said.

They were silent until Julien shot up from the couch.

"Oh, my God," he said.

"What?" she asked. "What is it?"

He blew out a heavy breath and sank back into the couch.

"That day when I was making the cheesecakes, I asked Esme to stir the filling for me while I took a phone call," he said.

Lumi stared at him. "Esme . . . the secretary?" she asked finally.

He nodded, pursing his lips.

"But . . . *oh*," she said, remembering what Julien had told her about her weird gifts. Esme was just a door away from him every day. There was no doubt in Lumi's mind that Esme had been watching him, hoping for a chance. Until Lumi came along, Esme probably thought she had one, and when it became obvious that she and Julien were becoming something other than co-chefs . . . "Oh, God."

He buried his head in his hands. "I had no idea," he said.

She reached over and rubbed his shoulder with the unburned hand. "No, of course you didn't. How could you know your girlfriend is some kind of food clairvoyant unless someone had told you?" she asked.

He shook his head within his hands, then peeked out from between his fingers, a slow smile spreading over his face. "Did you say girlfriend?" he asked.

"Yeah, I guess I did," she said. "There's a lot to figure out here."

"Like what?"

"Like Esme. How would I even go about accusing her? I'm sure she never imagined while she was stirring that filling that her resentment was going to go directly into my bloodstream," Lumi said.

"Argh, what a mess," Julien said. "If I had confronted her about the gifts, none of this would have happened."

Lumi shook her head. "We don't know that. It still could

have happened because she probably would still be thirsting anyway. And she'd likely be resentful of anyone who got close to you. She does have a right to her feelings . . . even if they suck."

Julien was silent, his expression unreadable. Suddenly, Lumi felt like she had been walking for miles. Her eyelids grew heavy too.

He noticed the change in her and put his hands on either side of her shoulders.

"Lumi, are you okay?" he asked.

"I just feel exhausted all of a sudden," she said.

He nodded. "That's understandable . . . this is a lot to take in. And you haven't had so much activity in a while. Do you want to take a nap?"

"We just took a nap." She laughed.

"So?" he asked. "I don't charge for naps."

She was about to say no, but a huge yawn erupted from her. "You know what, maybe just a few minutes," she said. She closed her eyes and leaned back against the couch.

Thirty minutes later, she opened them. Julien was by her side, reading a newspaper, the couch-side light turned down low.

"Julien?" she whispered, and he turned to her.

"Yes, love?" he asked.

"What time is it?"

"Ten," he said.

"I should go," she said, stretching as she stood up.

"You know, you don't need to, Lumi," he said, measuring his words.

Her breath caught slightly in her throat. "Um . . . yes, I should. I need to go home and shower."

"Oh! Didn't you shower already?"

"I was going to, until someone came along and started breaking down my door."

"Right . . . that. Well, I do have a shower here," he said.

"Oh, you do?" she asked, distracted.

"Yes, I got tired of bathing in the Hudson River after a while." He grinned. She rolled her eyes playfully.

He led her into the hall, which had been fit with hardwood flooring, and pushed open a white door with frosted glass. The bathroom was spotless and was as white as she expected. He grabbed a plush crimson towel from his linen closet and gave her a quick kiss on the forehead before closing the door behind him.

All alone, she slipped off her dress, careful not to drag it over the burns, and stood naked in front of the mirror. She scrutinized her upper body, from her face to her neck, to the swells of her breasts, to her belly. If she was honest with herself, the portion of her body covered by the burns was quite small. And the rest of her body looked and felt the same.

"Lumi. I forgot, that bathroom doesn't have any—"

He cracked the door open behind her.

"Soap."

35

JULIEN

Julien had meant it when he told himself to leave Lumi alone. But when he saw her standing there in the bathroom, the valley between her shoulder blades had its own special language for him. It spoke to him, told him something only he could understand. It made it impossible for him to remain neutral.

"Can we try, Lu? I'll be careful, so careful," he whispered.

"Okay," she whispered in return, flicking off the bathroom light before he whisked her away in his arms.

He lifted her up and carried her over the threshold into the master bedroom, and the symbolism of the act was not lost on him. With the flick of a switch, the room flooded with a tenuous light. He laid her down, gentle as a rose, on the edge of the bed.

From his vantage point, he could see the surprise in her face as she noticed that the master bedroom was a spectrum of navy, gray, and cream hues, different from the bright white that covered the rest of Julien's living and working spaces. He lay down behind her and then wrapped an arm around her waist, pulling her close to him until they were two spoons, cuddled together.

He planted a soft kiss on the delicate skin of her neck. She leaned her head away from him in response, opening that tender plane to him and giving him more space to do what he wanted. Seeing this, he continued moving down, his kisses becoming hungrier. He slid down her neck, and his heart stalled for a second when she responded to his kisses with a moan.

This moment was a long time in the making, and one he had ached for. The night in the kitchen had been fire, necessary to keep them both from spontaneously combusting. But he hadn't had the chance to take his time to make love to her the way he truly wanted to since he first laid eyes on her. The smell of gardenia and lime radiating from her neck pervaded all his senses as though it were a drug that blinded him to all but his desire.

From her neck he moved to her spine and followed that curve all the way down, one kiss at a time. He could feel the muscles in her back grow more relaxed under his lips. With his fingers, he traced the curve of her waist as his mouth blazed a feverish trail down the slope of her back. She exhaled softly, goose bumps announcing themselves on her skin.

Watching her arch her back toward him to receive more of his kisses knocked the wind out of him. A thought crossed his mind, and he smiled to himself with a glint in his eye. He pushed away from her and stood up behind her.

"Sorry," he lied. "I got a little carried away."

She turned to face him, eyeing him seductively. "Come back," she whispered.

She reached out to catch him by the hand and pulled him back into his previous position.

He looked at her face and could tell she wasn't thinking about anything besides her growing need for him. And that was exactly what he wanted. He still had on his cotton shirt and pants, and he peeled them off, tossing them over the side of the bed.

He could feel her pulse quicken as he pressed his chest into the bare skin of her back, his wiry red-gold hairs tickling its surface. She sighed and melted under his fingers as he traced the outlines of the scars on her chest.

Julien moved from the scars and cupped the mounds of her breasts in his hands, staying clear of the edges of the burn. Lumi sighed and leaned her head back against him, tangling him in her springy curls. She slid her hand back and molded it to the corner of his square jaw. Turning her head toward him, their mouths met. She pressed her lips to his, enough to absorb some of their heat but not enough to disturb her scars. They kissed delicately as he continued to caress her breasts.

"See, Lu," he whispered, remembering her expression when he found her looking in the mirror, "none of this has changed. These are still so beautiful."

He brushed the tip of her nipple with his thumb. The sensation caused her to shiver against him, encouraging him even more. He kissed her neck again and reached around to stroke the plane of her belly.

"*This* is all the same," he whispered, a smile playing in his voice. "And this is . . ."

He let out a low whistle as his fingers found her velvety wetness. He dipped one finger inside her, and she ground her backside against him as he deepened his exploring. With the feel of her on his fingers and the sound of her breath, which by now was coming in shallow pants, it was all he could do to not grab her by the hips and sink himself into her like he wanted to. He tried to distract his thoughts, to think of anything else besides the boundless expanse of beauty at his fingertips.

She was moving against his fingers by then, and in one movement she jerked her hips forward, freeing his hand from inside her.

"Julien . . . I want to feel you," she whispered in a thick, low voice.

This was his cue. He reached into his night table and pulled out a condom.

Forgetting himself, he bit down on her ear as he grabbed her by the hips and slowly plunged into her, causing her to gasp. The sensation of her wet heat enveloping him was so overpowering, he felt as if he was going to pass out. She found his hands and molded hers over his knuckles, hugging herself with his arms before releasing them so he could be free to move.

He was surrounding her on all sides. He kissed her neck before he reached down to caress her hardened little pearl while he thrusted. She reached back and laced her hands behind his head, her nails grazing the nape of his neck and digging in as he thrust deeper.

"Julien!" His name was a siren call in her throat. Her sudden climax rocked her entire body and her skin shimmered against him. Her sounds and the velvety feel of her contracting around him were more than enough to send him hopelessly over the edge, leaving all distracting thoughts in the dust. He groaned and dug his fingers into the ridges of her hipbones as he emptied himself into the depths of her core.

"Oh, Lu," he mumbled contentedly moments later as he

hugged her closer, pushing a little deeper into her although he was starting to go soft. "You're magnificent."

"Mm," she murmured in response, her long eyelashes dusting her cheeks, already drifting into a sated sleep. For the moment, that answer was enough.

36

LUMI

It was only after they had made love again in the morning that Lumi's thoughts turned to food.

"Damn," she muttered as her stomach rumbled louder than it had in a long time. Her appetite was coming back. She wondered if Julien's appetite was the same, as she looked his body up and down as he lay on his side next to her.

Minutes later, he was awake. He leaned toward Lumi and planted a kiss just below her navel. He got up from the bed, snatched the discarded clothes from last night off the floor, and folded them onto a chair before he jumped into the shower.

While he bathed, Lumi took the liberty to scrounge around his kitchen for breakfast. For the first time since this shitstorm had started, she felt like cooking.

While perusing the fridge and pantry, she found some maple sausage and flour to make crepes, and she thought that would pair nicely with the oranges from the bowl that sat on the counter. Her heart pounded as she lit the fire for the skillet, but to her relief, she made it through cooking breakfast without getting burned or fainting.

"I now reestablish my power in this place," she said aloud, echoing a mantra she had learned in a creative visualization class once. To her surprise, it felt fitting in this kitchen.

By the time Julien walked into the kitchen, his hair freshly washed and the picture of health and vigor, the table was set with crepes, browned sausage, and freshly squeezed orange juice.

"Wow," he murmured, his eyes widening. He had been in the shower for all of ten minutes.

She smiled sweetly back at him, taking a sip of juice from a straw anchored in the unscathed corner of her mouth. As they ate, her eyes landed on a framed photograph that sat on his kitchen island. A tall, broad-figured woman with a wide smile and purple wig stood on the bank of a crystalline river. Her smile was bright and enchanting, but there was something off about her face. When Lumi looked closer at the photo, she saw that the woman had no eyebrows.

She had her arms around two children: a little roly-poly red-haired girl and a boy with red curls tumbling every which way and a serious, almost severe look in his brown eyes even though his mouth was smiling. He held a fish dangling from a line, and he didn't look too invested in that fish. She felt a twinge in her heart.

Her eyes flitted from the photograph to Julien, who was still mowing through his breakfast with a blissfully singular focus. She waited until he had finished the last bite of crepe.

"Julien," she asked in a soft voice, "is that your mother?"

He glanced up, and his eyes followed her gaze to the photo. "Mm-hmm," he answered.

She paused. "Well, I love her taste in wigs."

He chuckled. "Yes, she was a live wire. She was going through her third round of chemotherapy there. Leukemia."

She reached across the table and brushed the palm of her hand over his. He turned his palm over, and she grabbed it and squeezed hard. With her silence, she encouraged Julien to go on.

"She died about three months after that photo was taken, just two days before my twelfth birthday."

"Oh, Julien, my God. I'm so sorry."

"It's okay, Lu. That's life, right?" He shrugged. "Still miss her every day."

His gaze grew distant.

"She taught me how to fish, since my father was too busy. Before she died, she was planning a fishing-themed birthday party. She had bought fishing poles, a cake that looked like it had a little fish swimming on its surface, tiny fishbowls with real goldfish inside of them. She loved parties. My father threw the lot of it out after the funeral and we never spoke of it again."

"He just threw it all away? Was he angry that she'd been doing that?"

"No, he just couldn't deal with her being gone. They'd been together since university. They loved each other deeply . . . and when she died, he turned into a bitter bastard. Nothing I could do was good enough for him. When Christophe turned eighteen, he decided we were old enough to be on our own. He moved to Paris and left us behind in the house we grew up in. I was fifteen."

"Lord, I can't imagine what that was like for you."

She stroked his arm with the palm of her other hand and traced the silver hook on his bracelet with one finger.

"Do you still like to fish?"

Julien shrugged, letting out a heavy sigh. "It's been a while."

He stood up to clear the table, and she followed suit. He turned to face her, looped an arm around her waist, and pulled her close to him. He kissed her, and his mouth stretched against hers to deepen the kiss, until he remembered her burns. He pulled away, and she rested her head on his chest. He stroked her hair with one hand, and as she let him hold her, she felt the tension in his body ease. He exhaled.

She raised her face to look up at him, and he came closer until his face was less than an inch from hers. He kissed the tops of her closed eyelids and, very delicately, the scarlet streak of red that the burn had left just under her eye.

"Maybe I'll stay home today," he murmured. "Gloria and the others can make do without me."

Lumi shook her head. "Julien, it's not good for us to get into this . . . bubble, where it's just me and you," she said.

"What else is there?" he asked, his eyes dreamy.

"Julien." She tried to sound stern but suspected it wasn't working. "Go to work. Handle your biz." She gave him a playful shove.

He shook himself. "Yeah, yes. I guess you're right," he said. "We're catering a graduation dinner at DAX tonight. I'll see you tomorrow?"

She nodded emphatically. "Yes. Sounds good." And with that, she picked up her purse to leave.

"Lumi?" he asked.

"Yes?"

He started to say something but bit his tongue. "Take care of yourself for me," he said.

The spa tub was deep, not so deep that it activated Rafelina's fear of drowning, but deep enough to wet Lumi's, Jenny's, and Rafelina's ponytails as they soaked in it. Halved lemons bobbed on the surface of the water. The spa room had been darkened and fitted with a violet light. A canvas dotted with thousands of tiny luminous points was stretched over the standard stucco ceiling, giving the impression of a starry sky. It had been three weeks since the kitchen incident. With caution, Lumi had agreed to do a spa day with her two best friends.

"I better taste like lemonade by the time I get out of here," Rafelina said.

Lumi splashed her and laughed, and Jenny gave Rafi a polite smile.

"It's nice to have both of you here," Lumi said. "I know you got to meet when I opened Caraluna, but it's been a while."

"It's nice to be here," Jenny said with a sigh, sinking farther into the warm water.

Lumi draped her burned hand and arm over the edge of the tub. With her other hand, she flicked away the lemons that floated over and bumped into her shoulders, sending them bobbing over to Rafelina. The steam rising off the water made her burns itch, but she wasn't going anywhere. She needed this.

"You're kind of freaking me out, ma," Rafelina said. "You seem strangely okay for what happened."

"It's okay. I'm okay." Lumi threw her head back and heaved a long breath. "I'm not okay. Of course I'm not okay. But I have to keep going. I'm not going back to the state of mind I was in after I lost Caraluna."

Jenny reached toward Lumi and patted her arm, while Rafelina put an arm around her shoulders. The tears spilled over, and Lumi allowed them.

"You're not going back to that, Lumi. You'll see. Everything will be just fine. You'll get through this," Jenny said.

Rafelina nodded and squeezed her shoulders. Lumi leaned her head back against Rafelina's arm and breathed deep, letting the steam and salts do their work.

On the edge of the tub, a tall, thin woman with a towel wrapped around her head cleared her throat. "Excuse me, are you ladies almost done? I'm waiting for my turn to become tea. Also, you're doing it wrong. You're supposed to brush your skin while you're in there."

"Hmm . . . dead skin and lemon tea? Not a winning combo in my book. Let's get out of here," Rafelina said.

They stood up, wrapped their white spa towels around their bodies, and walked down the tiled steps to the locker room. Rafelina spied the infrared sauna and stepped away from Lumi and Jenny.

"Do you mind if I check that out real quick?" she asked.

"Not at all. I'd better not, but I'll wait for you in the locker room. You should go too, Jenn."

Jenny gave her a nod. "Thanks, Lumi."

Lumi watched them disappear behind a heavy pine door across from the spa tub, then trailed into the locker room. Aside from a kind-eyed woman folding disposable bras by the sinks, it was empty. She sat on one of the wooden benches between lockers, hugging her towel close to her body, and took a sip from the water bottle she held. There had been a bar set up with cucumber water, hibiscus tea, and copper cups at the entrance to the locker room, but she decided on plain bottled water. She'd learned it was best to limit outside information that could interfere with her senses when she found herself feeling open and relaxed.

The quiet time allowed her to check in with herself. Twenty minutes in the tub had left her feeling like jelly. Her skin tugged in the burned places, but more than causing pain, they itched. As she sipped the water, she noticed that her chest seemed to have grown more expansive; there was more space for her to breathe. In silence, she gave thanks for good friends and hot water, neither of which was a given.

37

LUMI

Evening fell over Manhattan, streaking the sky with pale orange, rose gold, and, finally, violet. Lumi was pulling on her jacket to go and walk the streets of Inwood to search for good pho when her door buzzer rang. She glanced up at the clock in surprise. She wasn't supposed to see Julien until the following day, and she hadn't made plans with her friends since she fell into this bubble of playing doctor the old-fashioned way with him.

A moment later, a knock came on her door. Julien stood before her. He smiled widely when he saw her, but she detected restlessness behind his smile.

"I know we said tomorrow, Lu, but I couldn't wait that long to see you."

She was secretly relieved. She had felt a dull ache all day, her body missing him in the places he had been. Plus, she could use his soothing touch after being itchy all day after the spa.

As she studied him, she detected an edge of irritation. She

reached forward to stroke the side of his face with her un-burned hand, letting the stubble prickle her palm. He laid his hand over hers and pressed it there, savoring the feel of her cool palm against his face.

"Everything okay?" she asked softly, searching his eyes.

"Yeah," he answered, breaking into another smile, "just kind of an irritating day at the office."

"What happened?" Lumi asked.

"Esme resigned," he said.

"Really?" she said.

Julien nodded. "Mm-hmm. Sent me an email. Didn't even come in to resign in person."

Lumi blew out the air she had been holding in. "Wow."

"Yep. Now I have no closure about what happened to you, and I also don't have a receptionist. Awesome," he said.

Lumi sighed. "I don't know what kind of closure we can ever have, babe. And trying to look for it makes me feel like I might go crazy, because I already know there's no way to find it. So you know what? We just have to say it is what it is and be thankful it wasn't worse. I can see, I can move, I can work. I need to keep looking forward because dwelling on the what-ifs doesn't help at all," she said.

Julien nodded, his mouth wide open. "I have nothing to say. You're right," he said.

"Well, I don't see what other way there is. Anyway! Can I get you a drink?" she asked.

"Sure," he said, and in a blink, she was back with two bourbons on the rocks in highball glasses.

"That's all I have right now," she said.

"It's perfect." He beamed at her as he sunk down into the

couch. He looped an arm around her waist, bringing her closer to him. "So, babe? We're in 'babe' territory now, I take it?"

She answered him with a playful eye roll. "You're just goofy."

He took a glass from her and savored the bourbon. After a few minutes, he felt his shoulders relax.

"That's better," he said. He settled a hand on her knee and then ran it up her thigh, caressing the fullness of it. Then he slid it down and away, playfully reaching out to tug on the hem of her jacket.

"I was just heading out to get some pho," she said.

He thought for a moment. "Lumi," he said, "I want to cook for you tonight."

Immediately she felt her chest constrict.

"I've been thinking about what you told me," he said, "and I think that if you taste what I make for you, you'll know for sure."

"I believe you," she said, and she did, although she still felt a little hesitant for him to cook for her so soon.

"Just let me cook for you tonight, please, Lu. If you don't like what you taste, you don't ever have to try my cooking again."

She half smiled as she remembered her vow to herself when she first started working at DAX.

"Please, babe," he whispered, leaning in to kiss her neck.

Goose bumps rose on Lumi's arms. She sighed in joking exasperation. "Fiiine."

He rewarded her with a brilliant smile, jumped up from the couch, and dashed to the kitchen. He searched through her refrigerator and found salmon fillets, fresh penne from Fairway, and some sliced pineapple.

"Can I use these?" he asked, holding up two small potted basil plants from the kitchen windowsill.

She nodded and watched him as he laid everything out on the countertop and began chopping. "What can I do?" she asked.

Julien gestured at her, thinking for a minute, a devilish grin playing on his lips. "You can change into something more comfortable and get ready for me," he said.

The feeling in the pit of her belly told her that was a fine idea.

By the time she had showered and changed into some soft lace pajamas, there was a full meal laid out on her kitchen table.

"Fresh pesto," she said. "And look at that. I was about to go out because I couldn't find anything to eat."

"See why you need me around?" he said as he winked.

There was also a bottle of pinot noir on the table that she hadn't noticed him bring in. She eyed it with a look of quizzical amusement.

"I always have a reserve," he said, smiling.

"In your sleeve?" she asked. She knew she didn't have any wine at home.

"This time, yes," he answered, as he uncorked the bottle and poured each of them a glass.

The penne had succulent bites of flaked salmon throughout, equally bathed in the fresh pesto he had whipped up. She saw him focus studiously on his plate as she took a forkful in her mouth. There was the full and creamy flavor of garlic, the tangy basil, and the savory morsels of fish. There were also some crackles of bright, sweet flavor—the pineapple. And then there was that deep, smoky aftertaste of sage again.

She stopped in her tracks. He glanced up, raising an eyebrow.

"Everything's excellent," she said, and he let out an audible sigh of relief. "It's just . . . I have to tell you something," Lumi added.

Julien encouraged her to go on with his eyes.

"You remember what I told you the other day, about the food and tastes?"

"Of course."

"Every time I eat your cooking, it tastes like sage to me. It doesn't matter what you put in it. I never tasted that before. And I can't figure out why," she blurted out, feeling relief at finally having gotten this off her chest.

A wistful look crinkled the corners of his eyes. "That's funny," he said. "When I was a child, my mother had an herb garden, and that's where she taught me how to plant. I was in charge of the sage and marjoram, and sometimes, when she wasn't looking, I would pick a few sage leaves and chew them."

"Hmm. That could be it."

"Could be, I have no idea. But there's something I can't wait anymore to tell you, and it's that I love you," he said.

Her breath caught in her throat, and her heart thrummed in her chest. That wasn't the answer she was expecting, but it was all she needed to hear and more. Though if she were to be truly honest with herself, she already knew.

"I love you too," she said.

A few months ago, she would never have imagined she would be saying it to a man. Especially not this one. But it had the ring of truth in her ears.

"I love you, Lumi," he whispered into her hair. He grasped

her hand, and she leaned in to kiss him. They had the rest of the dinner the next morning for breakfast.

"I brought you something," Julien said, setting a white cardboard bakery box down on Lumi's kitchen counter the following afternoon. The late May sun was resplendent, and the magnolia trees across the street by Kraft Field were fully bloomed, so much so that Lumi swore she could smell them from inside the apartment.

"Oh, honey, you shouldn't have," she joked, but nevertheless hastened over to open the lid. She gasped as she peeked in.

"Wow, Julien. White chocolate and caviar on . . . is that barley crostini?"

"Yup," he answered with a grin.

She picked one up and took a bite. "Delicious. You didn't make these, though."

He smiled. "You're right. It was Gloria," he said.

Lumi stared down at the crostini round, turning it this way and that, watching the light refract off the tiny, glossy roe bubbles. She felt his eyes on her.

"I miss working with you, Lu. I wish you would reconsider and come back to the kitchen. You know, just give it a chance."

She sighed. "Julien, I can't. *Especially* now. I can't work with you like we're just two chefs cooking together. And I also don't feel right to have you as a . . . boss type of figure anymore. Things are just too different now and I don't want to pretend."

They listened from inside the apartment as a taxi honked loudly down 218th Street.

Julien nodded slowly. "I understand. But you don't have to

pretend, Lu. Everyone knows by now. We're on the other side of that fence."

She covered her eyes with her hands.

"There's nothing wrong with that." He thought for a minute. "What if there was a third option?"

She looked up at him quizzically.

"What if we were to go into business together?" he asked.

Her eyes widened. "What do you mean? How would that even work?" she asked.

"Well," he mused, "I could close DAX for a few weeks. And then we could reopen it as something else."

"As what? You love DAX. And *you* worked very hard to create that for yourself. I'll be damned if I let you close it on my account. Besides, the clientele love DAX for what it is now. They know what to expect, they trust the quality. You have diners who come nightly because they want to eat classic French food but don't want to cook it themselves. If they can't order their favorite dishes anymore, do you think they'll still come?" she asked.

"Maybe some yes, maybe some no. But then, maybe others who don't come at all would be drawn in by something more inventive," he said.

Lumi frowned. "Would you even enjoy doing that?"

"With you, I would." He picked up a crusty bread round and licked a dollop of silken white chocolate off the jagged edge. "Or," he said, "I could sell some of my bonds, and with the proceeds we can open a new location that will be its own entity."

Her jaw dropped. "You'd do that?" she asked.

"That's the least of what I would do for you," he said, his

face completely serious as he crushed the tiny caviar bubbles between his tongue and the roof of his mouth.

She pursed her lips, holding back a laugh. "You're such an ass sometimes," she said, snapping a dish towel in his direction.

He leveled his gaze with hers. "Lumi, I'm serious about the business. I mean it. What do you think?" he asked, searching her face for any hints.

Lumi sighed, pausing for a moment. "Julien, it's more than I would've ever asked of you, but I have to be honest. I have something else in mind."

His eyes narrowed. "You want to reopen Caraluna, don't you?" he asked.

Lumi reached across the kitchen counter to lay her hand over his. "Yes, sort of. Not just reopen Caraluna but start a new venture. I've learned so much in the last few months that I think if I apply a DAX-type structure to my own restaurant, I could really have a chance this time."

Julien drew closer and laid an arm around her shoulders. "I know you miss your place, and the truth is that if you keep it closed, there will continue to be a hole here in Inwood where it used to be."

She looked at him in gratitude.

"So, how are you going to do it?" he asked.

She sighed and let her forehead fall into her palm. "I haven't figured that part out just yet," she said. "I still have bills from last season."

He nodded in understanding. "But you still have your restaurant license, right?"

"Yes, of course," she replied. "One thing I was thinking

was that I could put in a bid to cater some of the Summer Se-ries events at Lincoln Center."

Julien rubbed his chin between his thumb and his fore-finger. "That's not a bad idea at all. I did it two years ago. Sixty-five thousand for the summer."

"Pretty decent," she said.

"If you wanted to, you could cook everything at DAX on Saturday morning. This plan could help put a dent in those bills and still leave you with some start-up," he said.

"That would be amazing. Can I see the proposal you used to win the bid?" she asked.

"Of course. Just promise me, no ropa vieja and no swans in the flan."

"Ugh! Those were the bride's idea." She laughed and kissed him. Having her ideas heard wasn't half bad.

JULIEN'S PINEAPPLE PESTO
Makes 1 cup of pesto

2 cups fresh basil
2 cloves garlic
$\frac{1}{4}$ cup olive oil
2 tablespoons pine nuts
2 tablespoons parmesan cheese
$\frac{1}{2}$ cup crushed pineapple

Blend all the ingredients in a blender until smooth.

38

LUMI

Lumi was dabbing her scars with aloe when her phone vibrated with a text message. She expected it to be Julien telling her he was on his way over, as he'd been every day for the past three weeks since she came home from her accident.

"Oh!" she cried when the screen revealed that it was Richard.

Coming over in 10, mujer.

"Yikes," she said as she surveyed the sweaters, jackets, and jeans draped over her couch. She was glad Richard had thought to take the time and stop by, but if she had known he was coming by, she would've cleaned. She snatched the clothes up and stuffed them in the closet, closing the door tight. She wiped off the remaining aloe and braided her hair, lest Richard find her looking like an iguana had made a nest on her head.

Lumi unlatched the door and left it ajar, and a moment later, Richard slid through, Kramer-style.

"Querida!" he said, pulling her in for a hug. "Ooh . . . let me get a look at you."

With both arms he leaned her away from him, taking in the scars on her face.

"They look better than before and they already look flatter than in the photo you sent me. You've been taking good care of them, I can tell."

"Yeah," she said, "you know, just making sure they heal. They don't seem to be getting any lighter, though."

"So what, reina? They're yours," he said.

Lumi stifled a giggle, covering her mouth with her hand. "Well, what can I say," she said, "either I'm going to laugh about it or cry, and crying hurts my face, so . . ." She let her words trail off.

She noticed Richard held a gray neoprene sack in his hand.

"Whatcha got there?" she asked.

"Some vino, linda! Care for a glass?" He peeled back the sack and produced a bottle of cabernet.

Lumi glanced at the clock. "It's eleven," she said, giving him a pointed look.

Richard sighed. "Child, please. At this point, I have wine for blood. Where's the corkscrew in this place?"

He walked over to the kitchen cabinets, and she pointed to the one just above the stove. He gasped in delight as he stood before it.

"On second thought . . . girrrl! You have a greca! Let's make a little espresso first, then wine." He unscrewed the top of the espresso maker and held out his hand, gesturing for Lumi to bring the coffee.

"Now that's a plan I can get behind," she said. She lifted

a lilac earthenware jar off her kitchen counter and brought it to where he stood.

They made coffee together and sat down on opposite ends of the couch, sipping their demitasse cups in companionable silence.

"How are things at DAX?" she asked softly.

"They're okay." He shrugged. "Julien hasn't been normal since you appeared. Whatever you're giving him, keep giving it, because he's mostly off all of our cases now."

She raised her hand to hide the red from the blood that rushed to her cheeks. "What do you mean?" she asked.

Richard side-eyed her. "Oh, come on, Lumi. We all know by now."

She let out a heavy sigh. "Oh, God," she said.

"What? Don't be ashamed! If it can't be me, at least it's you."

They both laughed together, and Richard shook his head gently.

"He seems happy, though. In the seven years I've known him, I've never seen him happy like this."

Lumi looked up from her coffee and furrowed her brow. "Richard . . . oh, God, I shouldn't ask you this." She stared down into the depths of her coffee cup.

"I know what you're going to ask. No, he never brought any other chicks back to the kitchen," he said, giving her a pointed look. "Anyway, let's pop the cork on that wine."

He stood up and walked back to the kitchen to retrieve the object of his affection.

The door swung open. "Did somebody say wine?" Rafelina stuck her head in.

"Rafi!" Lumi exclaimed, and hopped up to embrace her friend.

"Oh, honey," Rafelina said, gently hugging her friend. She squeezed her closer and stopped dead when her gaze fell on the man in the kitchen.

"Ricardito, is that you?" she whispered. "Oh, my God!"

Richard had been facing the sink, and when he turned around his face lit up. "Rafelina!" He set the wine down and leaped over the kitchen stools to where they stood. "Ohhh!"

Without letting go of Lumi, Rafelina shifted her over to one side and hugged Richard with her other arm, tears streaming freely down her cheeks.

Lumi looked from one friend to the other, completely confused. "How . . . ?"

Richard turned to Lumi, his arm still around Rafelina. "Rafi was my best friend from nursery school to sixth grade."

Rafelina nodded, wiping her cheeks with a tissue. "We smoked our first cigarette together when we were eleven. And he's the one who taught me how to put on liquid eyeliner!"

"Oh, wow . . . good job! So what happened? Why'd you lose touch?" Lumi asked.

"My family moved to Boston the summer before seventh grade," Richard explained. "Back then I didn't know how to use the internet very well—"

"And I was a horrible letter writer," Rafelina added.

"And that was pretty much it," Richard finished. "Never forgot my first bestie, though!" he said, giving her shoulders a squeeze.

"Well, the good thing is we both know how to use the internet now." Rafelina laughed. "There'll be no reason not to stay in touch. In the meantime, how 'bout that wine?"

Richard poured the cabernet into three crystal goblets and pulled up a chair opposite the couch for Rafelina. Lumi sipped her wine through a straw as her two friends caught up on the past twenty years. After rounds of raucous laughter, the conversation gradually turned to Lumi and Richard's time working together at DAX.

"But really, Ricardito, don't you think it's strange what happened to Lumi?"

"Nothing is strange when a petty bitch is afoot."

Rafelina looked taken aback. "What do you mean?"

Richard leaned in closer. "I mean there is someone who had it out for Lumi since she began at DAX."

"Who?" Rafelina asked.

"Ms. Esmeralda Rincon." He rolled his eyes.

"Oh, yeah? What's her deal?"

"Well—wait. I need some background music to tell this story." He motioned with his chin in the direction of Lumi's stereo. Rafelina and Lumi exchanged an amused glance, and Lumi sent a playlist from her phone to her stereo. Sultry jazz notes flooded the apartment.

"Ahora sí. So yeah, Esme was receptionist for this other chef . . . what was his name? Verni?"

"Verdi?" Lumi couldn't help but gasp in shock.

"You know him, Lumi?" Richard asked.

She bit her lip and gave a sullen nod. "We've met."

"Well, she worked for him and apparently they were also, like, an item."

Upon hearing this, Lumi feared she would become ill.

"Is he hot?" Rafelina interjected, leaning forward and resting her chin onto her palm.

"If you like the Michelin Man, sweetie," Richard said.

Rafelina blinked her brown eyes. "Um . . . gotcha."

"Anyway, Verdi and Julien used to be friends. But one night, Verdi brought her to DAX for dinner. Gloria was there, and she said that it was a miracle Esme didn't faint when she saw Julien. When Esme heard he was looking for a receptionist, she applied for the job, and when she got it, what I heard is that she left Verdi a letter quitting her job and breaking up with him in the same note."

"Oh, God, that's horrible," Lumi said. So that was what Verdi meant about calling it even.

"Yep. Zero remorse. When she first started, she and Gloria were kinda friendly. Gloria told me that she would make 'joking' comments about having a five-year plan to marry Julien and become second in his company. She saw he wasn't interested in her, but she planned on wearing him down over time . . . who knows how," he said with pursed lips.

"Whoa, that's some heavy shit," Rafelina said, blowing out a breath.

"Jesus," Lumi said, leaning her forehead onto her palm.

"Yep. And now she quit DAX too, so who knows? Maybe she got a new job at the office of the Sexiest Man Alive. Either that or she just couldn't deal with this," he said, gesturing at Lumi from head to toe. "Anyway, you ladies up for some tapas? I need to put something in my stomach to soak up the wine, and there's a cute new place on 207th that would be perfect for catching up with my grade-school bestie and my kitchen buddy." He winked at them both.

Lumi and Rafelina shrugged and nodded, prompting Richard to toss Lumi a jacket. He and his glossy-haired newfound old friend linked arms on the way out of the apartment.

39

LUMI

The unusually balmy morning of May 27 found Lumi and Julien in bed at his apartment, catching some breeze from the fan. Lumi gazed at her reflection in the glass pane. Owing to the impeccable burn care she had received, her scars had flattened, and left in their place were swaths of different-colored skin: nearly bone white, rosy pink, swirls of an almost maroon color. They did not seem to be planning to get much lighter. But Lumi was getting used to them. Richard was right, they gave the impression that her face was painted. It could have been worse.

Giving herself a tiny smile, she turned back to Julien. "So, are you ready to turn thirty-nine tomorrow?" she asked.

Julien rolled over onto his stomach, burying his face in her breasts.

"Eh. Ready as I'll ever be," he replied. The air blowing in their direction undulated Lumi's curls across the silken pillowcase. He tilted his head up to kiss her and got up from the bed.

As he paced over to the dresser to grab his boxers from where they had landed the night before, a small note on a yellow Post-it caught his eye.

Shopping List

Whipped cream
Rope
Fishhooks
Leather ties

He let out a low whistle. "Planning a party, eh, Lu?" he exclaimed, clapping his hands and rubbing them together in anticipation.

Lumi was beet-red blushing. "Er . . . it might be a little different than what you're thinking."

Julien feigned a frown. "Is that set in stone? Because I like what I'm thinking." He lunged for her, grabbing her around the waist. They both fell back onto the bed, where he tickled her mercilessly.

"You're incorrigible," she sputtered between laughs. "And you weren't supposed to see that, so, um—just act surprised, 'kay?"

Julien looked at her with his bottomless brown eyes and playfully innocent expression. "It's forgotten," he said solemnly.

"Good."

"What's good?" he asked innocently.

"Oh, you." She swatted at him. The sound of her phone broke up the tickle attack. "Wait," she said, nearly panting. "It's Jenny."

Julien loosened his grip on her so she could answer the phone.

"Hey, Jenn . . . Yes, let's still meet at twelve . . . Mm-hmm. Yes. Exactly. Okay. Love ya." She hung up and took a deep breath, collecting her thoughts.

"I'm giving you thirty seconds to get up. After that, there will be no leaving here today," he murmured into her ear, stroking her belly.

"We better go then," she said. She tucked the note into her purse pocket.

"If we must, love. I'm going to get as much done as possible so I can take the day off tomorrow. Meet you at your place tonight?" he asked.

"Yes," she said. "Definitely my place."

He eyed her curiously but didn't ask any more questions. After all, he had agreed not to interfere with the surprise.

40

JULIEN

By ten thirty that night, Julien was at Lumi's door. The hours had flown by, and he couldn't wait to see her and what she had planned. If it was anything like that note hinted at, it was going to be his kind of night.

He knocked on the door, and to his surprise it swung open. Also to his surprise, the first thing he saw were blue lights that projected waves onto the walls. Julien gasped as he took in the sight of the living room and kitchen. A hundred tiny sequined fish hung on glittering hooks from the ceiling. Blue streamers simulating waves ran from one side of the living room to the other. He turned toward Lumi, who stood in the middle of all the fish and waves, a welcoming mermaid.

"Better late than never," she said shyly. "Happy birthday, Julien."

He wanted to speak, wanted to say many things, but the emotion was so thick in his throat that all he could do was pull her to him and shower her with kisses.

"I love you, mon coeur, I love you. You're the best," he whispered fervently, kissing all over her face, lightly over her scars. "Someone up there was looking out for me when they sent you to me."

A single tear escaped from his eye and traveled down his cheek, nearly falling to the ground before she could catch it with a kiss. She tightened her arms around him, smiling to herself.

"I made a cake too," she said, tugging him over to the kitchen counter where a square layered cake with diminutive goldfish and waves of turquoise buttercream sat pretty on a crystal plate. "Do you want some?"

Julien looked at her, and his eyes were glowing, his face effulgent.

"I would love to, but can we just sit for a minute, Lu? I feel a little . . ." He didn't complete the sentence, and he didn't need to. He sat down on the couch, her head on his chest, him holding her close to his heart. It was then that he decided not to wait any longer.

Rochelle stretched her wonderfully rounded arms, yawning as she traversed the aisle of the diamond store for the fifth time. "That birthday story is positively brilliant. But since when do you need someone to help you choose anything, you headstrong mule?" she asked, regarding her brother curiously.

"This is different, Ro," he answered tersely.

She eyed him askance. "Are you sure you'll be able to live with another human being?"

He glared at her. "Yes."

"I don't know. She leaves one dish in the sink and I think

there's going to be a headline in the *Daily News* about a pretty young chef found dead with a pillow over her face."

He cringed at the thought. He knew he would never hurt her and would happily maim whoever tried. If he ever ran into that Colton guy one day . . . He gritted his teeth. The free fall of his heart when she had told him that story was still in his muscle memory. She deserved so much better than that. And here was Rochelle, making frivolous jokes.

"You know what, maybe this was a bad idea after all," Julien snapped.

Rochelle heeled, seeing her teasing had gone further than she had wanted. She forced herself to take a deep breath. "I'm sorry. It's just that this whole thing feels so . . . alien to me. I was certain you were going to be alone forever."

"Well, can you understand the concept that a person can change? That life can change? I'm not the same man I was six or even three months ago. I'm not the same man I was . . . before her."

Rochelle willed herself not to roll her eyes. "You know, the truth is I'm a little jealous of her."

Julien's eyes shot up. "Well, if I'd known you wanted to marry me, I would have referred you to a therapist a lot sooner."

"Not about that, you idiot. I mean . . ." She sighed wistfully. "I want to be somebody's Lumi."

Julien studied her, frowned, and put his arm around her. "You will be, Ro. I'm convinced of it." He gave her shoulders a quick squeeze. "Now can you please help me choose?"

She leaned her head back onto his arm. "Yes. I will." And then in a whisper: "Maman would be proud of you, you know."

"Let's just hope she's watching and also forgives the grief I've given our father over the years."

Rochelle pursed her lips. "We can only hope. Now, look. Yoo-hoo!" she called to the bearded clerk at the register. "I'd like to see this rose gold art deco setting over here."

41

LUMI

One week after Julien's birthday, Lumi found herself being led on a stroll in Central Park at twilight.

"Come on, I want to get to the turtle pond before sunset," Julien said, practically dragging her by the elbow. She hadn't known Julien was such a turtle lover.

The grass gave way to the asphalt path as they traversed Sheep Meadow. When they reached the turtle pond, Lumi drew a sharp breath. The sun had begun to set, and its rosy beams illuminated the thousands of lily pads floating on the surface of the pond, giving it the appearance of being lit with myriad floating candles.

Turtles small and large alike poked their heads out of the mossy water, hoping for a stray morsel of bread. The chatter and song of the various bird species living in the trees added a mellifluous backdrop.

Lumi had twisted her hair into an oversized topknot. A few tendrils had escaped at the base and danced in the breeze. She looked over at Julien, and their eyes met. He looked slightly euphoric, and for some reason that made a tiny muscle she hadn't even known was there clench in her belly. She reached for his hand, and he took hers and squeezed it. He turned to her.

"Lumi," he began, "there's something I have to tell you, and something I have to ask you."

She felt the hairs stand up on end on her back and took a deep breath, her nostrils flaring, nodding for him to go on.

He took a deep breath and, seeming to draw courage from it, continued. "There's a part of what I want to say that I can't put into words." He sighed. "But what I feel for you is more than love. We're two sides of the same coin, Lu. I hate when people say stuff like this, but it rather feels like we share the same soul."

Lumi sucked in her breath.

"I was planning to wait a little longer to do this, but after that birthday party, I can't wait a day longer to tell you that I want, no, I *need* to be with you. Forever," he said.

He reached into his back pocket and pulled out a burgundy velvet box. He flipped back the lid, and there was a single pear-shaped diamond glittering on a smooth rose gold band.

"Lumi"—he smiled, the sun glinting off his perfect white teeth—"Will you marry me?"

Against her will, she froze. She had heard people say that in the moments before death they saw their life flash before their eyes, and she wondered if the inverse was true. In the seconds right before a new path opened up, could one see her future flash before her eyes?

Because her future with Julien did. Scenes of their life together stretched out before her in one cohesive and exquisite tapestry. Them living together, loving each other, working with each other—she swore that if she hadn't blinked too soon she would have better seen the image of a redheaded little boy snuggled on her chest.

And at the same time, she could hear the ugly, gnarled voices in her head. Some of them belonged to Inés and some of them were her own. They pointed out that Colton had been a great partner until they had agreed to get engaged. Julien was not Colton, and she couldn't imagine Julien changing like that. But, back then, she wouldn't have been able to imagine Colton changing either.

She wanted to think of a better answer to explain her inner conflict to him. But all she came up with was this: "Julien . . . it's beautiful. Can I think about it?"

Julien's moony smile gradually morphed into a blank stare. "What?" he asked in a tone barely above a whisper.

"I—I need to think about it," she stammered.

"Y-you don't want to marry me?" he asked, his voice hollow.

"It's not that—it's not you. It's . . . marriage."

He had been looking at the ring, and his glance shot up to her. "What?" he asked in disbelief.

"Marriage. I'm not sure it's a good idea."

"Why not? I love you, and you love me. What could be a better idea than melding every aspect of our lives?"

"That's not what marriage is. It ruins people's lives," she whispered in horror.

Julien looked startled. "Okay . . . wait. You think that marrying me would ruin your life?"

She shook her head vehemently. "Not just you. Getting married in general. I've seen it ruin too many relationships."

She sighed with a weight greater than her body. "We have such a good thing now, I love our relationship the way it is. Why ruin it by getting married?"

"But we're not talking about getting married in general. We're talking about you and me."

Her stomach clenched, and she felt herself starting to sweat.

Silence.

"I know what it is. You don't think I'm marriage material."

"What is marriage material?" she interrupted. "Who is marriage material? Although now that you say that . . . are you sure you're ready for something like this?"

He glared at her. "I can't believe this. You know, let's pretend this never happened and just go back to how we were before."

"We can't," she said. "Things will already be different."

"How can they not be different?" he asked. "After all we've been through, you still don't trust me."

She squeezed her eyes shut, holding back the tears. "It's not that, it's—"

"Right, it's marriage." He drew in a heavy breath. "I guess it just means something different to me. My parents . . . when my mother passed, it all went to shit, but growing up, watching that beautiful partnership they had, I wanted that, and nothing less."

"I'm happy for you. But I have no idea what that looks like."

"It looks like us, Lu."

She didn't answer. They stood in silence as their vacant gazes swept across the pond. Lumi noticed some dead fish floating belly-up along the edge that she hadn't spotted before.

"I had thought, had hoped, we were in a different place. You have the right to say no, obviously. But I will not lie, it hurts," Julien said.

Lumi winced.

They sat in silence from another stretch, and then he said, "I'm sorry to do this, but I really need to be alone right now."

"What? We can't just talk about this?" she asked.

"Maybe another time. Right now, I'd like to call it a day, but I'm also not leaving you here in the park by yourself," he said.

He turned his body in the direction of the nearest park exit and waited until she began following him to start walking. She trailed behind him until they reached the exit. It had been a long and winding path to the pond, and yet somehow it took only a few steps to get out to the east side.

"There," he said, his expression slightly dazed, unfocused.

All of a sudden, she felt fear seize her chest and heart. "Are—are you saying goodbye?" she asked.

"No. I just need a little time."

"Time for what?"

His face was overcast, and his expression didn't give away his meaning.

He turned away from her and fell in step with the passersby trudging down Fifth Avenue. She got the sudden urge to scream, and she hugged herself, shutting her eyes tightly to repress it. When she opened them, she was alone under a blazing streetlamp. The sun had finally set.

Lumi burst through the door of her apartment, not completely sure how she got there. She had stumbled into the subway, squinted her eyes against the world, and then she was there.

She rifled through drawers in her apartment, searching for something without knowing what she was looking for.

"Stop it. *Stop it!*" she screamed at herself, forcing herself to be still. She sat herself down on the velour couch. It didn't stop the room from spinning.

As she looked over her living room, the fish hanging from the ceiling were tiny daggers in her heart. They were her, hooked through the mouth with something that felt immovable. She felt a throbbing pain radiating from her mouth just looking at them, and suddenly she needed something, anything, to make the pain go away. She jumped up, ran over to the refrigerator, and snatched up cakes, cookies, pats of butter, apples, anything she could find.

She bit an apple, nothing. Cookie, nothing. She threw each one haphazardly across the kitchen when she found that they didn't give her what she was looking for. Then she found it in the back of her fridge: a chocolate pie that Julien had made her the week before. She stuck her hand straight into it, raised a glob of silky pudding to her lips, and licked the side of it.

She felt the familiar buzz that reminded her of him spreading from her lips to her face and all the way through her body, and she screamed, throwing the pie across the room as well. It hit the side of the wall that separated the kitchen and living room, splattering across the purple paint. In a frantic haze she pulled out her phone and called Julien. It rang and rang and rang. She cried, and sobs squeezed every ounce of air out of her body when he didn't answer.

42

JULIEN

Julien let the door slam behind him and tossed his keys onto the kitchen table. He pulled the ring box out of his pocket, holding it between two fingers as if it would burn him, and dropped it in a coffee jar, sealing the lid on tight. He sat down at the table and hung his head in his hands. The evening had gone the opposite of how he had envisioned it, and the worst part about it was that he hadn't been able to control his mouth. He winced as he thought about the things he had said to her. Just remembering them ripped into him, his words knives in his head. He had promised himself he would never say anything to hurt her, and he had failed miserably. He knew what came next.

Sure enough, his phone began to vibrate in his pocket. He pulled it out and groaned when he saw her name flashing on the screen.

"I can't hear this now, Lu," he said somberly, taking the phone and tossing it from where he sat in the kitchen onto the living room couch. He pressed his forehead into his knuckles and waited for the ringing to stop.

"Hey, Julien. What are you doing?" The hazy echo of Patrick's voice was enough to bring Julien back from wherever his mind had been before he picked up the phone.

"Oh, hey, Pat. Uh, nothing. Reading some résumé responses to the Craigslist ad I put out in search of a new receptionist." His hand tightened reflexively over his computer mouse.

"You're hiring a dude this time, right?"

Julien let out a hollow chuckle. "Heh, that's probably the best idea."

There was a lull in their conversation, and Julien embraced the silence without trying to fill it.

"You okay, man?" Patrick asked.

"Mm-hmm."

"No. Hold on a sec. I'm calling you on FaceTime."

Julien groaned inwardly but accepted the call and ignored the urge to cringe as Patrick's concerned expression came into view on the phone screen. His brown eyes appraised Julien's appearance.

"Julien, you look like you haven't shaved for three days," Patrick said at last.

"So what?" Julien replied. "Beards are in style, didn't you know?"

Patrick harrumphed under his breath. "So . . . you put an ad out for a sous chef too, right?"

At this Julien glared at him. "Excuse me?"

Patrick sighed, adjusting his collar as a way to avoid the

camera. "Look, man, I hate to be the one to tell you. You're a pretty sensible guy . . . *usually*. But Lumi told you she wasn't coming back to DAX, you're not even together anymore, and here you are, still waiting for her."

Julien listened, still as a statue.

"I mean, it's sad, I get it. We all want these things to work out, but we need to be honest with ourselves. Most of the time, they don't," Patrick said.

"Patrick?" Julien asked.

"Yes?"

"I really don't want to talk about it."

Patrick sighed. "Right. I'll leave you to it, then. If you want to do brunch this Saturday . . ."

Julien frowned, his nose wrinkling with the movement. "I'll let you know," he said in a hollow tone.

"Right. Talk to you soon, then," Patrick said. He closed out the video call, leaving Julien with more alone time than he already had.

43

LUMI

Lumi rang the bell and waited, smoothing the petals on the spring flower wreath that hung on the front door. After a moment, she heard Jenny unlatching the locks on the other side. "Hey, lady," Jenny said cheerfully as she opened the door, ushering her friend inside.

"Thanks, Jenn," Lumi replied.

"Come, have a seat," said Jenny, gesturing toward the rectangular dining table. Lumi sat and Jenny went to make some coffee.

There was a bowl of lemon meringues on the table, and Lumi plucked one out and examined it in the light. "Jenn, I'm taking one of these," she said, popping it into her mouth.

"Sure, lady," Jenny's voice drifted out from the kitchen.

Lumi pressed the sugar puff with her tongue and, finding it lacking, snatched a napkin and spit it out. She walked into the kitchen and tossed the napkin into the trash bin. Her eyes darted over to the cupboards and counters, landing on a box of chocolate cupcakes. She seized it.

"Can I try this? Do you mind?" she asked Jenny.

"Um . . . sure, hon," Jenny answered, watching as Lumi picked out a cupcake, bit into it, and then chucked it in the trash.

Lumi felt Jenny staring at her but couldn't stop.

"Lumi . . . what is it you're looking for?" Jenny said evenly.

Lumi froze, except for her fingers, which she hastily streaked across a napkin to remove a glob of chocolate frosting.

"Whatever it is . . . you're not going to find it in food," Jenny said softly.

"That's where you're wrong. I've got to go," she said, stumbling toward the door. "Talk to you soon, Jenn."

"But wait," Jenny gasped. "We didn't even have coffee!"

"I'm sorry," Lumi croaked. "I have to go."

"Lumi, why don't you just try calling him again? It's been a week."

The echo of Jenny's voice followed her, already halfway down the hallway. She shook her head, and with sad eyes she blew Jenny a kiss before she bounded down the stairs of the co-op.

44

JULIEN

At the end of a long night in the kitchen, the last thing Julien wanted to do was go home. Three weeks had passed since he had last spoken to Lumi, and still he couldn't bring himself to return her call. He saw her in his bed, on his couch, in his kitchen. The desire to touch her, to hold her, brought him pain that did not fade.

He turned off all the lights and sat in the metal chair. Their metal chair. Strange as it was—and he was fully aware that it was strange—he preferred to sit in the kitchen in the dark after closing time some nights.

The quiet spell between them had been unlike any other breakup or fight he'd ever had. He hadn't felt any desire to drown out the glaring echo of her absence with anything. No drinking, no nights out. He knew none of it would work, anyway.

Funny that for so long, he hadn't wanted to commit to any woman he met. And now that he finally met the one he pined for, she didn't want to commit to him. He wasn't laughing.

He looked out at the lights of the city, remembering a very different night when she had lain in his arms right there in that kitchen. She didn't know that he had awoken to find her dreaming, her breath rasping softly in her throat. She had made him into an entirely different person; if before that night someone had told him they saw someone's spirit shine through, he would have told them to lay off the acid. But that night with her sleeping safe in his arms, there was something beyond her body gently entwined with his in a way that could not be unwoven.

He had to ask himself why he was worried, that being the case. Immediately after that, he wanted to punch something. He was allowing himself to come undone mentally, the worst thing he could possibly do. He forced himself to get up, lock up, and step out into the night.

The beginning of summer was usually Julien's favorite part of the year, and yet this year it had felt joyless and hollow. Even so, the balmy evening air caressed his face and, in it, he could feel her. It seemed she wasn't so far away from him.

He made his way down Broadway, reached the front door of his building, and passed it, heading into the park instead. Rogelio was at the stone table, jaunty red cap cocked to the side, playing chess with a friend with round glasses and honey-colored locs.

"Dax," he said, acknowledging Julien with a nod. "You're next. But just letting you know, it could be a hot minute. Games can go long when you're this well matched." He winked at the woman across from him.

Julien nodded back and took a seat at the adjacent table to watch them play. Indeed, the game moved slowly. The woman seemed to anticipate Rogelio's every move, and she snatched up the spaces on the chessboard before he could move his pieces there. Likewise, Rogelio knew just how to block her when she tried to make a bold move forward. They chortled with glee when one blocked or frustrated the other. It was all part of the game, and they were in it, although maybe not to win it, at the rate they were going.

He couldn't watch them without thinking of Lumi. He couldn't imagine living the rest of his life this way, not being able to talk to her, not being able to tell her the insane things that had happened in his day, not being able to share it all with her. If marriage was all that was standing in the way, was it truly necessary?

For the first time in his life, he had the desire to have a family of his own . . . with her. He had envisioned himself having what his parents had once he found the right person, but he knew that wasn't the only way.

"I have been rude. This is Celeste, my partner of thirty-five years," Rogelio said.

Celeste smiled and bobbed in her seat.

Partners. His first impulse was to call Lumi, but he decided to sit with his thoughts, think about it a little more. It wasn't time yet, but the time would come. They would find a way, marriage or no marriage. He needed to be with her. He stood up, readying himself to leave.

"Not playing today, Dax?"

Julien shook his head. "Another day, my friend." He walked away as Celeste called a tie, and Rogelio leaned in for a kiss.

45

LUMI

The crackle of tiny featherlight feet stepping over plastic wrappers rankled Lumi's nerves as she tried to nap on the couch. She had exiled herself there, since every time she lay down on her bed she ended up retreating because she could feel Julien haunting her.

"Damn it," she muttered, "now I have a mouse in here to boot."

The fact remained that she just couldn't relax. Trying to begin the job search in the weeks since her argument with Julien had only compounded her anxiety. She still had not found a single thing to eat that would ease it, even a little. And the guilt . . . once again she found herself plagued by guilt when she remembered the hurt on his face.

And it was even worse because part of her had wanted to say yes, and it was not such a small part. She *did* want to be with him forever. She did want to wake up next to him every morning, knowing they could count on each other, finding little ways to make him smile. She loved all the things she imagined about their future life together. Having confined herself to her apartment, all that played over in her mind were those first days when she had come home from the hospital, when he came day after day to tend to her. And how he had believed in her dreams.

But the voices would not cease their whispers; their roots were too strong and had been twisted into her psyche for too long. She repeated a now-familiar pattern of taking out her phone, bringing up his name, staring at the screen, and then chucking the phone into a corner, covering her mouth with a pillow so she could scream out her frustration without her neighbors thinking someone was getting killed.

"Why am I even here anymore?" she sputtered aloud, surveying the crunched-up candy wrappers strewn across the floor.

She didn't have an answer. Barely seeing through her swimming eyes, she punched the numbers on her phone screen.

The first sound she heard was the melody of old-time Dominican merengue music and her mother yelling, "Ana, apagame esa vaina! Turn off the hot plate before the coffee bubbles out."

So her mother and aunt were still boiling espresso on the hot plate they had fashioned out of broken flat irons in the back room of the hair salon. It all was a siren song beckoning her with a single command.

"Aló? Salon AnaInés," her mother grunted into the phone.

"Mami?" she sniffled. "I'm coming home."

46

LUMI

Lumi sat on a folding chair in the matchbox-sized kitchen of the salon, making grilled cheese sandwiches with Wonder Bread as she boiled coffee on the makeshift hot plate. The comfort food of her childhood still did the trick, and making food with no thought to artistry was refreshing.

Her mother and aunt were happy to have her and, thankfully, had not asked too many questions. They had bought her plenty of bread and set her up in the guest bedroom. To Lumi's surprise, there hadn't been any "I told you sos," although she would have been remiss if she hadn't noticed that since the day her mother sat with her in the hospital, she had been a little more reserved than usual.

It was a slow afternoon at the usually bustling salon. Lumi flipped through the glossy hair-color books and tugged at the multihued swatches in fascination, grateful to be in a different and yet familiar environment. Anahilda sat in a salon chair, checking her text messages. Except for a few wrinkles, she had barely changed since Lumi was a child. If anything, the gentle crinkles that deepened around her eyes made her look well loved and well lived.

Inés didn't look too different either. Same clay-set features, same wiry copper curls tied up in a paisley bandanna to keep them out of her way while she worked. There was an element of comfort in that, and Lumi briefly wondered what her life would have been like if she had stayed in Miami.

New York was not the only place to cook. She could have gone to Johnson & Wales, apprenticed herself, and perhaps by now she'd be an executive chef with no responsibilities, no business to shoulder, and no debts.

She probably would never have met him. DAX was not the kind of place she would have gone for her own enjoyment. She would have never tasted of him, never known there was someone out there who had reserves of electric surges just for her. Lumi sighed loudly at her inner thoughts.

Anahilda heard and swiveled her salon chair toward her niece. "What is it, m'ija?" she asked gently.

"Oh, Tía." Lumi sighed.

Anahilda reached out to Lumi, smoothing the side of her arm. "Whatever it was, it must've been big for you to come back here to stay awhile. You didn't even come back when you got burned."

This was enough to open the floodgates. As Anahilda drew closer and put her arm around her, Inés inched over. Inés gingerly patted Lumi on the hand.

Unable to hold it in any longer, Lumi began to speak through her sobs. "There's this man."

Anahilda nodded knowingly. Lumi opted to leave out the detail that he had been her boss.

"We worked together at the place I told you about, where

I started after Caraluna. His smile—" She stopped abruptly. His smile had become a knife in her heart. "He cooked for me, and it did something to me that no one else's cooking has. It has a taste I've never found in anyone else's."

The two elder women exchanged glances.

"When I got burned, he came to take care of me every day," she sputtered, too pained to care what the ladies' opinion would be on that.

"That's nice," Inés said. Anahilda shot her a burning glance.

Lumi exhaled heavily. "He asked me to marry him," she said, her shoulders following a gravitational pull to the floor.

"And what's the problem, m'ija?" Anahilda asked.

"I know what marriage does to people," Lumi said in an almost whisper.

"Iluminada—" Inés began.

"No, don't tell me it's not that bad. It's what you guys have been teaching me all along."

"But, my daughter—"

"Mami, when I was young, you always said that marrying my father ruined your life. And the boyfriends, you said you would never marry any of them, even if one turned out good, which none of them did. You wouldn't give yourself to anyone in that way. You too," Lumi said in Anahilda's direction.

In front of her, Anahilda elbowed Inés in the fleshy pillow of her upper arm. "Inés, are you not going to tell her?"

"I don't know what you mean," Inés said, her gaze fixed on her hands, turning them over as if they were dry leaves in her lap.

Anahilda glared at her sister. "Even as you see how this lie is affecting her, you're not going to tell her the truth?"

Lumi's glance shot from her mother to her aunt and back again. "Mami," she began in a measured tone. "What is Tía talking about? What . . . *lie*?"

Inés sighed wearily. "Iluminada, there's something I need to tell you. Ehm." She cleared her throat awkwardly, staring at the base of the salon chair. "It's not entirely true that your father left us."

"What?" Lumi exclaimed.

Inés nodded sorrowfully. "He did go back to Santo Domingo, and it's true that I did not hear from him again. But it was after I left him."

Lumi shook her head, dazed by this new information. "What? *Why?*"

"I was twenty-one, and in my opinion, he just didn't want the same things out of life as I did. He was too much of a dreamer. He thought that being a line cook at the Miami Sheraton was going to get him places. After three years together, he still hadn't been able to save the money he promised me so we could open our own business. If I stayed with him, I was never going to have the life I wanted."

"Then why did you tell me all these years that he left us? And that men could not be trusted?" Lumi asked, her voice cracking.

"I did it to keep you safe," Inés blurted out. "I knew you'd be going out into the world on your own one day, and I needed to know you'd be wary enough to stay away from men. You know they only want one thing. I didn't want to see your youth and your beauty become another casualty of their wretched lust."

"And you would rather have had me grow up distrusting every man I met?" Lumi balked.

"Did it work out so bad? You went on to your fancy cooking school with no relationships or responsibilities holding you back."

The muscles in Lumi's chest knotted together, threatening her breathing. She turned to Anahilda. "And you, you thought it was a good idea to keep this from me too?"

Anahilda hung her head. "It wasn't my place to intervene."

"I see."

Lumi stood up, knocking over the folding chair and sending it clattering to the floor.

"Excuse me," she said. She bounded toward the door, mustering all the energy she could to slam it behind her.

She barreled down the streets of Little Havana, practically knocking into the passersby strolling and sipping their espressos at a leisurely pace. Two blocks down, she came to a panting stop in front of a little green cottage with lush arrangements of daisies, freesia, and tiger lilies in the window. Coming around the side of the cottage with a wrinkled garden hose was an elderly woman with kindly eyes set in a face that could have been shaped from clay.

"Doña Elia!" Lumi called.

Doña Elia glanced up from her garden. Her eyes lit up when her younger friend came into her line of sight.

"Ah, Lumi," she said, as she let the hose fall to the ground and puttered over to the picket fence. She unlatched the gate and Lumi stepped in. Doña Elia drew her close for a brief but affectionate hug. "Won't you come in?" she asked, walking toward the cottage.

The cottage was painted a cheery yellow on the inside, and there were two chairs in front of a desk amid the tables and baskets of flowers. "Would you like a glass of lemonade?" she asked.

Lumi nodded, and Doña Elia reached into a mini-fridge under her desk and pulled out two glasses of lemonade, already poured. Lumi took a sip and inhaled deeply. She felt strengthened and warmed despite the temperature of the beverage. It was a viscerally grounding feeling, like being connected to the helix of ancestor wisdom. She was so grateful she had run into the elder woman.

"Where's Don Emilio?" Lumi asked, remembering Doña Elia's husband, who was usually out front building tables while she arranged the flowers.

"Emilio died two years ago, m'ija," Doña Elia said.

"Oh. I'm so sorry," Lumi said in a hushed tone, ashamed that she hadn't known.

"It's okay. He was eighty-eight years old, and we had a long and wonderful life together."

Lumi looked up, startled, something having been awakened by the old woman's words.

Doña Elia left her desk and came closer, letting her weight sink into the white wrought-iron chair opposite Lumi. She struck a match and lit a persimmon-colored taper sitting in the center of the matching table in between them. Delicately, she traced the scars leading from the corner of Lumi's eye to the corner of her mouth.

"These look like they healed well," she said. "I heard what happened from your mother." She shook her head slowly. "It was a woman who caused this, m'ija. I've looked into the situation."

Lumi's stomach turned. "But why?" she answered.

Doña Elia sighed, settling into her chair. "I don't know. Most likely envy. In my eighty-six years, when I have seen women direct this kind of hatred at other women, it's almost always envy. But I will advise you one thing, m'ija—do not seek revenge. Justice is in the hands of the Creator of all that is."

Lumi nodded, slightly dazed.

Doña Elia peered into the tiny flame. "And as for the man . . . hmm . . ." She paused, her lips curving into a smile.

She reached for Lumi's hand and squeezed it.

"All is not lost, m'ija. Follow your senses," she said, raising an eyebrow. "The senses don't lie, and they'll lead you through all of . . . this." She made a circular motion around Lumi's head.

Lumi sighed and leaned her elbow on the table, supporting her head with it. "These past few weeks have been so full of chaos. First, everything with him . . . and now my mother. I come here to get away and get a little distance, and this is the time Mami chooses to tell me, 'Oh, guess what? The story with your father? Everything I taught you? Lies.'"

Doña Elia frowned and studied Lumi's exasperated features. "Your mother is a hard woman," she said simply, "and she has lived most of her life focusing on what she *doesn't* want. So . . . there's your example," she concluded cryptically.

She patted Lumi lightly on the hand.

"It's time for me to close the shop," she said, as she looked pointedly at the now-darkened windows. Lumi stood up slowly. Doña Elia drew her in for a hug again, but this time she held her there and said, "May all the love and light you need accompany you. Go with power, m'ija."

Lumi felt a lightening in her chest and squeezed her in return. Doña Elia smelled of incense and agua de florida, and Lumi found the fragrance comforting.

"Thank you, Doña Elia," she whispered back. "I'll see you soon."

Doña Elia nodded graciously. "Give my regards to your mother and Anahilda."

Lumi nodded and paced toward the door, bowing her head slightly to Doña Elia on the way out.

Across the street, there was a bus in the waiting station. Its sign read MIAMI BEACH. Lumi dashed across the street and hopped on, tossing some coins in the fare box, and grabbed a seat on the bus before the vehicle lurched into action. She watched the blur of stores and people of Calle Ocho whiz by, letting the aftertaste of Doña Elia's lemonade linger on her palate.

When the bus pulled up at Collins Avenue and Forty-First Street, she stepped off and took a narrow side path that led past an elegant hotel right up to the boardwalk. She could see there were still people on the sand and she decided to walk down to the water. She slipped off her sandals and carried them with her, dangling them from one of her fingers.

She inhaled the sea air deeply and let it wash over her, tossing her curls every which way. She let the breeze caress her and allowed all thoughts to rush out from her and into the waves, past the breakers. In that moment, there was no need to find answers, she just wanted to be.

When the cool breeze turned cold and the last families and couples with dogs packed up and left the beach bare, she knew what she would do. She had a call to make. She fished her phone out of her pocket as she walked back to the bus stop and pulled up her contacts.

"Corazón! I thought you forgot about me."

As soon as she heard Richard's melodious voice, she could not help but smile. "Mi amor." She blew a kiss into the phone. "Listen, I'm going to need your help with something."

By the time Lumi got back to Inés's, the cicadas in the front yard were chirping at full pitch. She appraised the exterior of the ranch-style home she had grown up in. There was a shutter coming loose that she hadn't noticed before, and in the upper left-hand corner, the paint was beginning to peel. The facade had become dingier in the stretch of several hours.

The lights were dimmed, so she supposed her mother and Anahilda had already retired to bed. She stepped into the compact kitchen for a glass of water and found Inés sitting at the dinette table, folding cotton dinner napkins into minute squares. When she got them down to matchbox size, she shook the napkins loose and started again.

Lumi took a seat at the table, and Inés kept folding, un-folding, and refolding, her gaze focused on the cotton squares. As the silence stretched on, Lumi remembered her glass of water. As she retrieved the water pitcher, a low voice came from behind her back.

"I told you why I did what I did."

Lumi whirled around, and Inés was still staring at her nap-kins. She approached the table with caution. She studied the lines on her mother's face, the way her eyes bore into the table, and her arms tingled with the urge to hug her. Instead, she asked in a near whisper, "Mami, why did you assume I would judge you?"

Inés shook her head. "I don't know, m'ija. I guess because almost everyone else did."

"Did you love him, Mami?"

Inés let out a long sigh that sounded like she had been holding it in for the past thirty years. "Yes," she said, "yes, I did." The last words came out like she was fighting not to swallow them. "I loved him, but our decisions made us face life before we were ready."

She drew another long breath.

"I was sure I had done right by you, but now . . . I'm not so sure anymore. I'm sorry."

Lumi reached out to squeeze her mother's hand, and to her surprise, Inés looked up at her and squeezed back, her brown eyes shining in the dim light.

"Mami," Lumi said, "I'm going back."

Inés gave her a small nod. "You do what you have to do, m'ija. As if you were ever going to do anything else," she said, smiling.

This was the closest she would get to her mother's blessing, and she knew it, and that was huge.

"I'll start packing," Lumi said softly. She laid a light kiss on her mother's forehead and went to her room to grab her suitcase.

47

LUMI

The subway crawled toward 116th Street early on a July morning. The Fulton Fish Market was Lumi's favorite, but it was eight o'clock and Fulton closed at seven. She had planned to take a bus at 155th Street until she realized she was too late. She opted to just stay on the subway, remembering Ocean Wave Seafood on 116th. It wasn't Fulton, but it would have to do.

Lumi wore a white T-shirt, distressed jeans that barely hung on by a stitch, and a beige linen scarf with gilded threads that billowed under her chin as she walked toward the market.

The frigid air hit her full blast as she stepped in. She spotted a few spiny crustaceans on ice and was relieved to see their claws were tightly bound with thick rubber bands. A single lobster would do the trick. She stepped into line behind the woman waiting at the counter. As she stared at the back of the woman's head, her heart thudded in her chest as she recognized the honey-blond hair with black roots.

"Esme?"

Esme whipped her head around. "Lumi?" Her face blanched.

What was Esme doing at the fish market at eight o'clock in the morning? Would it be too obvious if Lumi turned on her heel and hightailed it back to the subway station?

Instead, she took a deep breath and settled herself. "Wow. I wasn't sure I would ever see you again," Lumi said. "What brings you here?"

Esme fidgeted with her jacket cuffs and shifted her weight from side to side. "This is my neighborhood. My mother's church is having a model biblical meal today at noon," she said.

Lumi wrinkled her brow in curiosity. "What's that?"

Esme smiled a small grin. "They prepare and share a meal made of the same foods Jesus and his disciples ate in the Bible."

"Ah." Lumi leaned her shoulder against the glass of the display case, and Esme did the same.

"And you?"

"I . . . came to buy some lobster."

An uncomfortable silence stretched between the two women until Lumi spoke again.

"Esme, what happened? Why did you leave?" Lumi asked.

Esme returned a sorrowful glance. "There wasn't much room for growth in my position."

"I see."

Esme stared down at her fingernails. "And also, I couldn't help feeling like somehow I was responsible . . . for what happened to you. I just didn't want to be there anymore after that."

Lumi bit her lip. Should she tell her she most likely was? She released her lip and managed a small nod.

"I never meant to hurt anyone," Esme said. And then: "I heard you two are together now."

Lumi sighed. "No, we're not, not anymore. Argh—it's complicated."

"Well, I hope it works out for you," Esme said.

"What?!"

"You heard me."

Lumi swallowed. "You're not, well, jealous?"

"You love him," Esme said simply.

"What?"

Esme nodded. "My mom and her church have helped me through this a lot. I was obsessed. I thought it was the same thing, but now I'm starting to see that love is something else . . . I just wanted to get what I wanted."

"Which was?"

"Well, I wanted him and the life that came with it. I saw his charm and that he was successful. Like, big-time successful in ways I was afraid I could never be, and I wanted it for myself."

Lumi nodded. If she could allow herself to cry in a fish market for the woman across from her, she would. She didn't understand obsession too well, but she understood what it felt like to feel small. She understood what it felt like to feel so lackluster that you thought you could only shine by borrowing someone else's light. The part of Esme's spiel that made her saddest was how far from the truth that was. She couldn't call Esme a friend, but she could see she was organized, determined, and got things done. She could use all that in her own favor.

"And now?" Lumi asked.

"Now, I'm rethinking that. I suck at cooking, but I love the restaurant ambiance and I'm not terrible at administration," Esme said.

"No, you're good at it."

Esme managed a grin. "I'm going to see where that takes me."

The fishmonger appeared and handed Esme a paper bag stuffed to the top with parcels. Esme thanked him and leaned away from the display case.

"Take care, Lumi. And I'm so sorry for what happened to you."

Lumi reached out and squeezed her shoulder, touching her for the first time. "Hey. We're good."

As Esme went her way, Lumi found herself genuinely hoping it went well for Esme.

She returned to the fishmonger, who was ready to take her order.

"Hi. I'll have this one on the left."

48

JULIEN

It was a Thursday afternoon, and the muggy July air pressed up against every window in Manhattan, including those of DAX. The staff labored in a bored lull, until a high-pitched scream punctuated the thick silence. Julien looked up briefly from his paperwork, then shrugged and turned his gaze back downward. He was careful not to look at the stack of papers covered in zany arrows and loopy script in purple ink. Even so, he cringed as they briefly crossed his line of vision.

"Ahhh!" A second scream rattled the glass panes of the office.

"What the hell?" he said, pushing back his chair and trudging toward the hallway. The first thing he saw was a lobster scuttling down the hall toward him.

"Again?" he said. "I swear to God, I'm making a new rule in this kitchen: whoever loses a lobster has to put it down their pants after I catch it."

As the lobster came within grabbing distance, he noticed that it had a slip of gold paper tied to its tail with a purple ribbon. He reached forward and deftly snatched the paper, which was folded in quarters. He let the lobster run free, claws snapping, into his office, and closed the door behind him to keep it contained.

He unfolded the note and was greeted by her loopy script right away.

Dear Julien,

For the past month, my soul has not been at ease. I've been eating Wonder Bread out of a bag, if that tells you anything. I can't get used to not seeing you, not touching you, not hearing you, not having you close to me.

When I started working at DAX, it was humiliating for me. Not because of you, but because my own business, my own dream, had failed. You being the way you are, I promised myself I wasn't going to taste of you . . . but once I did, I couldn't get enough and that has stayed constant. But what we have goes far beyond that, which I understood more than ever after I got burned.

You defied every expectation I had. You made sure I healed, and you carried me through it. I don't know how I would've done it without you. Although those times were painful, they showed me that what we have is real. You

asked me if I was afraid that you were not
marriage material, but in these weeks that
I've had to myself, I realized that deep down,
I was afraid that it was me who was not
marriage material. I was afraid to just let go
and trust that things can work out well.

When you asked me to marry you, images
of what our life could be together
came alive in my mind's eye. And they
didn't feel like silly imaginings; they
felt like a window into the future.

I'm so sorry that I hurt you in the
muddle of all these fears and feelings.
I miss you more than you know.

Love,
Lumi

"Well . . . damn," Julien said. He leaned against the wall of
the hallway and rested the note on his knee. He turned it over
and found something written on the back:

P.S. I'll be in the wine closet if you
can find it in your heart to see me. If
not, I'll still be in there, drinking your
best wines to drown out my sorrows
at having lost a love like yours.

He grinned and slowly ambled into the kitchen, where the staff was studiously focused on their endeavors. Only Richard looked up and gave Gloria a quick nudge before he looked back at his wine list. Julien shook his head knowingly as he marched over to the wine closet, its doors wide open. He shut them behind him as he entered.

Lumi was sitting on the metal kitchen chair against the farthest merlot wall, a bottle of 1947 D'Orsay burgundy in her hand and a bouquet of orange tiger lilies in her arms.

"You're here," she said.

Julien leaned against the doorway, his eyes meeting hers. "I figured this was a relative proposition."

She thought for a moment. "You mean, the longer you took to think about it, the more bottles of wine you would lose?"

"Mm-hmm." He nodded. "Was I right?"

She pursed her lips to keep from smiling. "Pretty much, yes," she said. "Where's the lobster?"

"Tearing my office to shreds as we speak."

She shrugged apologetically, holding out the bouquet. "These reminded me of you."

He hesitated a moment, then reached past the flowers and pulled her to him.

"Oh, Lumi." He sighed.

"I'm sorry," she said. "Will you please forgive me?"

He nodded. "Lumi, I could never stay mad at you." He smoothed her hair. "I'm sorry for the things I said too."

She shook her head. "Don't even mention it. I would have said a lot worse in your position, probably. About the question—"

"It's okay, love, we don't have to talk about it. I've done a lot of thinking and . . . we don't need that to be together."

"You—you don't want to marry me anymore?"

"It's not that. It's just—let's forget the whole thing happened. I don't want it to come between us."

"It doesn't need to. I do want to marry you, Julien. I was just so afraid. I meant everything I said that day. It wasn't you. I did a lot of thinking over the past three weeks too, and I have a lot of news to share with you. A lot. But we have time. Bottom line is I don't want to live in the shadow of the past and others' fears for the rest of my life, much less have them stand in the way of me and you making a wonderful life together. *Our* wonderful life together."

He squeezed both her hands, beaming.

"I hope you still have the ring and didn't do something crazy like throw it in some bushes."

"Of course I still have it," he said softly.

"Well, can we do this again?" she asked, gazing up at him hopefully.

"Are you sure?"

"Yes, I'm sure," she said, hearing the resolve in her own words.

He went to the safe and came back to the wine closet. He opened the box, and the ring sparkled under the small round ceiling lights.

"Ms. Santana, will you marry me?" he asked.

"Yes," she said, and she knew she meant it.

Behind them, Richard, Gloria, and the dishwashers broke out into whooping cheers. Julien reached out and enfolded Lumi in a joyous embrace. This time, neither of them cared who saw them kissing. Filled with melodious laughter, the kitchen opened late that day.

EPILOGUE

ONE YEAR LATER

Lumi fastened the final string of decorative star lights to the wall. With a flourish, she hung turquoise and cream ribbons from the dining room ceiling, running them across until the spools were bare. On each table, of which there were twelve, she placed a blooming butter-hued orchid in a jeweled turquoise vase.

She had settled on a new color scheme for her new restaurant, simply named Lumi's Kitchen: shades that reminded her of the ocean. The sea always helped her regroup and rejuvenate, and her hope was that her place would do the same for her customers. The sole pop of purple was a cheery painting she hung on the door to the kitchen, a river scene that she and Julien had painted together at a wine-and-paint party she'd convinced him to host weekly at DAX.

When the entire room was adorned, she laid down her stapler and tape roll and darted into the kitchen. There he was, his freckled face flushed. Julien was standing at the island, dicing asparagus with a gleaming chef's knife. She drank in the sunlight of the smile he gave her when she came in, until a knock on the service door caused her to turn her head.

She and Julien exchanged a glance before he answered it. A bubbly young woman with springy black hair and several packages wrapped in sheaths of butcher paper stood in the doorway, eyes on Julien.

"Delivery for Lumi's Kitchen, can you sign?" she asked.

"Nope!" Julien responded with cheer in his voice. "I am just the vegetable cutter. That's the head chef over there." He nodded his head in Lumi's direction.

The deliverywoman glanced from Julien to Lumi's glittering rose gold engagement ring to Lumi, who took the packages, signed with a smile, and thanked the woman before showing her back to the door.

Magda came into the kitchen, giving both Lumi and Julien a small wave before she picked up the last missing table settings. She had just about jumped ship at her other job when she heard Lumi was opening a new restaurant in Inwood. The rest of the employees were new: men and women Lumi had connected with while she was doing her pre-opening events at Lincoln Center. They all understood her vision and had the experience needed to help her push it forward.

The door from the dining room opened again, and this time it was Inés and Anahilda.

"There's a line forming out front, m'ija," Inés said, and Anahilda nodded in confirmation, her face effusive.

Lumi took a deep breath. "Thanks, Ma and Tía, but we're not ready yet."

She peeked into the dining room and saw that all the tables were set. Then she did a final once-over of each station in the kitchen. She had a separate prep station for each food group, and the wine closet would be set up as soon as she received her liquor license.

Magda stuck her head in the doorway. "Ready yet? We have about twenty people in line. The *Time Out New York* article must have really helped."

Lumi's chest started to constrict, but she took a deep breath. A warm hand squeezed hers, and she leaned her head onto Julien's shoulder.

"No, we're not ready yet. Everyone, I need just a moment alone in the kitchen. I'll be right out," Lumi said.

Julien and Magda nodded and quickly stepped out.

Lumi stood at the kitchen island and bowed her head, resting it on her laced fingers. She thought of Doña Elia and what she would say at a moment like this. Before she knew it, the words were coming to her.

"Thank you. Thank you. Thank you," she whispered, and then rested her hands at her sides. Only six syllables, and they covered all she needed to express.

"Okay. Now we're ready," she said as she stepped into her new dining room, her family, both born to and made, by her side. "Let them come in."

She opened the door to greet her new customers, and one by one, they filed into the dining room, taking in the blooming orchids, the tinkly jazz piano harmonizing with a tambora in the background, and the luscious aromas that pervaded the space.

For her first dinner, she had chosen a coq au vin marinated in mamajuana liquor, a simple mango-cilantro salad, and yuca frites with a garlic reduction and a dusting of Caille bacon.

The dessert was an apple ratatouille, a dish she had created by slicing red and green apple varieties that she then baked in a cinnamon-sugar sauce.

She served the first plate herself and watched as the diners' faces lit up with the first bite. Tables continued to fill up through the night, and the diners oohed and aahed over the marriage of flavors gracing their palates in this vibrant new space.

At the end of the night, Lumi was wiped but so, so grateful. She washed the dishes herself as Julien swept and saw the others out until it was just them left in the restaurant. She pulled up a chair in the middle of the dining room and he dragged two next to her, one for her to put her feet up on and one for him to sit on.

"That was a great first night. You were something to watch, cooking and stirring and greeting and serving. I'm proud of you."

"I couldn't have done it without you." She coursed one foot up his leg and rested it in his lap, where he grasped her ankle and began to rub it.

"This is nothing compared to what I want to give you, what I want to share with you."

"I know," she said. And she did. It was a truth rooted into the best-hidden places within her. And it made her heart glow to think that she too had something to share, something so vast it had no limits.

They would have to do their best to make it fit in their lifetimes.

LUMI'S COQ AU VIN IN MAMAJUANA
Serves 4

4 whole chicken legs
juice of 1 lime
$\frac{1}{2}$ cup mamajuana (Dominican liquor made
  of red wine, rum, herbs, roots, and honey)
$\frac{1}{2}$ teaspoon black pepper
salt, to taste
oregano, to taste
sage, to taste
2 tablespoons cooking oil
1 red onion
6 cloves garlic
$\frac{1}{4}$ cup cilantro, diced
1 green pepper, diced
3 stalks celery, diced
$\frac{1}{3}$ cup carrots, diced
$2\frac{1}{2}$ cups red wine
2 tablespoons butter
1 tablespoon brown sugar
1 tablespoon tomato paste

Separate the chicken thighs from the drumsticks and skin if desired. "Wash" the chicken with the lime juice and drain. Marinate the chicken for at least 2 hours in the salt, seasonings (which include the garlic, onion, cilantro, pepper, celery, carrots), and mamajuana. Remove the chicken from the marinade, reserving the liquid. Heat the butter on medium-high in an iron Dutch oven. Sprinkle the sugar into the butter and allow to brown. When the sugar is bubbling, add the chicken and brown on each side for 2 minutes. Add the reserved marinade and cook on low heat for 1 hour, stirring occasionally so the chicken does not stick to the bottom of the pot. After about 50 minutes, add the tomato paste and stir until dissolved.

MANGO-CILANTRO SALAD
Serves 8

4 ripe mangoes
1 medium red onion
olive oil, to taste
red wine vinegar, to taste
$1/4$ cup cilantro, diced

Chop the mangoes into chunks and dice the onion as small as possible. Toss in the olive oil and red wine vinegar. The mango should be moistened by the oil and vinegar but not swimming in it. Garnish with the cilantro.

LUMI'S APPLE "RATATOUILLE"
Serves 12

$1/2$ cup butter, plus more for the baking dish
3 red apples, mixed varieties

3 green apples, mixed varieties

3 tablespoons cinnamon

$\frac{1}{2}$ cup sugar

$\frac{1}{4}$ cup lemon juice

Preheat the oven to 350 degrees Fahrenheit. Grease the bottom of a 9-inch baking dish with a dab of butter. Slice the apples into $\frac{1}{8}$-inch slices and layer over one another in the dish. Melt the butter on low heat in a small saucepan. Add the cinnamon and sugar and stir into a viscous mixture. When these elements are well combined, remove from the heat and pour over the apples. Sprinkle with the lemon juice and bake for 30 minutes or until golden.

AUTHOR'S NOTE

Please note that all of Lumi's recipes represent her own brand of Dominican fusion cuisine, which consists of fusion twists from all over and/or traditional dishes cooked according to her eclectic tastes. For those interested in getting to know traditional Dominican cuisine, I recommend separate research.

ACKNOWLEDGMENTS

Thank you to my editor, Amber Oliver. Thank you for sitting with Lumi and seeing her heart, and for all your thoughtful comments and suggestions.

Thank you to Maria Cardona, Nick Owen, Ms. Anna Soler-Pont, Ellie Laing, and everyone at the Pontas Agency for believing in me and for your guidance.

Many thanks to my critique partners, Maribel L. and Sarah S., for reading along as I wrote and providing opinions, prayers, and edits.

To Coralie Moss, Taralynn Moore, Felicia Grossman, Sheena D., and Claire F., who beta read and gave me superstar feedback. And to all the ladies of RChat who were there with virtual chocolate, hugs, and on-the-spot CP talks.

Katie McCoach, for your insights on the first fifty pages.

Vanya, Larry, Kanitta, Anna M., Kat, Noura, thank you for the love.

To Maribel B., for teaching a scattered teenager to cook.

ACKNOWLEDGMENTS

To my parents for a lot, including passing on a passion for storytelling, making sure there was always an abundance of books in our house, and "hiring" me to write stories.

To CTB for the cupcakes, encouragement, and for the often hilarious culinary stories, and CB for his solidarity.

To my husband, Joel, thank you for your love, for lighting my way and celebrating with me. Also, this book probably would not have gotten finished if you didn't wake me up at 5 A.M. to write and filter out distractions when I was editing.

I thank our children for giving me the heart-fuel and fire necessary to move forward.

And thank you, reader, for coming along on Lumi's journey with me.

ABOUT THE AUTHOR

Yaffa S. Santos was born and raised in New Jersey. A solo trip to the Dominican Republic in her teenage years changed her relationship to her Dominican heritage and sparked a passion for cooking and its singular ability to bring people together. Yaffa is a graduate of Sarah Lawrence College, where she studied writing and visual art. She has lived in New York City, Philadelphia, and Santo Domingo, and now lives in Florida with her family.

P.S.

About the author

About the book

Read on

Insights,
Interviews
& More . . .

Meet Yaffa S. Santos

YAFFA S. SANTOS WAS BORN AND raised in New Jersey. A solo trip to the Dominican Republic in her teenage years changed her relationship to her Dominican heritage and sparked a passion for cooking and its singular ability to bring people together. Her debut novel, *A Taste of Sage*, combines her interests in the romance genre and the art of cooking. Yaffa is a graduate of Sarah Lawrence College, where she studied writing and visual art. She has lived in New York, Philadelphia, and Santo Domingo, and now lives in Florida with her family. ⟳

A Q&A with Yaffa S. Santos

What was your writing process like for A Taste of Sage?

The majority of the novel was written between 5–7 A.M., before my children got up for school. I wrote the very first scene in August 2015. When I was a child, I would do this thing for fun where I would interview myself, family members, and friends, asking them their favorite color, food, activity, etc. I did this for Lumi before I wrote any scenes for her.

What is your favorite part of the novel?

The novel combines many elements I enjoy such as cooking, the romance and women's fiction genres, and thinking about what lies beyond the five senses.

What is your favorite recipe in the book?

It's hard to choose just one. Maybe sancocho because it has a grounding effect on me. Writing the recipes was a process of cooking and then writing down what I was doing, since I learned from watching others. It should be known that I am an enthusiast and home cook, but *not* a professional or expert. ▶

A Q&A with Yaffa S. Santos *(continued)*

If you had only one chance to impress someone with your cooking, what dish would you make?

Probably rabo encendido (oxtail).

What media (books, tv, movies, etc.) did you use as a resource when writing this book?

I read *Like Water for Chocolate* by Laura Esquivel about twenty years ago. It was the first time I got an inkling that a novel could focus on cooking and even contain recipes.

The book *Levente no. Yolayorkdominicanyork* by Josefina Báez inspired me because it brought back memories of living in Upper Manhattan.

What are you reading at the moment?

Dominicana by Angie Cruz.

What are you working on next?

I would like to work on a happy ending for Esme. I wouldn't be surprised if I came up with another project along the way, though. ❧

A Behind the Book
Essay on *A Taste of Sage*

I BEGAN WRITING *A TASTE OF SAGE* WITH the idea of a woman chef living and working in New York City, but it became important to me that there also be an aspect of the story that extended beyond the five senses. I'd long had an interest in the idea of tasting food and feeling a connection to the cook beyond what was immediately available to the five senses.

Some of my curiosity was triggered by comments my son would make as a small child. He is on the autism spectrum, and he would say things like "This song is orange" or "This pizza tastes angry." At first, they didn't make sense to me, and then I wondered, what if these are facts on another plane of reality outside the five senses, and I just don't perceive them because I'm not attuned to that information?

In a similar/familial vein, my husband has a long-standing pet peeve where he will not eat a meal he feels was cooked by an angry person or a person in a bad mood. It made me think.

It was also important to me that the protagonist be a Dominican American ▶

chef, because I wanted her to represent Dominican cuisine, which has not often had a spotlight in American novels. The representation has grown since I started this project—Adriana Herrera's *American Dreamer* is a notable example—but at the time I began in 2015, there was less that I was aware of. I was also inspired by stories my sister told me about the larger-than-life personalities she encountered in culinary school. I lived in Inwood and Washington Heights, New York City, during my twenties, and that became the inspiration for basing Lumi's home and restaurant in Inwood.

As far as where Julien and DAX came into the picture, French food is often upheld as a culinary standard, which is one of the reasons I chose it. Lumi is so creative, and she loves to innovate. Going into a traditional French restaurant where she is not allowed to do that was one of the hardest and most frustrating challenges she could have, professionally.

I also wanted to create a scenario where Dominican fusion cuisine would be presented on the same level as French food, and not on a sort of hierarchy where one is practical and one is elegant.

Why Is Julien French Canadian?

When I was in college, my husband and I lived in Westchester County, New York. It wasn't too long of a drive to Montreal, and we drove up for weekends quite a bit. I developed a fondness for the city, and I wanted it to be tied into the book.

Having Julien be French Canadian was a way to explain why he would have an emotional investment in a traditional French restaurant that sticks to tradition with a capital T, but for me it also separated his identity from that of the French chef stereotype that tends to pop up in American media.

Where did the idea for Julien and Esme come from?

Julien and Esme came from another project, a short story challenge I was invited to participate in by one of my critique partners. I had started shaping Lumi's character but was planning on keeping the two projects separate. But the more Lumi's arc was revealed to me, it became clear she was going to have a sojourn at another restaurant while she got her business back together. ▶

A Behind the Book Essay *(continued)*

When I was thinking about what kind of people she would encounter there, I thought of Julien's character and my first thought was, "But they would hate each other." And then, "Ooh, they would hate each other!" It came together from there.

I am excited that the book is out now, and it is a dream come true. It has been a long road to here for me personally. I hope readers enjoy Lumi's journey as much as I did. She has come to feel like a best friend to me, and I'm proud of her progress! ᴄᴡ

Yaffa's Favorite Dishes

IN *A TASTE OF SAGE*, LUMI AND JULIEN whip up a bevy of delectable dishes throughout the novel that are sure to leave readers' mouths watering. As the author of such a delicious novel, Yaffa has included some of her own favorite dishes below!

1. Pollo guisado with moro de habichuelas negras (chicken stew and rice with black beans). This is my go-to for when I want to make something relatively quickly that I know my whole family will eat.
2. Sancocho
3. Chivo y chenchén (stewed goat with cracked corn)
4. My mom's salmon with quinoa and coconut
5. Key lime pie. Living in Florida has only compounded this. ∾

Discover great authors, exclusive offers, and more at hc.com.